REX STOUT

D0032671

In
the Best
Families

*Introduction
by Patricia Sprinkle*

BANTAM BOOKS
NEW YORK • TORONTO • LONDON • SYDNEY • AUCKLAND

CRIME LIME ™ A NERO WOLFE MYSTERY

This edition contains the complete text
of the original hardcover edition.
NOT ONE WORD HAS BEEN OMITTED.

IN THE BEST FAMILIES

A Bantam Crime Line Book / published by arrangement with
The Viking Press, Inc.

PUBLISHING HISTORY

Viking Press edition published September 1950
Dollar Mystery Guild edition published January 1951
Bantam edition published October 1953
New Bantam edition / September 1962
Bantam reissue edition / February 1995

This book appeared in condensed form in the
MONTREAL STANDARD and the NEWARK EVENING NEWS

CRIME LINE and the portrayal of a boxed "cl" are trademarks of Bantam
Books, a division of Bantam Doubleday Dell Publishing Group, Inc.

ISBN 0-553-27776-6

Published simultaneously in the United States and Canada

Bantam Books are published by Bantam Books, a division of Bantam Doubleday
Dell Publishing Group, Inc. Its trademark, consisting of the words "Bantam
Books" and the portrayal of a rooster, is Registered in U.S. Patent and Trademark
Office and in other countries. Marca Registrada. Bantam Books, 1540 Broadway,
New York, New York 10036.

PRINTED IN THE UNITED STATES OF AMERICA

OPM   10 9 8 7 6 5

Introduction

I first met Nero Wolfe in 1954, when I was ten years old.

My father, a Presbyterian pastor with an eclectic taste in literature, was bedridden that long, hot, coastal North Carolina summer and had sent an urgent note to the librarian: *Please let Patti check out books for me.* It was a great honor, and a great responsibility.

Each Friday evening Mother and I made the five-mile trip into Wilmington. While she bought groceries at the local Colonial, I tiptoed from the children's section to the grown-up shelves and savored titles, trying to pick books that would help my daddy feel better. I don't know if it was his preference or my own, but I usually wound up with an armful of mysteries.

During the twilit rides home, secluded in my backseat nest of brown-paper bags, I dipped into Daddy's books, for it was—and still is—constitutionally impossible for me to ride five miles with an unopened book. One evening I discovered an enormous spider of a detective who waited amid his orchids for cases to come to him. When I was ten, spiders were fascinating. So was Nero Wolfe.

As an adult, I see other reasons why Nero Wolfe tickled my ten-year-old's fancy. For one thing, he was fat—so fat he overflowed his chair. He drank beer. Nobody in my daddy's congregation admitted to drinking anything stronger than Pepsi. He sassed (insulted) people and got away with it. He got away with being a picky eater, too, and he never did anything he didn't want to do. Nero Wolfe was the grown-up this child yearned to be!

All through that stultifying summer, while Mother worried and Daddy dyed white sheets gold with sweat-soaked pajamas, I devoured stories about Nero Wolfe—including *In the Best Families*. I neither noticed nor cared who wrote them; at that age I assumed all authors were dead people.

By autumn Daddy was well, I was sent back to the library's children's section, and Nero Wolfe was stored on the mental shelves of my childhood reserved for Forbidden Fruit. I forgot all about him.

During the next thirty-eight years, I discovered dead Englishwomen writers and fell in love with whodunits. I tried a few hard-boiled American books but found them long on violence and profanity, short on conversation, puzzle, and plot. I concluded I didn't like American mystery authors, especially male ones.

Then, in the strange workings of Providence, which sometimes decrees that we shall become what we profess to eschew, in 1988 I myself became an American mystery author. In 1992 I was confined to bed with hepatitis, reduced to reading whatever other people brought me. Among one stack of offerings were three books by an unfamiliar author, Rex Stout.

Only when I had read everything else within reach did I finally open *The Mother Hunt*. There, in paragraph two, with that keen joy reserved for the recovery of dear things we've forgotten we've lost, I found my old friend Nero Wolfe!

He was just as fat, just as sassy, just as picky, just as adamantly immobile, and just as delightful as he'd been nearly forty years before.

In his creator, however, I found something astonishing and far more subtle: the standards by which I still judge all mystery writing and toward which I strive in my own.

In the Best Families illustrates where I learned to prefer detectives who are intelligent, cultured, nonviolent, and shrewd rather than those who lead with their fists or their gonads. Thugs and master criminals may use firearms and explosives. Archie Goodwin may feel more comfortable with a gun under his armpit. Nero Wolfe, however, invariably acts —as he instructs Goodwin in this case—"in the light of experience as guided by intelligence."

Stout presumes intelligent readers as well. A random opening of this novel turns up words like *shamus, scrutinized,* and *echelons,* and a master criminal who explains to Archie Goodwin that "a basic requirement for continued success in illicit enterprises is a sympathetic understanding of the limitation of the human nervous system." No wonder my vocabulary increased dramatically the summer I met Nero Wolfe!

No wonder, too, that I subsequently found hardboiled detectives immature and boring. No one taught by Stout to appreciate urbane maturity would ever confuse "adult" with mere prurience or repetitive profanity. I believe it was by Stout that I was first convinced, as one of my own characters would later say, that a writer who depends on frequent profanity needs a larger vocabulary.

In the Best Families also shows why I have always thought mysteries ought to be funny. Not slapstick, add-it-to-the-plot funny, but intrinsic-to-the-character funny. Stout taught me irony by creating a famous detective who, at the end of a case, calls his chef before he calls the police. And while, as a child, I scarcely noticed Archie Goodwin, I absorbed the bite and personality behind lines like "I solemnly assured her that we rarely notified the press when someone requested an appointment on business" and "[His] eyes were the result of an error on the assembly line. They had been intended for a shark and someone got careless."

Finally, Rex Stout's books explain why I continue to believe that no matter how well drawn the characters, they cannot carry a mystery without a clever, well-contrived plot. *In the Best Families* twists and turns as Wolfe's new client immediately gets murdered, Wolfe's kitchen is bombed, and Wolfe decamps, leaving Archie to deal with a master criminal. Then Archie himself is embroiled in the criminal organization by a seamy Californian, and— No, read it yourself! See if you, like me, find it fascinating, clever, and wholly satisfying.

—**Patricia Sprinkle**

In the
Best Families

Chapter 1

It was nothing out of the ordinary that Mrs. Barry Rackham had made the appointment with her finger pressed to her lips. That is by no means an unusual gesture for people who find themselves in a situation where the best they can think of is to make arrangements to see Nero Wolfe.

With Mrs. Barry Rackham the shushing finger was only figurative, since she made the date speaking to me on the phone. It was in her voice, low and jerky, and also in the way she kept telling me how confidential it was, even after I solemnly assured her that we rarely notified the press when someone requested an appointment on business. At the end she told me once more that she would have preferred to speak to Mr. Wolfe himself, and I hung up and decided it rated a discreet routine check on a prospective client, starting with Mr. Mitchell at the bank and Lon Cohen at the *Gazette*. On the main point of interest; could she and did she pay her bills, the news was favorable: she was worth a good four million and maybe five. Calling it four, and assuming that Wolfe's bill for services rendered would come to only half of it, that would be enough to pay my current salary—

as Wolfe's secretary, trusted assistant, and official gnat—for a hundred and sixty-seven years; and in addition to that, living as I did there in Wolfe's house, I also got food and shelter. So I was fixed for life if it turned out that she needed two million bucks' worth of detective work.

She might have at that, judging from the way she looked and acted at 11:05 the next morning, Friday, when the doorbell rang and I went to let her in. There was a man on the stoop with her, and after glancing quickly east and then west she brushed past him and darted inside, grabbed my sleeve, and told me in a loud whisper, "You're not Nero Wolfe!"

Instantly she released me, seized the elbow of her companion to hurry him across the sill, and whispered at him explosively, "Come in and shut the door!" You might have thought she was a duchess diving into a hock shop.

Not that she was my idea of a duchess physically. As I attended to the door and got the man's hat and topcoat hung on the rack, I took them in. She was a paradox—bony from the neck up and ample from the neck down. On her chin and jawbone and cheekbone the skin was stretched tight, but alongside her mouth and nose were tangles of wrinkles.

As I helped her off with her fur coat I told her, "Look, Mrs. Rackham. You came to consult Nero Wolfe, huh?"

"Yes," she whispered. She nodded and said right out loud, "Of course."

"Then you ought to stop trembling if you can. It makes Mr. Wolfe uneasy when a woman trembles because he thinks she's going to be hysterical, and he might not listen to you. Take a deep breath and try to stop."

"You were trembling all the way down here in the car," the man said in a mild baritone.

"I was not!" she snapped. That settled, she turned to me. "This is my cousin, Calvin Leeds. He didn't want me to come here, but I brought him along anyhow. Where's Mr. Wolfe?"

I indicated the door to the office, went and opened it, and ushered them in.

I have never figured out Wolfe's grounds for deciding whether or not to get to his feet when a woman enters his office. If they're objective they're too complicated for me, and if they're subjective, I wouldn't know where to start. This time he kept his seat behind his desk in the corner near a window, merely nodding and murmuring when I pronounced names. I thought for a second that Mrs. Rackham was standing gazing at him in reproach for his bad manners, but then I saw it was just surprised disbelief that he could be that big and fat. I'm so used to the quantity of him that I'm apt to forget how he must impress people seeing him for the first time.

He aimed a thumb at the red leather chair beyond the end of his desk and muttered at her, "Sit down, madam."

She went and sat. I then did likewise, at my own desk, not far from Wolfe's and at right angles to it. Calvin Leeds, the cousin, had sat twice, first on the couch toward the rear and then on a chair which I moved up for him. I would have guessed that both he and Mrs. Rackham had first seen the light about the same time as the twentieth century, but he could have been a little older. He had a lot of weather in his face with its tough-looking hide, his hair had been brown but was now more gray, and with his medium size and weight he looked and moved as if all his inside springs were still sound and lively. He had taken Wolfe in, and the surroundings too, and now his eyes were on his cousin.

Mrs. Rackham spoke to Wolfe. "You couldn't very well go around finding out things. Could you?"

"I don't know," he said politely. "I haven't tried for years, and I don't intend to. Others go around for me." He gestured at me. "Mr. Goodwin, of course, and others as required. You need someone to go around?"

"Yes." She paused. Her mouth worked. "I think I do. Provided it can be done safely—I mean, without anyone knowing about it." Her mouth worked some more. "I am bitterly ashamed—having at my age, for the first time in my life—having to go to a private detective with my personal affairs."

"Then you shouldn't have come," Leeds said mildly.

"Then you have come too soon," Wolfe told her.

"Too soon? Why?"

"You should have waited until it became so urgent or so intolerable that it would cause you no shame to ask for help, especially for one as expensive as me." He shook his head. "Too soon. Come back if and when you must."

"Hear that, Sarah?" Leeds asked, but not rubbing it in.

Ignoring him, she leaned forward and blurted at Wolfe, "No, I'm here now. I have to know! I have to know about my husband!"

Wolfe's head jerked around to me, to give me a look intended to scorch. But I met his eye and told him emphatically, "No, sir. If it is, she fibbed. I told her we wouldn't touch divorce or separation evidence, and she said it wasn't."

He left me and demanded, "Do you want your husband followed?"

"I—I don't know. I don't think so—"

"Do you suspect him of infidelity?"

"No! I don't!"

Wolfe grunted, leaned back in his chair, squirmed to get comfortable, and muttered, "Tell me about it."

Mrs. Rackham's jaw started to quiver. She looked at Leeds. His brows went up, and he shook his head, not as a negative apparently, but merely leaving it to her. Wolfe let out a grunt. She moved her eyes to him and said plaintively, "I'm neurotic."

"I am not," Wolfe snapped, "a psychiatrist. I doubt if—"

She cut him off. "I've been neurotic as long as I can remember. I had no brother or sister and my mother died when I was three, and my father didn't enjoy my company because I was ugly. When he died —I was twenty then—I cried all during the funeral service, not because he was dead but because I knew he wouldn't have wanted me so close to him all that time—in the church and driving to the cemetery and there at the grave."

Her jaw started to quiver again, but she clamped it and got control. "I'm telling you this because it's no secret anyway, and I want you to understand why I must have help. I have never been sure exactly why my first husband married me, because he had money of his own and didn't really need mine, but it wasn't long until he hated looking at me just as my father had. So I—"

"That isn't true, Sarah," Calvin Leeds objected. "You imagined—"

"Bosh!" she quashed him. "I'm not that neurotic! So I got a divorce with his consent and gratitude, I think, though he was too polite to say so, and I hurried it through because I didn't want him to know I was pregnant. Soon after the divorce my son was born, and that made complications, but I kept him—I kept him and he was mine until he went to war. He never showed the slightest sign of feeling about my looks the way my father and my husband had. He was never embarrassed about me. He liked being with me. Didn't he, Calvin?"

"Of course he did," Leeds assured her, apparently meaning it.

She nodded and looked thoughtful, looking into space and seeing something not there. She jerked herself impatiently back to Wolfe. "I admit that before he went away to war, he got married, and he married a very beautiful girl. It is not true that I wished he had taken one who resembled me, even a little bit, but naturally I couldn't help but see that he had gone to the other extreme. Annabel is very beautiful. It made me proud for my son to have her— it seemed to even my score with all the beautiful women I had known and seen. She thinks I hate her, but that is not true. People as neurotic as I am should not be judged by normal standards. Not that I blame Annabel, for I know perfectly well that when the news came that he had been killed in Germany her loss was greater than mine. He wasn't mine any longer then, he was hers."

"Excuse me," Wolfe put in politely but firmly. "You wanted to consult me about your husband. You say you're divorced?"

"Certainly not! I—" She caught herself up. "Oh. This is my second husband. I only wanted you to understand."

"I'll try. Let's have him now."

"Barry Rackham," she said, pronouncing the name as if she held a copyright on it, or at least a lease on subsidiary rights. "He played football at Yale and then had a job in Wall Street until the war came. At the end of the war he was a major, which wasn't very far to get in nearly four years. We were married in 1946—three years and seven months ago. He is ten years younger than I am."

Mrs. Barry Rackham paused, her eyes fixed on Wolfe's face as if challenging it for comment, but the challenge was declined. Wolfe merely prodded her with a murmur.

"And?"

"I suppose," she said as if conceding a point, "there is no one in New York who does not take it for granted that he married me simply for my money. They all know more about it than I do, because I have never asked him, and he is the only one that knows for sure. I know one thing: it does not make him uncomfortable to look at me, I know that for sure because I'm very sensitive about it, I'm neurotic about it, and I would know it the first second he felt that way. Of course he knows what I look like, he knows how ugly I am, he can't help that, but it doesn't annoy him a particle, not even—"

She stopped and was blushing. Calvin Leeds coughed and shifted in his chair. Wolfe closed his eyes and after a moment opened them again. I didn't look away from her because when she blushed I began to feel a little uncomfortable myself, and I wanted to see if I could keep her from knowing it.

But she wasn't interested in me. "Anyway," she went on as the color began to leave, "I have kept things in my own hands. We live in my house, of course, town and country, and I pay everything, and

there are the cars and so on, but I made no settle-
ment and arranged no allowance for him. That didn't
seem to me to be the way to handle it. When he
needed cash for anything he asked for it and I gave it
to him freely, without asking questions." She made a
little gesture, a flip of a hand. "Not always, but
nearly always. The second year it was more than the
first, and the third year more again, and I felt he was
getting unreasonable. Three times I gave him less
than he asked for, quite a lot less, and once I refused
altogether—I still asked no questions, but he told me
why he needed it and tried to persuade me; he was
very nice about it, and I refused. I felt that I must
draw the line somewhere. Do you want to know the
amounts?"

"Not urgently," Wolfe muttered.

"The last time, the time I refused, it was fifteen
thousand dollars." She leaned forward. "And that
was the last time. It was seven months ago, October
second, and he has not asked for money since, not
once! But he spends a great deal, more than for-
merly. For all sorts of things—just last week he gave
a dinner, quite expensive, for thirty-eight men at the
University Club. I have to know where he gets it. I
decided that some time ago—two months ago—and I
didn't know what to do. I didn't want to speak to my
lawyer or banker about a thing like this, or in fact
anybody, and I couldn't do it myself, so I asked my
cousin, Calvin Leeds." She sent him a glance. "He
said he would try to find out something, but he
hasn't."

We looked at Leeds. He upturned a palm.

"Well," he said, half apology and half protest, "I'm
no trained detective. I asked him straight, and he
just laughed at me. You didn't want anyone else to

get a hint of it, that you were curious about money he wasn't getting from you, so I was pretty limited in my asking around. I did my best, Sarah, you know I did."

"It seems to me," Wolfe told her, "that Mr. Leeds had one good idea—asking him. Have you tried that yourself?"

"Certainly. Long ago. He told me that an investment he had made was doing well."

"Maybe it was. Why not?"

"Not with my husband." She was positive. "I know how he is with money. It isn't in him to make an investment. Another thing: he is away more now. I don't know where he is as much as I used to. I don't mean weeks or even days, just an afternoon or evening—and several times he has had an appointment that he couldn't break when I wanted him to—"

Wolfe grunted, and she was at him. "I know! You think I feel that I've bought him and I own him! That's not it at all! All I really want is to be like a wife, just any wife—not beautiful and not ugly, not rich and not poor—just a wife! And hasn't a wife a right to know the source of her husband's income— isn't it her *duty* to know? If you had a wife wouldn't you *want* her to know?"

Wolfe made a face. "I can tell you, madam, what I *don't* want. I don't want this job. I think you're gulling me. You suspect that your husband is swindling you, either emotionally or financially, and you want me to catch him at it." He turned to me. "Archie. You'll have to change that formula. Hereafter, when a request comes for an appointment, do not say merely that we will not undertake to get divorce or separation evidence. Make it clear that we will not engage to expose a husband for a wife, or a wife for a

husband, under any camouflage. May I ask what you
are doing, Mrs. Rackham?"

She had opened her brown leather handbag and
taken out a checkfold and a little gold fountain pen.
Resting the checkfold on the bag, she was writing in
it with the pen. Wolfe's question got no reply until
she had finished writing, torn out the check, returned
the fold and pen to the bag, and snapped the bag
shut. Then she looked at him.

"I don't want you to expose my husband, Mr.
Wolfe." She was holding the check with her thumb
and fingertip. "God knows I don't! I just want to
know. You're not ugly and afraid and neurotic like
me, you're big and handsome and successful and not
afraid of anything. When I knew I had to have help
and my cousin couldn't do it, and I wouldn't go to
anyone I knew, I went about it very carefully. I
found out all about you, and no one knows I did, or at
least why I did. If my husband is doing something
that will hurt me that will be the end; but I don't
want to expose him, I just have to know. You are the
greatest detective on earth, and you're an honest
man. I just want to pay you for finding out where
and how my husband is getting money, that's all. You
can't possibly say you won't do it. Not possibly!"

She left her chair and went to put the check on
his desk in front of him. "It's for ten thousand dollars, but that doesn't mean I think that's enough.
Whatever you say. But don't you dare say I want to
expose him! My God—expose him?"

She had my sympathy up to a point, but what
stuck out was her basic assumption that rich people
can always get anything they want just by putting
up the dough. That's enough to give an honest work-
ingman, like a private detective for instance, a pain

in three places. The assumption is of course sound in some cases, but what rich people are apt not to understand is that there are important exceptions.

This, however, was not one of them, and I hoped Wolfe would see that it wasn't. He did. He didn't want to, but the bank account had by no means fully recovered from the awful blow of March fifteenth, only three weeks back, and he knew it. He came forward in his chair for a glance at the check, caught my eye and saw how I felt about it, heaved a sigh, and spoke.

"Your notebook, Archie. Confound it."

Chapter 2

The following morning, Saturday, I was in the office typing the final report on a case which I will not identify by name because it was never allowed to get within a mile of a newspaper or a microphone. We were committed on Mrs. Rackham's job, since I had deposited her check Friday afternoon, but no move had been made yet, not even a phone call to any of the names she had given us, because it was Wolfe's idea that first of all we must have a look at him. With Wolfe's settled policy of never leaving his house on business, and with no plausible excuse for getting Barry Rackham to the office, I would have to do the looking, and that had been arranged for.

Mrs. Rackham had insisted that her husband must positively not know or even suspect that he was being investigated, and neither must anyone else, so the arrangements for the look were a little complicated. She vetoed my suggestion that I should be invited to join a small week-end gathering at her country home in Westchester, on the ground that someone would probably recognize the Archie Goodwin who worked for Nero Wolfe. It was Calvin Leeds who offered an amendment that was adopted. He had a little place of his own at the edge of her estate, where he raised dogs, called Hillside Kennels. A month ago one of his valuable dogs had been poisoned, and I was to go there Saturday afternoon as myself, a detective named Archie Goodwin, to investigate the poisoning. His cousin would invite him to her place, Birchvale, for dinner, and I would go along.

It was a quiet Saturday morning in the office, with Wolfe up in the plant rooms as usual from nine to eleven, and I finished typing the report of a certain case with no interruptions except a couple of phone calls which I handled myself, and one for which I had to give Wolfe a buzz—from somebody at Mummiani's on Fulton Street to say that they had just got eight pounds of fresh sausage from Bill Darst at Hackettstown, and Wolfe could have half of it. Since Wolfe regards Darst as the best sausage maker west of Cherbourg, he asked that it be sent immediately by messenger, and for heaven's sake not with dry ice.

When, at 11:01, the sound of Wolfe's elevator came, I got the big dictionary in front of me on my desk, opened to H, and was bent over it as he entered the office, crossed to his oversized custom-built chair, and sat. He didn't bite at once because his mind was elsewhere. Even before he rang for beer he asked, "Has the sausage come?"

Without looking up I told him no.

He pressed the button twice—the beer signal—leaned back, and frowned at me. I didn't see the frown, absorbed as I was in the dictionary, but it was in his tone of voice.

"What are you looking up?" he demanded.

"Oh, just a word," I said casually. "Checking up on our client. I thought she was illiterate, her calling you handsome—remember? But, by gum, it was merely an understatement. Here it is, absolutely kosher: 'Handsome: moderately large.' For example it gives 'a handsome sum of money.' So she was dead right, you're a handsome detective, meaning a moderately large detective." I closed the dictionary and returned it to its place, remarking cheerfully, "Live and learn!"

It was a dud. Ordinarily that would have started him tossing phrases and adjectives, but he was occupied. Maybe he didn't even hear me. When Fritz came from the kitchen with the beer, Wolfe, taking from a drawer the gold bottle opener that a pleased client had given him, spoke.

"Fritz, good news. We're getting some of Mr. Darst's sausage—four pounds."

Fritz let his eyes gleam. "Ha! Today?"

"Any moment." Wolfe poured beer. "That raises the question of cloves again. What do you think?"

"I'm against it," Fritz said firmly.

Wolfe nodded. "I think I agree. I *think* I do. You may remember what Marko Vukcic said last year—and by the way, he must be invited for a taste of this. For Monday luncheon?"

"That would be possible," Fritz conceded, "but we have arranged for shad with roe—"

"Of course." Wolfe lifted his glass and drank, put it down empty, and used his handkerchief on his lips. That, he thought, was the only way for a man to scent a handkerchief. "We'll have Marko for the sausage at Monday dinner, followed by duck Mondor." He leaned forward and wiggled a finger. "Now about the shallots and fresh thyme: there's no use depending on Mr. Colson. We might get diddled again. Archie will have to go—"

At that point Archie had to go answer the doorbell, which I was glad to do. I fully appreciate, mostly anyhow, the results of Wolfe's and Fritz's powwows on grub when it arrives at the table, but the gab often strikes me as overdone. So I didn't mind the call to the hall and the front door. There I found a young man with a pug nose and a package, wearing a cap that said, "Fleet Messenger Service." I signed the slip, shut the door, started back down the hall, and was met not only by Fritz but by Wolfe too, who can move well enough when there's something he thinks is worth moving for. He took the package from me and headed for the kitchen, followed by Fritz and me.

The small carton was sealed with tape. In the kitchen Wolfe put it on the long table, reached to the rack for a knife, cut the tape, and pulled the flaps up. My reflexes are quick, and the instant the hissing noise started I grabbed Wolfe's arm to haul him back, yelling at Fritz, "Watch out! Drop!"

Wolfe can move all right, considering what he has to move. He and I were through the open door into the hall before the explosion came, and Fritz came bounding after, pulling the door with him. We all kept going, along the short stretch of hall to the office door, and into the office. There we stopped dead. No explosion yet.

"Come back here!" Wolfe commanded.

"Be quiet," I commanded back, and dropped to my hands and knees and made it into the hall. There I stopped to sniff, crawled to within a yard of the crack under the kitchen door, and sniffed again.

I arose, returned to the office on my feet, and told

them, "Gas. Tear gas, I think. The hissing has stopped."

Wolfe snorted.

"No sausage," Fritz said grimly.

"If it had been a trigger job on a grenade," I told him, "there would have been plenty of sausage. Not for us, of us. Now it's merely a damn nuisance. You'd better sit here and chat a while."

I marched to the hall and shut the door behind me, went and opened the front door wide, came back and stood at the kitchen door and took a full breath, opened the door, raced through and opened the back door into the courtyard, ran back again to the front. Even there the air current was too gassy for comfort, so I moved out to the stoop. I had been there only a moment when I heard my name called.

"Archie!"

I turned. Wolfe's head with its big oblong face was protruding from a window of the front room.

"Yes, sir," I said brightly.

"Who brought that package?"

I told him Fleet Messenger Service.

When the breeze through the hall had cleared the air I returned to the kitchen and Fritz joined me. We gave the package a look and found it was quite simple: a metal cylinder with a valve, with a brass rod that had been adjusted so that when the package was opened so was the valve. There was still a strong smell, close up, and Fritz took it to the basement. I went to the office and found Wolfe behind his desk, busy at the phone.

I dropped into my chair and dabbed at my runny eyes with my handkerchief. When he hung up I asked, "Any luck?"

"I didn't expect any," he growled.

"Right. Shall I call a cop?"

"No."

I nodded. "The question was rhetorical." I dabbed at my eyes some more, and blew my nose. "Nero Wolfe does not call cops. Nero Wolfe opens his own packages of sausage and makes his own enemies bite the dust." I blew my nose again. "Nero Wolfe is a man who will go far if he opens one package too many. Nero Wolfe has never—"

"The question was not rhetorical," Wolfe said rudely. "That is not what rhetorical means."

"No? I asked it. I meant it to be rhetorical. Can you prove that I don't know what rhetorical means?" I blew my nose. "When you ask me a question, which God knows is often, do I assume—"

The phone rang. One of the million things I do to earn my salary is to answer it, so I did. And then a funny thing happened. There is absolutely no question that it was a shock to me to hear that voice, I know that, because I felt it in my stomach. But partly what makes a shock a shock is that it is unexpected, and I do not think the sound of that voice in my ear was unexpected. I think that Wolfe and I had been sitting there talking just to hear ourselves because we both expected, after what had happened, to hear that voice sooner or later—and probably sooner.

What it said was only, "May I speak to Mr. Wolfe, please?"

I felt it in my stomach, sharp and strong, but damned if I was going to let him know it. I said, but not cordially, "Oh, hello there, if I get you. Was your name Duncan once?"

"Yes. Mr. Wolfe, please."

"Hold the wire." I covered the transmitter and told Wolfe, "Whosis."

"Who?" he demanded.

"You know who from my face. Mr. X. Mr. Z. Him."

With his lips pressed tight, Wolfe reached for his phone. "This is Nero Wolfe."

"How do you do, Mr. Wolfe." I was staying on, and the hard, cold, precise voice sounded exactly as it had the four previous times I had heard it, over a period of three years. It pronounced all its syllables clearly and smoothly. "Do you know who I am?"

"Yes." Wolfe was curt. "What do you want?"

"I want to call your attention to my forbearance. That little package could have been something really destructive, but I preferred only to give you notice. As I told you about a year ago, it's a more interesting world with you in it."

"I find it so," Wolfe said dryly.

"No doubt. Besides, I haven't forgotten your brilliant exposure of the murderer of Louis Rony. It happened then that your interest ran with mine. But it doesn't now, with Mrs. Barry Rackham, and that won't do. Because of my regard for you, I don't want you to lose a fee. Return her money and withdraw, and two months from today I shall send you ten thousand dollars in cash. Twice previously you have disregarded similar requests from me, and circumstances saved you. I advise strongly against a repetition. You will have to understand—"

Wolfe took the phone from his ear and placed it on the cradle. Since the effect of that would be lost if my line stayed open, I did likewise, practically simultaneously.

"By God, we're off again," I began. "Of all the rotten—"

"Shut up," Wolfe growled.

I obeyed. He rested his elbows on his chair arms, interlaced his fingers in front of where he was roundest, and gazed at a corner of his desk blotter. I did not, as a matter of fact, have anything to say except that it was a lousy break, and that didn't need saying. Wolfe had once ordered me to forget that I had ever heard the name Arnold Zeck, but whether I called him Zeck or Whosis or X, he was still the man who, some ten months ago, had arranged for two guys with an SM and a tommy gun to open up on Wolfe's plant rooms from a roof across the street, thereby ruining ten thousand dollars' worth of glass and equipment and turning eight thousand valuable orchid plants into a good start on a compost heap. That had been intended just for a warning.

Now he was telling us to lay off of Barry Rackham. That probably meant that without turning a finger we had found the answer to Mrs. Rackham's question—where was her husband getting his pocket money? He had got inside the circle of Arnold Zeck's operations, about which Wolfe had once remarked that all of them were illegal and some of them were morally repulsive. And Zeck didn't want any snooping around one of his men. That was almost certainly the sketch, but whether it was or not, the fact remained that we had run smack into Zeck again, which was fully as bad as having a gob of Darst sausage turn into a cylinder of tear gas.

"He likes to time things right, damn him," I complained. "He likes to make things dramatic. He had someone within range of this house to see the package being delivered, and when I left the front door

open and then went and stood on the stoop that
showed that the package had been opened, and as
soon as he got the word he phoned. Hell, he might
even—"

I stopped because I saw that I was talking to myself. Wolfe wasn't hearing me. He still sat gazing at
the corner of the blotter. I shut my trap and sat and
gazed at him. It was a good five minutes before he
spoke.

"Archie," he said, looking at me.

"Yes, sir."

"How many cases have we handled since last
July?"

"All kinds? Everything? Oh, forty."

"I would have thought more. Very well, say forty.
We crossed this man's path inadvertently two years
ago, and again last year. He and I both deal with
crime, and his net is spread wide, so that may be
taken as a reasonable expectation for the future:
once a year, or in one out of forty cases that come to
us, we will run into him. This episode will be repeated." He aimed a thumb at the phone. "That thing
will ring, and that confounded voice will presume to
dictate to us. If we obey the dictate we will be main-
taining this office and our means of livelihood only by
his sufferance. If we defy it we shall be constantly in
a state of trepidant vigilance, and one or both of us
will probably get killed. Well?"

I shook my head. "It couldn't be made plainer. I
don't care much for either one."

"Neither do I."

"If you got killed I'd be out of a job, and if I got
killed you might as well retire." I glanced at my
wristwatch. "The hell of it is we haven't got a week
to decide. It's twelve-twenty, and I'm expected at

the Hillside Kennels at three o'clock, and I have to eat lunch and shave and change my clothes. That is, if I go. If I go?"

"Precisely," Wolfe sighed. "That's point two. Two years ago, in the Orchard case, I took to myself the responsibility of ignoring this man's threat. Last year, in the Kane case, I did the same. This time I don't want to and I won't. Basic policy is my affair, I know that, but I am not going to tell you that in order to earn your pay you must go up there today and look at Mr. Rackham. If you prefer, you may phone and postpone it, and we'll consider the matter at greater length."

I had my brows raised at him. "I'll be damned. Put it on me, huh?"

"Yes. My nerve is gone. If public servants and other respected citizens take orders from this man, why shouldn't I?"

"You damn faker," I said indulgently. "You know perfectly well that I would rather eat soap than have you think I would knuckle under to that son of a bitch, and I know that you would rather put horse-radish on oysters than have me think you would. I might if you didn't know about it, and you might if I didn't know about it, but as it is we're stuck."

Wolfe sighed again, deeper. "I take it that you're going?"

"I am. But under one condition, that the trepidant vigilance begins as of now. That you call Fritz in, and Theodore down from the plant rooms, and tell them what we're up against, and the chain bolts are to be kept constantly on both doors, and you keep away from windows, and nothing and no one is to be allowed to enter when I'm not here."

"Good heavens," he objected sourly, "that's no way to live."

"You can't tell till you try it. In ten years you may like it fine." I buzzed the plant rooms on the house phone to get Theodore.

Wolfe sat scowling at me.

Chapter 3

When, swinging the car off the Taconic State Parkway to hit Route 100, my dash clock said only 2:40, I decided to make a little detour. It would be only a couple of miles out of my way. So at Pines Bridge I turned right, instead of left across the bridge. It wouldn't serve my purpose to make for the entrance to the estate where EASTCREST was carved on the great stone pillar, since all I would see there was a driveway curving up through the woods, and I turned off a mile short of that to climb a bumpy road up a hill. At the top the road went straight for a stretch between meadows, and I eased the car off onto the grass, stopped, and took the binoculars and aimed them at the summit of the next hill, somewhat higher than the one I was on, where the roof and upper walls of a stone mansion showed above the trees. Now, in early April, with no leaves yet, and with binoculars, I could see most of the mansion and even something of the surrounding grounds, and a couple of men moving about.

That was Eastcrest, the legal residence of the illegal Arnold Zeck—but of course there are many ways of being illegal. One is to drive through a red

light. Another is to break laws by proxy only, for
money only, get your cut so it can't be traced, and
never try to buy a man too cheap. That was what
Zeck had been doing for more than twenty years—
and there was Eastcrest.

All I was after was to take a look, just case it
from a hilltop. I had never seen Zeck, and as far as I
knew Wolfe hadn't either. Now that we were headed
at him for the third time, and this time it might be
for keeps, I thought I should at least see his roof and
count his chimneys. That was all. He had been too
damn remote and mysterious. Now I knew he had
four chimneys, and that the one on the south wing
had two loose bricks.

I turned the car around and headed down the hill,
and, if you care to believe it, I kept glancing in the
mirror to see if something showed up behind. That
was how far gone I was on Zeck. It was not healthy
for my self-respect, it was bad for my nerves, and I
was good and tired of it.

Mrs. Rackham's place, Birchvale, was only five
miles from there, the other side of Mount Kisco, but I
made a wrong turn and didn't arrive until a quarter
past three. The entrance to her estate was adequate
but not imposing. I went on by, and before I knew it
there was a neat little sign on the left:

HILLSIDE KENNELS
Doberman Pinschers

The gate opening was narrow and so was the
drive, and I kept going on past the house to a bare
rectangle in the rear, not very well graveled, and
maneuvered into a corner close to a wooden building.
As I climbed out a voice came from somewhere, and

then a ferocious wild beast leaped from behind a bush and started for me like a streak of lightning. I froze except for my right arm, which sent my hand to my shoulder holster automatically.

A female voice sounded sharp in command. "Back!"

The beast, ten paces from me, whirled on a dime, trotted swiftly to the woman who had appeared at the edge of the rectangle, whirled again and stood facing me, concentrating with all its might on looking beautiful and dangerous. I could have plugged it with pleasure. I do not like dogs that assume you're guilty until you prove you're innocent. I like democratic dogs.

A man had appeared beside the woman. They advanced.

She spoke. "Mr. Goodwin? Mr. Leeds had to go on an errand, but he'll be back soon. I'm Annabel Frey." She came to me and offered a hand, and I took it.

This was my first check on an item of information furnished us by Mrs. Rackham, and I gave her an A for accuracy. She had said that her daughter-in-law was very beautiful. Some might have been inclined to argue it, for instance those who don't like eyes so far apart or those who prefer pink skin to dark, but I'm not so finicky about details. The man stepped up, and she pronounced his name, Hammond, and we shook. He was a stocky middle-aged specimen in a bright blue shirt, a tan jacket, and gray slacks—a hell of a combination. I was wearing a mixed tweed made by Fradick, with an off-white shirt and a maroon tie.

"I'll sit in my car," I told them, "to wait for Mr. Leeds. With the livestock around loose like that."

She laughed. "Duke isn't loose, he's with me. He wouldn't have touched you. He would have stopped three paces off, springing distance, and waited for me. Don't you like dogs?"

"It depends on the dog. You might as well ask if I like lemon pie. With a dog who thinks of space between him and me only in terms of springing distance, my attitude is strictly one of trepidant vigilance."

"My Lord." She blinked long lashes over dark blue eyes. "Do you always talk like that?" The eyes went to Hammond. "Did you get that, Dana?"

"I quite agree with him," Hammond declared, "as you know. I'm not afraid to say so, either, because it shows the lengths I'll go to, to be with you. When you opened his kennel and he leaped out I could feel my hair standing up."

"I know," Annabel Frey said scornfully. "Duke knows too. I guess I'd better put him in." She left us, speaking to the dog, who abandoned his pose and trotted to her, and they disappeared around a corner of the building. There was a similarity in the movements of the two, muscular and sure and quick, but sort of nervous and dainty.

"Now we can relax," I told Hammond.

"I just can't help it," he said, irritated. "I'm not strong for dogs anyhow, and with these . . ." He shrugged. "I'd just as soon go for a walk with a tiger."

Soon Annabel rejoined us, with a crack about Hammond's hair. I suggested that if they had something to do I could wait for Leeds without any help, but she said no.

"We only came to see you," she stated impersonally. "That is, I did, and Mr. Hammond went to the length of coming along. Just to see you, even if you are Archie Goodwin, I wouldn't cross the street; but

I want to watch you work. So many things fall short of the build-up, I want to see if a famous detective does. I'm skeptical already. You look younger than you should, and you dress too well, and if you really thought that dog might jump you, you should have done something to—where did that come from? Hey!"

Sometimes I fumble a little drawing from my armpit, but that time it had been slick and clean. I had the barrel pointed straight up. Hammond had made a noise and an involuntary backward jerk.

I grinned at her. "Showing off. Okay? Want to try it? Get him and send him out from behind that same bush, with orders to take me, and any amount up to two bits, even, that he won't reach me." I returned the gun to the holster. "Ready?"

She blinked. "You mean you *would?*"

Hammond giggled. He was a full-sized middle-aged man and he looked like a banker, and I want to be fair to him, but he giggled. "Look out, Annabel," he said warningly. "He might."

"Of course," I told her, "you would be in the line of fire, and I've never shot a fast-moving dog, so we would both be taking a risk. Only I don't like you being skeptical. Stick around and you'll see."

That was a mistake, caused by my temperament. It is natural and wholesome for a man of my age to enjoy association with a woman of her age, maid, wife, or widow, but I should have had sense enough to stop to realize what I was getting in for. She had said that she had come to watch me work, and there I was asking for it. As a result, I had to spend a solid hour pretending that I was hell bent to find out who had poisoned one of Leeds' dogs when I didn't care a hang. Not that I love dog-poisoners, but that wasn't what was on my mind.

When Calvin Leeds showed up, as he did soon in an old station wagon with its rear taken up with a big wire cage, the four of us made a tour of the kennels and the runs, with Leeds briefing me, and me asking questions and making notes, and then we went in the house and extended the inquiry to aspects such as the poison used, the method employed, the known suspects, and so on. It was a strain. I had to make it good, because that was what I was supposed to be there for, and also because Annabel was too good-looking to let her be skeptical about me. And the dog hadn't even died! He was alive and well. But I went to it as if it were the biggest case of the year for Nero Wolfe and me, and Leeds got a good fifty bucks' worth of detection for nothing. Of course nobody got detected, but I asked damn good questions.

After Annabel and Hammond left to return to Birchvale next door, I asked Leeds about Hammond, and sure enough he was a banker. He was a vice-president of the Metropolitan Trust Company, who handled affairs for Mrs. Rackham—had done so ever since the death of her first husband. When I remarked that Hammond seemed to have it in mind to handle Mrs. Rackham's daughter-in-law also, Leeds said he hadn't noticed. I asked who else would be there at dinner.

"You and me," Leeds said. He was sipping a highball, taking his time with it. We were in the little living room of his little house, about which there was nothing remarkable except the dozens of pictures of dogs on the walls. Moving around outside, there had been more spring to him than to lots of guys half his age; now he was sprawled on a couch, all loose. I was reminded of one of the dogs we had come upon during our tour, lying in the sun at the door of its kennel.

"You and me," he said, "and my cousin and her husband, and Mrs. Frey, whom you have met, and Hammond, and the statesman, that's seven—"

"Who's the statesman?"

"Oliver A. Pierce."

"I'm intimate with lots of statesmen, but I never heard of him."

"Don't let him know it." Leeds chuckled. "It's true that at thirty-four he has only got as far as state assemblyman, but the war made a gap for him the same as for other young men. Give him a chance. One will be enough."

"What is he, a friend of the family?"

"No, and that's one on him." He chuckled again. "When he was first seen here, last summer, he came as a guest of Mrs. Frey—that is, invited by her—but before long either she had seen enough of him or he had seen enough of her. Meanwhile, however, he had seen Lina Darrow, and he was caught anyhow."

"Who's Lina Darrow?"

"My cousin's secretary—by the way, she'll be at dinner too, that'll make eight. I don't know who invited him—my cousin perhaps—but it's Miss Darrow that gets him here, a busy statesman." Leeds snorted. "At his age he might know better."

"You don't think much of women, huh?"

"I don't think of them at all. Much or little." Leeds finished his drink. "Look at it. Which would you rather live with, those wonderful animals out there, or a woman?"

"A woman," I said firmly. "I haven't run across

her yet, there are so many, but even if she does turn out to be a dog I hope to God it won't be one of yours. I want the kind I can let run loose." I waved a hand. "Forget it. You like 'em, you can have 'em. Mrs. Frey is a member of the household, is she?"

"Yes," he said shortly.

"Mrs. Rackham keeping her around as a souvenir of her dead son? Being neurotic about it?"

"I don't know. Ask her." Leeds straightened up and got to his feet. "You know, of course, that I didn't approve of her going to Nero Wolfe. I went with her only because she insisted on it. I don't see how any good can come of it, but I think harm might. I don't think you ought to be here, but you are, and we might as well go on over and drink their liquor instead of mine. I'll go and wash up."

He left me.

Chapter 4

Having been given by Leeds my choice of driving over—three minutes—or taking a trail through the woods, I voted for walking. The edge of the woods was only a hundred yards to the rear of the kennels. It had been a warm day for early April, but now, with the sun gone over the hill, the sharp air made me want to step it up, which was just as well because I had to, to keep up with Leeds. He walked as if he meant it. When I commented on the fact that we ran into no fence anywhere, neither in the woods nor in the clear, he said that his place was merely a little corner of Mrs. Rackham's property which she had let him build on some years ago.

The last stretch of our walk was along a curving gravel path that wound through lawns, shrubs, trees, and different-shaped patches of bare earth. Living in the country would be more convenient if they would repeal the law against paths that go straight from one place to another place. The bigger and showier the grounds are, the more the paths have to curve, and the main reason for having lots of bushes and things is to compel the paths to curve in order to get through the mess. Anyhow, Leeds and I finally got to the house, and entered without ringing or knocking, so apparently he was more or less a member of the household too.

All six of them were gathered in a room that was longer and wider than Leeds' whole house, with twenty rugs to slide on and at least forty different things to sit on, but it didn't seem as if they had worked up much gaiety, in spite of the full stock of the portable bar, because Leeds and I were greeted as though nothing so nice had happened in years. Leeds introduced me, since I wasn't supposed to have met Mrs. Rackham, and after I had been supplied with liquid, Annabel Frey gave a lecture on how I worked. Then Oliver A. Pierce, the statesman, wanted me to demonstrate by grilling each of them as suspected dog poisoners. When I tried to beg off they insisted, so I obliged. I was only so-so.

Pierce was a smooth article. His manner was, of course, based on the law of nature regulating the attitude of an elected person toward everybody old enough to vote, but his timing and variations were so good that it was hard to recognize it, although he was only about my age. He was also about my size, with broad shoulders and a homely honest face, and a draw on his smile as swift as a flash bulb. I made a note to look up whether I lived in his assembly district. If he got the breaks the only question about him was how far and how soon.

If in addition to his own equipment and talents he acquired Lina Darrow as a partner, it would probably be farther and sooner. She was, I would have guessed, slightly younger than Annabel Frey— twenty-six maybe—and I never saw a finer pair of eyes. She was obviously underplaying them, or rather what was back of them. When I was questioning her she pretended I had her in a corner, while her eyes gave it away that she could have waltzed all around me if she wanted to. I didn't know whether she thought she was kidding somebody, or was just practicing, or had some serious reason for passing herself off as a flub.

Barry Rackham had me stumped and also annoyed. Either I was dumber than Nero Wolfe thought I was, and twice as dumb as I thought I was, or he was smarter than he looked. New York was full of him, and he was full of New York. Go into any Madison Avenue bar between five and six-thirty and there would be six or eight of him there: not quite young but miles from being old; masculine all over except the fingernails; some tired and some fresh and ready, depending on the current status; and all slightly puffy below the eyes. I knew him from A to Z, or thought I did, but I couldn't make up my mind whether he knew what I was there for, and that was the one concrete thing I had hoped to get done. If he knew, the question whether he was on Zeck's payroll was answered; if he didn't, that question was still open.

And I still hadn't been able to decide when, at the dinner table, we had finished the dessert and got up to go elsewhere for coffee. At first I had thought he couldn't possibly be wise, when I had him sized up for a dummy who had had the good luck to catch Mrs. Rackham's eye somewhere and then had happened to take the only line she would fall for, but further observation had made me reconsider. His handling of his wife had character in it; it wasn't just yes or no. At the dinner table he had an exchange with Pierce about rent control, and without seeming to try he got the statesman so tangled up he couldn't wiggle loose. Then he had a good laugh, took the other side of the argument, and made a monkey out of Dana Hammond.

I decided I'd better start all over.

On the way back to the living room for coffee, Lina Darrow joined me. "Why did you take it out on me?" she demanded.

I said I didn't know I had.

"Certainly you did. Trying to indict me for dog poisoning. You went after me much harder than you did the others." Her fingers were on the inside of my arm, lightly.

"Certainly," I conceded. "Nothing new to you, was it? A man going after you harder than the others?"

"Thanks. But I mean it. Of course you know I'm just a working girl."

"Sure. That's why I was tougher with you. That, and because I wondered why you were playing dumb."

The statesman Pierce broke us up then, as we entered the living room, and I didn't fight for her. We collected in the neighborhood of the fireplace for coffee, and there was a good deal of talk about nothing, and after a while somebody suggested television, and Barry Rackham went and turned it on. He and Annabel turned out lights. As the rest of us got settled in favorably placed seats, Mrs. Rackham left us. A little later, as I sat in the semi-darkness scowling at a cosmetic commercial, some obscure sense told me that danger was approaching and I jerked my head around. It was right there at my elbow: a Doberman pinscher, looking larger than normal in that light, staring intently past me at the screen.

Mrs. Rackham, just behind it, apparently misinterpreting my quick movement, spoke hastily and loudly above the noise of the broadcast. "Don't try to pat him!"

"I won't," I said emphatically.

"He'll behave," she assured me. "He loves television." She went on with him, farther forward. As they passed Calvin Leeds the affectionate pet halted for a brief sniff, and got a stroke on the head in response. No one else was honored.

Ninety minutes of video got us to half-past ten, and got us nothing else, especially me. I was still on the fence about Barry Rackham. Television is raising hell with the detective business. It used to be that a social evening at someone's house or apartment was a fine opportunity for picking up lines and angles, moving around, watching and talking and listening; but with a television session you might as well be home in bed. You can't see faces, and if someone does make a remark you can't hear it unless it's a scream, and you can't even start a private inquiry, such as finding out where a young widow stands now on skepticism. In a movie theater at least you can hold hands.

However, I did finally get what might have been a nibble. The screen had been turned off, and we had all got up to stretch, and Annabel had offered to drive Leeds and me home, and Leeds had told her that we would rather walk, when Barry Rackham moseyed over to me and said he hoped the television hadn't bored me too much. I said no, just enough.

"Think you'll get anywhere on your job for Leeds?" he asked, jiggling his highball glass to make the ice tinkle.

I lifted my shoulders and let them drop. "I don't know. A month's gone by."

He nodded. "That's what makes it hard to believe."

"Yeah, why?"

"That he would wait a month and then decide to blow himself to a fee for Nero Wolfe. Everybody knows that Wolfe comes high. I wouldn't have thought Leeds could afford it." Rackham smiled at me. "Driving back tonight?"

"No, I'm staying over."

"That's sensible. Night driving is dangerous, I think. The Sunday traffic won't be bad this time of year if you leave early." He touched my chest with a forefinger. "That's it, leave early." He moved off.

Annabel was yawning, and Dana Hammond was looking at her as if that was exactly what he had come to Birchvale for, to see her yawn. Lina Darrow was looking from Barry Rackham to me and back again, and pretending she wasn't looking anywhere with those eyes. The Doberman pinscher was standing tense, and Pierce, from a safe ten feet—one more than springing distance—was regarding it with an expression that gave me a more sympathetic feeling for him than I ever expected to have for a statesman.

Calvin Leeds and Mrs. Rackham were also looking at the dog, with a quite different expression.

"At least two pounds overweight," Leeds was saying. "You feed him too much."

Mrs. Rackham protested that she didn't.

"Then you don't run him enough."

"I know it," she admitted. "I will from now on, I'll be here more. I was busy today. I'll take him out now. It's a perfect night for a good walk—Barry, do you feel like walking?"

He didn't. He was nice about it, but he didn't. She broadened the invitation to take in the group, but there were no takers. She offered to walk Leeds and me home, but Leeds said she would go too slow, and he should have been in bed long ago since his rising time was six o'clock. He moved, and told me to come on if I was coming.

We said good night and left.

The outdoor air was sharper now. There were a few stars but no moon, and alone with no flashlight I would never have been able to keep that trail through the woods and might have made the Hillside Kennels clearing by dawn. For Leeds a flashlight would have been only a nuisance. He strode along at the same gait as in the daytime, and I stumbled at his heels, catching my toes on things, teetering on roots and pebbles, and once going clear down. I am not a deerstalker and don't want to be. As we approached the kennels Leeds called out, and the sound came of many movements, but not a bark. Who wants a dog, let alone thirty or forty, not even human enough to bark when you come home?

Leeds said that since the poisoning he always took a look around before going to bed, and I went on in the house and up to the little room where I had put my bag. I was sitting on the bed in pajamas, scratching the side of my neck and considering Barry Rackham's last-minute remarks, when Leeds entered downstairs and came up to ask if I was comfortable. I told him I soon would be, and he said good night and went down the short hall to his room.

I opened a window, turned out the light, and got into bed; but in three minutes I saw it wasn't working. My practice is to empty my head simultaneously with dropping it on the pillow. If something sticks and doesn't want to come out I'll give it up to three minutes but no more. Then I act. This time, of course, it was Barry Rackham that stuck. I had to decide that he knew what I was there for or that he didn't, or, as an alternative, decide definitely that I wouldn't try to decide until tomorrow. I got out of bed and went and sat on a chair.

It may have taken five minutes, or it could have been fifteen; I don't know. Anyhow it didn't accomplish anything except getting Rackham unstuck from my head for the night, for the best I could do was decide for postponement. If he had his guard up, so far I had not got past it. With that settled, I got under the covers again, took ten seconds to get into position on a strange mattress, and was off this time. . . .

Nearly, but not quite. A shutter or something began to squeak. Calling it a shutter jerked me back part way, because there were no shutters on the windows, so it couldn't be that. I was now enough awake to argue. The sound continued, at brief intervals. It not only wasn't a shutter, it wasn't a squeak. Then it was a baby whining; but it wasn't, because it came from the open window, and there were no babies out there. To hell with it. I turned over, putting my back to the window, but the sound still came, and I had been wrong. It was more of a whimper than a whine. Oh, nuts.

I rolled out of bed, switched on a light, went down the hall to Leeds' door, knocked on it, and opened it.

"Well?" he asked, full voice.

"Have you got a dog that whimpers at night?"

"Whimpers? No."

"Then shall I go see what it is? I hear it through my window."

"It's probably—turn on the light, will you?"

I found the wall switch and flipped it. His pajamas were green with thin white stripes. Giving me a look which implied that here was one more reason for disapproving of my being there, he padded past me into the hall and on into my room, me following. He stood a moment to listen, crossed and stuck his head out the window, pulled it in again, and this time went by me with no look at all and moving fast. I followed him downstairs and to the side door, where he pushed a light switch with one hand while he opened the door with the other, and stepped across the sill.

"By God," he said. "All right, Nobby, all right."

He squatted.

I take back none of my remarks about Doberman pinschers, but I admit that that was no time to expand on them, nor did I feel like it. The dog lay on its side on the slab of stone with its legs twitching, trying to lift its head enough to look at Leeds; and from its side that was up, toward the belly and midway between the front and hind legs, protruded the chased silver handle of a knife. The hair around was matted with blood.

The dog had stopped whimpering. Now suddenly it bared its teeth and snarled, but weakly.

"All right, Nobby," Leeds said. He had his palm against the side, forward, over the heart.

"He's about gone," he said.

I discovered that I was shivering, decided to stop, and did.

"Pull the knife out of him?" I suggested. "Maybe—"

"No. That would finish him. I think he's finished anyhow."

He was. The dog died as Leeds squatted there and I stood not permitting myself to shiver in the cold night breeze. I could see the slender muscular legs stretch tight and then go loose, and after another minute Leeds took his hand away and stood up.

"Will you please hold the door open?" he asked. "It's off plumb and swings shut."

I obliged, holding it wide and standing aside to let him through. With the dog's body in his arms, he crossed to a wooden bench at one side of the little square hall and put the burden down. Then he turned to me. "I'm going to put something on and go out and look around. Come or stay, suit yourself."

"I'll come. Is it one of your dogs? Or—"

He had started for the stairs, but halted. "No. Sarah's—my cousin's. He was there tonight, you saw him." His face twitched. "By God, look at him! Getting here with that knife in him! I gave him to her two years ago; he's been her dog for two years, but when it came to this it was me he came to. By God!"

He went for the stairs and up, and I followed. Over the years there have been several occasions when I needed to get some clothes on without delay, and I thought I was fast, but I was still in my room with a shoe to lace when Leeds' steps were in the hall again and he called in to me, "Wait downstairs. I'll be back in a minute."

I called that I was coming, but he didn't halt. By the time I got down to the little square hall he was gone, and the outside door was shut. I opened it and stepped out and yelled, "Hey, Leeds!"

His voice came from somewhere in the darkness. "I said wait!"

Even if he had decided not to bother with me there was no use trying to dash after him, with my handicap, so I settled for making my way around the corner of the house and across the graveled rectangle to where my car was parked. Getting the door unlocked, I climbed in and got the flashlight from the dash compartment. That put me, if not even with Leeds for a night outdoors in the country, at least a lot closer to him. Relocking the car door, I sent the beam of the flash around and then switched it off and went back to the side door of the house.

I could hear steps, faint, then louder, and soon Leeds appeared within the area of light from the hall's window. He wasn't alone. With him was a dog, a length ahead of him, on a leash. As they approached I courteously stepped aside, but the dog ignored me completely. Leeds opened the door and they entered the hall, and I joined them.

"Get in front of her," Leeds said, "a yard off, and stand still."

I obeyed, circling.

"See, Hebe."

For the first time the beast admitted I was there. She lifted her head at me, then stepped forward and smelled my pants legs, not in haste. When she had finished Leeds crossed to where the dead dog lay on the bench, made a sign, and Hebe went to him.

Leeds passed his fingertips along the dead dog's belly, touching lightly the smooth short hair. "Take it, Hebe."

She stretched her sinewy neck, sniffed along the course his fingertips had taken, backed up a step, and looked up at him.

"Don't be so damn sure," Leeds told her. He pointed a finger. "Take it again."

She did so, taking more time for it, and again looked up at him.

"I didn't know they were hounds," I remarked.

"They're everything they ought to be." I suppose

Leeds made some signal, though I didn't see it, and the dog started toward the door, with her master at the other end of the leash. "They have excellent scent, and this one's extraordinary. She's Nobby's mother."

Outside, on the slab of stone where we had found Nobby, Leeds said, "Take it, Hebe," and when she made a low noise in her throat as she tightened the leash, he added, "Quiet, now. I'll do the talking."

She took him, with me at their heels, around the corner of the house to the graveled space, across that, along the wall of the main outbuilding, and to a corner of the enclosed run. There she stopped and lifted her head.

Leeds waited half a minute before he spoke. "Bah. Can't you tell dogs apart? Take it!"

I switched the flashlight on, got a reprimand, and switched it off. Hebe made her throat noise again, got her nose down, and started off. We crossed the meadow on the trail to the edge of the woods and kept going. The pace was steady but not fast; for me it was an easy stroll, nothing like the race Leeds had led me previously. Even with no leaves on the trees it was a lot darker there, but unless my sense of direction was completely cockeyed we were sticking to the trail I had been over twice before.

"We're heading straight for the house, aren't we?" I asked.

For reply I got only a grunt.

For the first two hundred yards or so after entering the woods it was a steady climb, not steep, and then a leveling off for another couple hundred of yards to the start of the easy long descent to the edge of the Birchvale manicured grounds. It was at about the middle of the level stretch that Hebe suddenly went crazy. She dashed abruptly to one side, off the trail, jerking Leeds so that he had to dance to keep his feet, then whirled and came back into him, with a high thin quavering noise not at all like what she had said before.

Leeds spoke to her sharply, but I don't know what he said. By then my eyes had got pretty well accommodated to the circumstances. However, I am not saying that there in the dark among the trees, at a distance of twenty feet, I recognized the blob on the ground. I do assert that at the instant I pressed the button of the flashlight, before the light came, I knew already that it was the body of Mrs. Barry Rackham.

This time I got no reprimand. Leeds was with me as I stepped off the trail and covered the twenty feet. She was lying on her side, as Nobby had been, but her neck was twisted so that her face was nearly upturned to the sky, and I thought for a second it was a broken neck until I saw the blood on the front of her white sweater. I stooped and got my fingers on her wrist. Leeds picked up a dead leaf, laid it on her mouth and nostrils, and asked me to kneel to help him keep the breeze away.

When we had gazed at the motionless leaf for twenty seconds he said, "She's dead."

"Yeah." I stood up. "Even if she weren't, she would be by the time we got her to the house. I'll go—"

"She is dead, isn't she?"

"Certainly. I'll—"

"By God." He got erect, coming up straight in one movement. "Nobby and now her. You stay here—" He took a quick step, but I caught his arm. He jerked loose, violently.

I said fast, "Take it easy." I got his arm again, and he was trembling. "You bust in there and there's no telling what you'll do. Stay here and I'll go—"

He pulled free and started off.

"Wait!" I commanded, and he halted. "But first get a doctor and call the police. Do that first. I'm going to your place. We left that knife in the dog, and someone might want it. Can't you put Hebe on guard here?"

He spoke, not to me but to Hebe. She came to him, a darting shadow, close to him. He leaned over to touch the shoulder of the body of Mrs. Barry Rackham and said, "Watch it, Hebe." The dog moved alongside the body, and Leeds, with nothing to say to me, went. He didn't leap or run, but he sure was gone. I called after him, "Phone the police before you kill anybody!" stepped to the trail, and headed for Hillside Kennels.

With the flashlight I had no trouble finding my way. This time, as I approached, the livestock barked plenty, and, hoping the kennel doors were all closed tight, I had my gun out as I passed the runs and the buildings. Nothing attacked me but noise, and that stopped when I had entered the house and closed the door. Apparently if an enemy once got inside it was then up to the master.

Nobby was still there on the bench, and the knife was still in him. With only a glance at him in passing, I made for the little living room, where I had previously seen a phone on a table, turned on a light, went to the phone, and got the operator and gave her a number. As I waited a look at my wristwatch showed me five minutes past midnight. I hoped Wolfe hadn't forgotten to plug in the line to his room when he went up to bed. He hadn't. After the ring signal had come five times I had his voice.

"Nero Wolfe speaking."

"Archie. Sorry to wake you up, but I need orders. We're minus a client. Mrs. Rackham. This is a quick guess, but it looks as if someone stabbed her with a knife and then stuck the knife in a dog. Anyhow, she's dead. I've just—"

"What is this?" It was almost a bellow. "Flummery?"

"No, sir. I've just come from where she's lying in the woods. Leeds and I found her. The dog's dead too, here on a bench. I don't—"

"Archie!"

"Yes, sir."

"This is insupportable, under the circumstances."

"Yes, sir, all of that."

"Is Mr. Rackham out of it?"

"Not as far as I know. I told you we just found her."

"Where are you?"

"At Leeds' place, alone. I'm here guarding the knife in the dog. Leeds went to Birchvale to get a doctor and the cops and maybe to kill somebody. I can't help it. I've got all the time in the world. How much do you want?"

"Anything that might help."

"Okay, but in case I get interrupted here's a question first. On two counts, because I'm here working for you and because I helped find the body, they're going to be damn curious. How much do I spill? There's no one on this line unless the operator's listening in."

A grunt and a pause. "On what I know now, everything about Mrs. Rackham's talk with me and the purpose of your trip there. About Mrs. Rackham and Mr. Leeds and what you have seen and heard there, everything. But you will of course confine yourself strictly to that."

"Nothing about sausage?"

"Absolutely nothing. The question is idiotic."

"Yeah, I just asked. Okay. Well, I got here and met dogs and people. Leeds' place is on a corner of Mrs. Rackham's property, and we walked through the woods for dinner at Birchvale. There were eight of us at dinner. . . ."

I'm fairly good with a billiard cue, and only Saul Panzer can beat me at tailing a man or woman in New York, but what I am best at is reporting a complicated event to Nero Wolfe. With, I figured, a probable maximum of ten minutes for it, I covered all the essentials in eight, leaving him two for questions. He had some, of course. But I think he had the picture well enough to sleep on when I saw the light of a car through the window, told him good-by, and hung up. I stepped from the living room into the little hall, opened the outside door, and was standing on the stone slab as a car with STATE POLICE painted on it came down the narrow drive and stopped. Two uniformed public servants piled out and made for me. I only hoped neither of them was my pet Westchester hate, Lieutenant Con Noonan, and had my hope granted. They were both rank-and-file.

One of them spoke. "Your name Goodwin?"

I conceded it. Dogs had started to bark.

"After finding a dead body you went off and came here to rest your feet?"

"I didn't find the body. A dog did. As for my feet, do you mind stepping inside?"

I held the door open, and they crossed the threshold. With a thumb I called their attention to Nobby, on the bench.

"That's another dog. It had just crawled here to die, there on the doorstep. It struck me that Mrs. Rackham might have been killed with that knife before it was used on the dog, and that you guys would be interested in the knife as is, before somebody took it to slice bread with, for instance. So when Leeds went to the house to phone I came here. I have no corns."

One of them had stepped to the bench to look down at Nobby. He asked, "Have you touched the knife?"

"No."

"Was Leeds here with you?"

"Yes."

"Did he touch the knife?"

"I don't think so. If he did I didn't see him."

The cop turned to his colleague. "We won't move it, not now. You'd better stick here. Right?"

"Right."

"You'll be getting word. Come along, Goodwin."

He marched to the door and opened it and let me pass through first. Outdoors he crossed to his car, got in behind the wheel, and told me, "Hop in."

I stood. "Where to?"

"Where I'm going."

"I'm sorry," I said regretfully, "but I like to know where. If it's White Plains or a barracks, I would need a different kind of invitation. Either that or physical help."

"Oh, you're a lawyer."

"No, but I know a lawyer."

"Congratulations." He leaned toward me and

spoke through his nose. "Mr. Goodwin, I'm driving to Mrs. Rackham's house, Birchvale. Would you care to join me?"

"I'd love to, thanks so much," I said warmly and climbed in.

Chapter 5

The rest of that night, more than six hours, from half-past midnight until well after sunrise, I might as well have been in bed asleep for all I got out of it. I learned only one thing, that the sun rises on April ninth at 5:39, and even that wasn't reliable because I didn't know whether it was a true horizon.

Lieutenant Con Noonan was at Birchvale, among others, but his style was cramped.

Even after the arrival of District Attorney Cleveland Archer himself, the atmosphere was not one of singleminded devotion to the service of justice. Not that they weren't all for justice, but they had to keep it in perspective, and that's not so easy when a prominent wealthy taxpayer like Mrs. Barry Rackham has been murdered and your brief list of suspects includes (a) her husband, now a widower, who may himself now be a prominent wealthy taxpayer, (b) an able young politician who has been elected to the state assembly, (c) the dead woman's daughter-in-law, who may possibly be more of a prominent wealthy taxpayer than the widower, and (d) a vice-president of a billion-dollar New York bank. They're

all part of the perspective, though you wish to God
they weren't so you could concentrate on the other
three suspects: (e) the dead woman's cousin, a
breeder of dogs which don't make friends, (f) her secretary, a mere employee, and (g) a private dick from
New York whose tongue has needed bobbing for
some time. With a setup like that you can't just take
them all down to White Plains and tell the boys to
start chipping and save the pieces.

Except for fifteen minutes alone with Con
Noonan, I spent the first two hours in the big living
room where we had looked at television, having for
company the members of the family, the guests, five
members of the domestic staff, and two or more of-
ficers of the law. It wasn't a bit jolly. Two of the female servants wept intermittently. Barry Rackham
walked up and down, sitting occasionally and then
starting up again, speaking to no one. Oliver Pierce
and Lina Darrow sat on a couch conversing in under-
tones, spasmodically, with him doing most of the
talking. Dana Hammond, the banker, was jumpy.
Mostly he sat slumped, with his chin down and his
eyes closed, but now and then he would arise slowly
as if something hurt and go to say something to one
of the others, usually Annabel or Leeds. Leeds had
been getting a blaze started in the fireplace when I
was ushered in, and it continued to be his chief concern. He got the fire so hot that Annabel moved
away, to the other side of the room. She was the
quietest of them, but from the way she kept her jaw
clamped I guessed that it wasn't because she was the
least moved.

One by one they were escorted from the room for
a private talk and brought back again. It was when
my turn came, not long after I had arrived, that I

found Lieutenant Noonan was around. He was in a smaller room down the hall, seated at a table, looking harassed. No doubt life was hard for him—born with the instincts of a Hitler or Stalin in a country where people are determined to do their own voting. The dick who took me in motioned me to a chair across the table.

"You again," Noonan said.

I nodded. "That's exactly what I was thinking. I haven't seen you since the time I didn't run my car over Louis Rony."

I didn't expect him to wince, and he didn't. "You're here investigating that dog poisoning at Hill-side Kennels."

I had no comment.

"Weren't you?" he snapped. "If you're answering questions."

"Oh, I beg your pardon. I didn't know it was a question. It sounded more like a statement."

"You are investigating the dog poisoning?"

"I started to. I spent an hour at it there with Leeds, before we came here to dinner."

"So he said. Make any progress?"

"Nothing remarkable. For one thing, I had kibitzers, which is no help. Mrs. Frey and Mr. Hammond."

"Did you all come over here together?"

"No. Leeds and I came about an hour after Mrs. Frey and Mr. Hammond left."

"Did you drive?"

"Walked. He walked and I ran."

"You ran? Why?"

"To keep up with him."

Noonan smiled. He has the meanest smile I know of except maybe Boris Karloff. "You get your comedy from the comics, don't you, Goodwin?"

"Yes, sir."

"Tell me about the dinner here and afterwards. Make it as funny as you can."

I took ten minutes for it, as much as I had had for Wolfe, but getting interrupted with questions. I stuck to facts and gave them to him straight. When we came to the end he went back and concentrated on whether all of them had heard Mrs. Rackham say she was going for a walk with the dog, as of course they had since she had issued a blanket invitation for company. Then I was sent back to the living room, and it was Lina Darrow's turn in the preliminaries. I wondered if she would play dumb with him as she had with me.

It was as empty a stretch of hours as I have ever spent. I might as well have been a housebroken dog; no one seemed to think I mattered, and I was not in a position to tell them how wrong they were. At one point I made a serious effort to get into a conversation, making the rounds and offering remarks, but got nowhere. Dana Hammond merely gave me a look, without opening his trap. Oliver Pierce didn't even look at me. Lina Darrow mumbled something and turned away. Calvin Leeds asked me what they had done with Nobby's remains, nodded and frowned at my answer, and went to put another log on the fire. Annabel Frey asked me if I wanted more coffee, and when I said yes apparently didn't hear me. Barry Rackham, whom I tackled at the far end of the room, was the most talkative. He wanted to know whether anyone had come from the District Attorney's office. I said I didn't know. He wanted to know the name of the cop in the other room who was asking questions, and I told him Lieutenant Con

Noonan. That was my longest conversation, two whole questions and answers.

I did get in one piece of detection, somewhat later, when finally District Attorney Cleveland Archer made an appearance. As he came into the room and made himself known and everybody moved to approach him, I took a look at his shoes and saw that he had undoubtedly been in the woods to inspect the spot where Mrs. Rackham's body was found. Likewise Ben Dykes, the dean of the Westchester County dicks, who was with him. That made me feel slightly better. It would have been a shame to stick there the whole night without detecting a single damn thing.

After a few preliminary words to individuals Archer spoke to them collectively. "This is a terrible thing, an awful thing. It is established that Mrs. Rackham was stabbed to death out there in the woods—and the dog that was with her. We have the knife that was used, as you know—it has been shown to you—one of the steak knives that are kept in a drawer here in the dining room—they were used by you at dinner last evening. We have statements from all of you, but of course I'll have to talk further with you. I won't try to do that now. It's after three o'clock, and I'll come back in the morning. I want to ask whether any of you has anything to say to me now, anything that shouldn't wait until then." His eyes went over them. "Anyone?"

No sound and no movement from any quarter. They sure were a chatty bunch. They just stood and stared at him, including me. I would have liked to relieve the tension with a remark or question, but didn't want to remind him that I was present.

However, he didn't need a reminder. After all the

others, including the servants, had cleared out, Leeds and I were moving toward the door when Ben Dykes' voice came. "Goodwin!"

Leeds kept going. I turned.

Dykes came to me. "We want to ask you something."

"Shoot."

District Attorney Archer joined us, saying, "In there with Noonan, Ben."

"Him and Noonan bring sparks," Dykes objected. "Remember last year at Sperling's?"

"I'll do the talking," Archer stated, and led the way to the hall and along to the smaller room where Noonan was still seated at the table, conferring with a colleague—the one who had brought me from Hillside Kennels. The colleague moved to stand against the wall. Noonan arose, but sat down again when Archer and Dykes and I had pulled chairs up.

Archer, slightly plumper than he had been a year ago, with his round red face saggy and careworn by the stress of an extremely bad night for him, put his forearms on the table and leaned at me.

"Goodwin," he said earnestly but not offensively, "I want to put something up to you."

"Suits me, Mr. Archer," I assured him. "I've never been ignored more."

"We've been busy. Lieutenant Noonan has of course reported what you told him. Frankly, I find it hard to believe. Almost impossible to believe. It is well known that Nero Wolfe refuses dozens of jobs every month, that he confines himself to cases that interest him, and that the easiest and quickest way to interest him is to offer him a large fee. Now I—"

"Not the only way," I objected.

"I didn't say it was. I know he has standards—

even scruples. Now I can't believe that he found anything interesting in the poisoning of a dog—certainly
not interesting enough for him to send you up here
over a weekend. And I doubt very much if Calvin
Leeds, from what I know of him, is in a position to
offer Wolfe a fee that would attract him. His cousin,
Mrs. Rackham, might have, but she did not have the
reputation of throwing money around carelessly—
rather the contrary. We're going to ask Wolfe about
this, naturally, but I thought I might save time by
putting it up to you. I appeal to you to cooperate
with us in solving this dastardly and cowardly murder. As you know, I have a right to insist on it; knowing you and Wolfe as I do, I prefer to appeal to you
as to a responsible citizen and a man who carries a
license to work in this state as a private detective. I
simply do not believe that you were sent up here
merely to investigate the poisoning of a dog."

They were all glaring at me.

"I wasn't," I said mildly.

"IIa, you weren't!"

"Hell, no. As you say, Mr. Wolfe wouldn't be interested."

"So you lied, you punk," Noonan gloated.

"Wrong, as usual." I grinned at him. "You didn't
ask me what I was sent here for or even hint that
you would like to know. You asked if I was investigating the dog poisoning, and I told you I spent an
hour at it, which I did. You asked if I had made any
progress, and I told you nothing remarkable. Then
you wanted to know what I had seen and heard here,
and I told you, in full. It was one of the bummest and
dumbest jobs of questioning I have ever run across,
but you may learn in time. The first—"

Noonan blurted, "Why, you goddam—"

"I'll handle it," Archer snapped at him. Back to me: "You might have supplied it, Goodwin."

"Not to him," I said firmly. "I tried supplying him once and he was displeased. Anyway, I doubt if he would have understood it."

"See if I can understand it."

"Yes, sir. Mrs. Rackham phoned Thursday afternoon and made an appointment to see Mr. Wolfe. She came yesterday morning—Friday—at eleven o'clock, and had Leeds with her. She said that it had been her custom, since marrying Rackham three years and seven months ago, to give him money for his personal use when he asked for it, but that he kept asking for bigger amounts, and she began giving him less than he asked for, and last October second he wanted fifteen grand, and she refused. Gave him zero. Since then, the past seven months, he had asked for none and got none, but in spite of that he had gone on spending plenty, and that was what was biting her. She hired Mr. Wolfe to find out where and how he was getting dough, and I was sent up here to look him over and possibly get hold of an idea. I needed an excuse for coming here, and the dog poisoning was better than average." I fluttered a hand. "That's all."

"You say Leeds was with her?" Noonan demanded.

"That's partly what I mean," I told Ben Dykes, "about Noonan's notion of how to ask questions. He must have heard me say she had Leeds along."

"Yeah," Dykes said dryly. "But don't be so damn cute. This is not exactly a picnic." He spoke to Noonan. "Leeds didn't make any mention of this?"

"He did not. Of course I didn't ask him."

Dykes stood up and asked Archer, "Hadn't I better send for him? He went home."

Archer nodded, and Dykes went. "Good God," Archer said with feeling, not to Noonan or me, so probably to the People of the State of New York. He sat biting his lip a while and then asked me, "Was that all Mrs. Rackham wanted?"

"That's all she asked for."

"Had she quarreled with her husband? Had he threatened her?"

"She didn't say so."

"Exactly what did she say?"

That took half an hour. For me it was simple, since all I had to use was my memory, in view of the instructions from Wolfe to give them everything but the sausage. Archer didn't know what my memory is capable of, so I didn't repeat any of Mrs. Rackham's speeches verbatim, though I could have, because he would have thought I was dressing it up. But when I was through he had it all.

Then I was permitted to stay for the session with Leeds, who had arrived early in my recital but had been held outside until I was done. At last I was one of the party, but too late to hear anything that I didn't already know. With Leeds, who was practically one of the family, they had to cover not only his visit with his cousin to Wolfe's office, but also the preliminaries to it, so he took another half-hour more. He himself had no idea, he said, where Rackham had been getting money. He had learned nothing from the personal inquiry he had undertaken at his cousin's request. He had never heard, or heard of, any serious quarrel between his cousin and her husband. And so on. As for his failure to tell Noonan of the visit to Wolfe's office and the real reason for

my presence at Birchvale, he merely said calmly that
Noonan hadn't asked and he preferred to wait until
he was asked.

District Attorney Archer finally called it a night,
got up and stretched, rubbed his eyes with his fingertips, asked Dykes and Noonan some questions and
issued some orders, and addressed me. "You're staying at Leeds' place?"

I said I hadn't stayed there much so far, but my
bag was there.

"All right. I'll want you tomorrow—today."

I said of course and went out with Leeds. Ben
Dykes offered to give us a lift, but we declined.

Together, without conversation, Leeds and I
made for the head of the trail at the edge of the
woods, giving the curving paths a miss. Dawn had
come and was going; it was getting close to sunrise.
The breeze was down and the birds were up, telling
about it. The pace Leeds set, up the long easy slope
and down the level stretch, was not quite up to his
previous performances, which suited me fine. I was
not in a racing mood, even to get to a bed.

Suddenly Leeds halted, and I came abreast of
him. In the trail, thirty paces ahead, a man was getting up from his hands and knees to face us. He
called, "Hold it! Who are you?"

We told him.

"Well," he said, "you'll have to keep off this section of trail. Go around. We're just starting on it.
Bright and early."

We asked how far, and he said about three hundred yards, to where a man had started at the other
end. We stepped off the trail, to the right into the
rough, and got slowed down, though the woods were
fairly clean. After a couple of minutes of that I asked

Leeds if he would know the spot, and he said he would.

Soon he stopped, and I joined him. I would have known it myself, with the help of a rope they had stretched from tree to tree, making a large semicircle. We went up to the rope and stood looking.

"Where's Hebe?" I asked.

"They had to come for me to get her. She's in Nobby's kennel. He won't be needing it. They took him away."

We agreed, without putting it in words, that there was nothing there we wanted, and resumed our way through the woods, keeping off the trail until we reached the scientist at the far end of the forbidden section, who not only challenged us but had to be persuaded that we weren't a pair of bloodthirsty liars. Finally he was bighearted enough to let us go on.

I was glad they had taken Nobby away, not caring much for another view of the little hall with that canine corpse on the bench. Otherwise the house was as before. Leeds had stopped at the kennels. I went up to my room and was peeling off the pants I had pulled on over my pajamas when I was startled by a sudden dazzling blaze at the window. I crossed to it and stuck my head out: it was the sun showing off, trying to scare somebody. I glanced at my wrist and saw 5:39, but as I said, maybe it wasn't a true horizon. Not lowering the window shade, I went and stretched out on the bed and yawned as far down as it could go.

The door downstairs opened and shut, and there were steps on the stairs. Leeds appeared at my open door, stepped inside, and said, "I'll have to be up and around in an hour, so I'll close your door."

I thanked him. He didn't move.

"My cousin paid Mr. Wolfe ten thousand dollars. What will he do now?"

"I don't know, I haven't asked him. Why?"

"It occurred to me that he might want to spend it, or part of it, in her interest. In case the police don't make any headway."

"He might," I agreed. "I'll suggest it to him."

He still stood, as if there was something else on his mind. There was, and he unloaded it.

"It happens in the best families," he stated distinctly and backed out, taking the door with him.

I closed my eyes but made no effort to empty my head. If I went to sleep there was no telling when I would wake up, and I intended to phone Wolfe at eight, fifteen minutes before the scheduled hour for Fritz to get to his room with his breakfast tray. Meanwhile I would think of something brilliant to do or to suggest. The trouble with that, I discovered after some poking around, was that I had no in. Nobody would speak to me except Leeds, and he was far from loquacious.

I have a way of realizing all of a sudden, as I suppose a lot of people do, that I made a decision some time back without knowing it. It happened that morning at 6:25. Looking at my watch and seeing that that was where it had got to, I was suddenly aware that I was staying awake, not so I could phone Wolfe at eight o'clock, but so I could beat it the hell out of there as soon as I was sure Leeds was asleep; and I was now as sure as I would ever be.

I got up and shed my pajamas and dressed, not trying to set a record but wasting no time, and, with my bag in one hand and my shoes in the other, tiptoed to the hall, down the stairs, and out to the stone slab. While it wasn't Calvin Leeds I was escaping from, I thought it desirable to get out of Westchester County before anyone knew I wasn't upstairs asleep. Not a chance. I was seated on the stone slab tying the lace of the second shoe when a dog barked, and that was a signal for all the others. I scrambled up, grabbed the bag, ran to the car and unlocked it and climbed in, started the engine, swung around the graveled space, and passed the house on my way out just as Leeds emerged through the side door. I stepped on the brake, stuck my head through the window, yelled at him, "Got an errand to do, see you later!" and rolled on through the gate and into the highway.

At that hour Sunday morning the roads were all mine, the bright new sun was at my left out of the way, and it would have been a pleasant drive if I had been in a mood to feel pleased. Which I wasn't. This was a totally different situation from the other two occasions when we had crossed Arnold Zeck's path and someone had got killed. Then the corpses had been Zeck's men, and Zeck, Wolfe, and the public interest had all been on the same side. This time Zeck's man, Barry Rackham, was the number one suspect, and Wolfe had either to return his dead client's ten grand, keep it without doing anything to earn it, or meet Zeck head on. Knowing Wolfe as I did, I hit eighty-five that morning rolling south on the Sawmill River Parkway.

The dash clock said 7:18 as I left the West Side Highway at Forty-sixth Street. I had to cross to Ninth Avenue to turn south. It was as empty as the country roads had been. Turning right on Thirty-fifth Street, I went on across Tenth Avenue, on nearly to

Eleventh, and pulled to the curb in front of Wolfe's old brownstone house.

Even before I killed the engine I saw something that made me goggle—a sight that had never greeted me before in the thousands of times I had braked a car to a stop there.

The front door was standing wide open.

Chapter 6

My heart came up. I swallowed it down, jumped out, ran across the sidewalk and up the seven steps to the stoop and on in. Fritz and Theodore were there in the hall, coming to me. Their faces were enough to make a guy's heart pop right out of his mouth.

"Airing the house?" I demanded.

"He's gone," Fritz said.

"Gone where?"

"I don't know. During the night. When I saw the door was open—"

"What's that in your hand?"

"He left them on the table in his room—for Theodore and me, and one for you—"

I snatched the pieces of paper from his trembling hand and looked at the one on top. The writing on it was Wolfe's.

> Dear Fritz:
> Marko Vukcic will want your services. He should pay you at least $2000 a month.
> My best regards. . . .
> Nero Wolfe

I looked at the next one.

Dear Theodore:
Mr. Hewitt will take the plants and will need your help with them. He should pay you around $200 weekly.

My regards. . . .
Nero Wolfe

I looked at the third one.

AG:
Do not look for me.

My very best regards and wishes. . . .
NW

I went through them again, watching each word, told Fritz and Theodore, "Come and sit down," went to the office, and sat at my desk. They moved chairs to face me.

"He's gone," Fritz said, trying to convince himself.

"So it seems," I said aggressively.

"You know where he is," Theodore told me accusingly. "It won't be easy to move some of the plants without damage. I don't like working on Long Island, not for two hundred dollars a week. When is he coming back?"

"Look, Theodore," I said, "I don't give a good goddam what you like or don't like. Mr. Wolfe has always pampered you because you're the best orchid nurse alive. This is as good a time as any to tell you that you remind me of sour milk. I do not know where Mr. Wolfe is nor if or when he's coming back.

To you he sent his regards. To me he sent his very best regards and wishes. Now shut up."

I shifted to Fritz. "He thinks Marko Vukcic should pay you twice as much as he does. That's like him, huh? You can see I'm sore as hell, his doing it like this, but I'm not surprised. To show you how well I know him, this is what happened: not long after I phoned him last night he simply wrote these notes to us and walked out of the house, leaving the door open—you said you found it open—to show anyone who might be curious that there was no longer anyone or anything of any importance inside. You got up at your usual time, six-thirty, saw the open door, went up to his room, found his bed empty and the notes on the table. After going up to the plant rooms to call Theodore, you returned to his room, looked around, and discovered that he had taken nothing with him. Then you and Theodore stared at each other until I arrived. Have you anything to add to that?"

"I don't want to work on Long Island," Theodore stated.

Fritz only said, "Find him, Archie."

"He told me not to."

"Yes—but find him! Where will he sleep? What will he eat?"

I got up and went to the safe and opened it, and looked in the cash drawer, where we always kept a supply for emergency expenses. There should have been a little over four thousand bucks; there was a little over a thousand. I closed the safe door and twirled the knob, and told Fritz, "He'll sleep and eat. Was my report accurate?"

"Not quite. One of his bags is gone, and pajamas,

toothbrush, razor, three shirts, and ten pairs of socks."

"Did he take a walking stick?"

"No. The old gray topcoat and the old gray hat."

"Were there any visitors?"

"No."

"Any phone calls besides mine?"

"I don't know about yours. His extension and mine were both plugged in, but you know I don't answer when you're out unless he tells me to. It rang only once, at eight minutes after twelve."

"Your clock's wrong. That was me. It was five after." I went and gave him a pat on the shoulder. "Okay. I hope you like your new job. How's chances for some breakfast?"

"But Archie! His breakfast . . ."

"I could eat that too. I drove forty miles on an empty stomach." I patted him again. "Look, Fritz. Right now I'm sore at him, damn sore. After some griddle cakes and broiled ham and eight or ten eggs in black butter and a quart of coffee, we'll see. I think I'll be even sorer than I am now, but we'll see. Is there any of his favorite honey left that you haven't been giving me lately? The thyme honey?"

"Yes—some. Four jars."

"Good. I'll finish off with that on a couple of hot cakes. Then we'll see how I feel."

"I would never have thought—" Fritz's voice had a quaver, and he stopped and started over again. "I would never have thought this could happen. What is it, Archie?" He was practically wailing. "What is it? His appetite has been good."

"We were going to repot some Miltonias today," Theodore said dismally.

I snorted. "Go ahead and pot 'em. He was no help

anyhow. Beat it and let me alone. I've got to think.
Also I'm hungry. Beat it!"

Theodore, mumbling, shuffled out. Fritz, following him, turned at the door. "That's it, Archie. Think.
Think where he is while I get your breakfast."

He left me, and I sat down at my desk to do the
thinking, but the cogs wouldn't catch. I was too mad
to think. "Don't look for me." That was him to a T.
He knew damn well that if I should ever come home
to find he had vanished, the one activity that would
make any sense at all would be to start looking for
him, and here I was stopped cold at the take-off. Not
that I had no notion at all. That was why I had left
Leeds' place without notice and stepped it up to
eighty-five getting back: I did have a notion. Two
years had passed since Wolfe had told me, "Archie,
you are to forget that you know that man's name. If
ever, in the course of my business, I find that I am
committed against him and must destroy him, I shall
leave this house, find a place where I can work—and
sleep and eat if there is time for it—and stay there
until I have finished."

So that part was okay, but what about me? On
another occasion, a year later, he had said to five
members of a family named Sperling, in my presence, "In that event he will know it is a mortal encounter, and so will I, and I shall move to a base of
operations which will be known only to Mr. Goodwin
and perhaps two others." Okay. There was no argument about the mortal encounter or about the move.
But I was the Mr. Goodwin referred to, and here I
was staring at it—"Don't look for me." Where did
that leave me? Certainly the two others he had had
in mind were Saul Panzer and Marko Vukcic, and I
didn't even dare to phone Saul and ask a couple of

discreet questions; and besides, if he had let Saul in and left me out, to hell with him. And what was I supposed to say to people—for instance, people like the District Attorney of Westchester County?

That particular question got answered, partly at least, from an unexpected quarter. When I had finished with the griddle cakes, ham, eggs, thyme honey, and coffee, I went back to the office to see if I was ready to quit feeling and settle down to thinking, and was working at it when I became aware that I was sitting in Wolfe's chair behind his desk. That brought me up with a jerk. No one else, including me, ever sat in that chair, but there I was. I didn't approve of it. It seemed to imply that Wolfe was through with that chair for good, and that was a hell of an attitude to take, no matter how sore I was. I opened a drawer of his desk to check its contents, pretending that was what I had sat there for, and was starting a careful survey when the doorbell rang.

Going to answer it, I took my time because I had done no thinking yet and therefore didn't know my lines. Seeing through the one-way glass panel in the front door that the man on the stoop was a civilian stranger, my first impulse was to let him ring until he got tired, but curiosity chased it away and I opened the door. He was just a citizen with big ears and an old topcoat, and he asked to see Mr. Nero Wolfe. I told him Mr. Wolfe wasn't available on Sundays, and I was his confidential assistant, and could I help. He thought maybe I could, took an envelope from a pocket, extracted a sheet of paper, and unfolded it.

"I'm from the *Gazette*," he stated. "This copy for

an ad we got in the mail this morning—we want to be sure it's authentic."

I took the paper and gave it a look. It was one of our large-sized letterheads, and the writing and printing on it were Wolfe's. At the top was written:

Display advertisement for Monday's *Gazette*, first section, two columns wide, depth as required. In thin type, not blatant. Send bill to above address.

Below the copy was printed by hand:

MR. NERO WOLFE
ANNOUNCES HIS RETIREMENT
FROM THE DETECTIVE BUSINESS
TODAY, APRIL 10, 1950

Mr. Wolfe will not hereafter be available. Inquiries from clients on unfinished matters may be made of Mr. Archie Goodwin. Inquiries from others than clients will not receive attention.

Beneath that was Wolfe's signature. It was authentic all right.

Having learned it by heart, I handed it back. "Yeah, that's okay. Sure. Give it a good spot."

"It's authentic?"

"Absolutely."

"Listen, I want to see him. Give me a break! Good spot hell; it's page one if I can get a story on it."

"Don't you believe your own ads? It says that Mr. Wolfe will not hereafter be available." I had the door swung to a narrow gap. "I never saw you before, but

Lon Cohen is an old friend of mine. He gets to work at noon, doesn't he?"

"Yes, but—"

"Tell him not to bother to phone about this. Mr. Wolfe is not available, and I'm reserved for clients, as the ad says. Watch your foot, here comes the door."

I shut it and put the chain bolt on. As I went back down the hall Fritz emerged from the kitchen and demanded, "Who was that?"

I eyed him. "You know damn well," I said, "that when Mr. Wolfe was here you would never have dreamed of asking who was that, either of him or of me. Don't dream of it now, anyway not when I'm in the humor I'm in at present."

"I only wanted—"

"Skip it. I advise you to steer clear of me until I've had a chance to think."

I went to the office and this time took my own chair. At least I had got some instructions from Wolfe, though his method of sending them was certainly roundabout. The ad meant, of course, that I wasn't to try to cover his absence; on the contrary. More important, it told me to lay off the Rackham thing. I was to handle inquiries from clients on unfinished matters, but only from clients; and since Mrs. Rackham, being dead, couldn't inquire, that settled that. Another thing—apparently I still had my job, unlike Fritz and Theodore. But I couldn't sign checks, I couldn't—suddenly I remembered something. The fact that I hadn't thought of it before indicates the state I was in. I have told, in my account of another case of Wolfe's, how, in anticipation of the possibility that some day a collision with Arnold Zeck would drive him into a foxhole, he had instructed me to put fifty thousand dollars in cash in a safe deposit box over in Jersey, and how I obeyed instructions. The idea was to have a source of supply for the foxhole; but anyway, there it was, fifty grand, in the box rented by me under the name I had selected for the purpose. I was sitting thinking how upset I must have been not to have thought of that before when the phone rang and I reached for it.

"Nero Wolfe's office, Archie Goodwin speaking."

I thought it proper to use that, the familiar routine, since according to Wolfe's ad he wouldn't retire until the next day.

"Archie?" A voice I knew sounded surprised. "Is that you, Archie?"

"Right. Hello, Marko. So early on Sunday?"

"But I thought you were away! I was going to give Fritz a message for you. From Nero."

Marko Vukcic, owner and operator of Rusterman's Restaurant, the only place where Wolfe really liked to eat except at home, was the only man in New York who called Wolfe by his first name. I told him I would be glad to take a message for myself.

"Not from Nero exactly," he said. "From me. I must see you as soon as possible. Could you come here?"

I said I could. There was no need to ask where, since the only place he could ever be found was the restaurant premises, either on one of the two floors for the public, in the kitchen, or up in his private quarters.

I told Fritz I was going out and would be back when he saw me.

As I drove crosstown and up to Fifty-fourth Street, I was around eighty per cent sure that within a few minutes I would be talking with Wolfe. For him it would be hard to beat that for a foxhole—the place that cooked and served the best food in America, with the living quarters of his best and oldest friend above it. Even after I had entered at the side door, as arranged, ascended the two flights of stairs, seen the look on Marko's face as he welcomed me, felt the tight clasp of his fingers as he took my hands in his, and heard his murmured, "My friend, my poor young friend!"—even then I thought he was only preparing dramatically to lead me to Wolfe in an inner room.

But he wasn't. All he led me to was a chair by a window. He took another one, facing me, and sat with his palms on his knees, his head cocked a little to one side as usual.

"My friend Archie," he said sympathetically. "It is my part to tell you exactly certain things. But before I do that I wish to tell you a thing of my own. I wish to remind you that I have known Nero a much longer time than you have. We knew each other as boys in another country—much younger than you were that day many years ago when you first saw him and went to work for him. He is my old and dear friend, and I am his. So it was natural that he should come to me last night."

"Sure," I agreed. "Why not?"

"You must feel no pique. No *courroux*."

"Okay. I'll fight it down. What time did he come?"

"At two o'clock in the night. He was here an hour, and then left. That I am to tell you, and these things. Do you want to write them down?"

"I can remember them if you can. Shoot."

Marko nodded. "I know of your great memory. Nero has often spoken of it." He shut his eyes and in a moment opened them again. "There are these five things. First, the plants. He telephoned Mr. Hewitt last night, and tomorrow Mr. Hewitt will arrange for the plants to be moved to his place, and also for Theodore to go there to work. Second—"

"Am I to list the plants? Do the records go too?"

"I don't know. I can say only what I was told to say. That's all about the plants. Perhaps Mr. Hewitt can tell you. Second, that is Fritz. He will work here, and I will pay him well. I will see him today and arrange the details. Of course he is unhappy?"

"He thinks Mr. Wolfe will starve to death."

"But naturally. If not that, something else. I have always thought it a folly for him to be a detective. Third—I am third. I have a power of attorney. Do you want to see it?"

"No, thanks, I'll take your word for it."

"It is in there locked up. Nero said it is legal, and he knows. I can sign checks for you. I can sign anything. I can do anything he could do."

"Within certain limits. You can't—" I waved a hand. "Forget it. Fourth?"

"Fourth is the house. I am to offer the house and its contents for sale. On that I have confidential instructions."

I goggled at him. "Sell the house *and* contents?"

"Yes. I have private instructions regarding price and terms."

"I don't believe it."

His shoulders went up and down. "I told Nero you would think I was lying."

"I don't think you're lying. I just don't believe it. Also the bed and other articles in my room are my property. Must I move them out today or can I wait until tomorrow?"

Marko made a noise that I think was meant for

sympathy. "My poor young friend," he said apologetically, "there is no hurry at all. Selling a house is not
like selling a lamb chop. You will, I suppose, continue
to live there for the present."

"Did he say I should?"

"No. But why shouldn't you? That is my own
thought, and it brings us to the fifth and last thing:
the instructions Nero gave me for you."

"Oh, he did. That was thoughtful. Such as?"

"You are to act in the light of experience as
guided by intelligence."

He stopped. I nodded. "That's a cinch, I always
do. And specifically?"

"That's all. Those are your instructions." Marko
upturned his palms. "That's all about everything."

"You call that instructions, do you?"

"I don't. He did." He leaned to me. "I told him,
Archie, that his conduct was inexcusable. He was
standing ready to leave, after telling me those five
things and no more. Having no reply, he turned and
went. Beyond that I know nothing, but nothing."

"Where he went? Where he is? No word for me at
all?"

"Nothing. Only what I have told you."

"Hell, he's gone batty, like lots of geniuses," I declared, and got up to go.

Chapter 7

I drove around for two solid hours, mostly in the park. Now and then, for a change of scene, I left the park for a patrol of the avenues.

I hadn't been able to start thinking in the house, and it might work better on the move. Moreover, I didn't want any more just then of Fritz or Theodore, or in fact of anybody but me. So, in the light of experience and guided by intelligence, I drove around. Somewhere along the way I saw clearly what my trouble was: I was completely out of errands for the first time in years. How could I decide what to do when I had nothing to do? I now believed that the reason I never drove farther north than One Hundred and Tenth Street, nor farther south than Fourteenth Street during those two hours, was that I thought Wolfe was probably somewhere within those limits and I didn't want to leave them.

When I did leave them it wasn't voluntary. Rolling down Second Avenue in the Seventies, I had stopped for a red light abreast of a police car on my left. Just as the light was changing, the cop on my side stuck his head out and called, "Pull over to the curb."

Flattered at the attention as any motorist would be, I obeyed. The police car came alongside, and the cop got out and invented another new phrase. "Let me see your license."

I got out and handed it to him, and he took a look.

"Yeah, I thought I recognized you." He handed the license back, walked around the front of my car to the other side, got in beside me, and suggested, "Let's go to the Nineteenth Precinct. Sixty-seventh east of Lexington."

"That's one idea," I admitted. "Or what's wrong with the Brooklyn Botanical Gardens, especially on Easter? I'll toss you for it."

He was unmoved. "Come on, Goodwin, come on. I know you're a card. I've heard all about you. Let's go."

"Give me one reason, good or bad. If you don't mind?"

"I don't know the reason. All I know is the word that came an hour ago, to pick you up and take you in. Maybe you shouldn't have left the infant on the church steps on Easter Day."

"Of course not," I agreed. "We'll go get it."

I eased away from the curb into traffic, with the police car trailing behind. Our destination, the Nineteenth Precinct Station, was not new to me. That was where I had once spent most of a night, conversing with Lieutenant Rowcliff, the Con Noonan of the New York Police Department.

After escorting me in to the desk and telling the sergeant about it, my captor had a point to make. His name was not John F. O'Brien, it was John R. O'Brien. He explained to the sergeant that he had to insist on it because last year one of his heroic acts had been credited to John F., and once was enough, and he damn well wanted credit for spotting a wanted man on the street. That attended to, he bade me a pleasant good-by and left. Meanwhile the sergeant was making a phone call. When he hung up he looked at me with a more active interest.

"Westchester wants you," he announced. "Leaving the scene of a crime and leaving jurisdiction. Want to drag it out?"

"It might be fun, but I doubt it. What happens if I don't?"

"There's a Westchester man downtown. He's on his way up here to take you."

I shook my head. "I'll fight like a cornered rat. I know fourteen lawyers all told. Ten to one he has no papers. This is one of those brotherly acts which I do not like. You're on a spot, Sergeant."

"Don't scare me to death. If he has no papers I'll send you downtown and let them handle it."

"Yeah," I admitted, "that would let you out. But we can make it simpler for both of us if you care to. Get the Westchester DA on the phone and let me talk to him. I'll even pay for the call."

At first he didn't like the idea and then he did. I think what changed his mind was the chance of picking up a piece of hot gossip on the murder of the month. He had to be persuaded, but when I told him the DA would be at the Rackham place and gave him the number, that settled it. He put the call in. However, he covered. When he got the number he made it clear that he merely wanted to offer the DA an opportunity to speak to Archie Goodwin if he wished to. He did. I circled the railing to get to the desk and took the phone.

"Mr. Archer?"

"Yes! This is—"

"Just a minute!" I said emphatically. "Whatever you were going to say this is, I double it. It's an outrage. It—"

"You were told to stay here, and you sneaked away! You left—"

"I was not told to stay there. You asked me if I was staying at Leeds' place, and I said my bag was there, and you said you would want me today, and I said of course. If I had stayed at Leeds' place I might have been permitted seven hours' sleep. I decided to do something else with the seven hours, and they're not up yet. But you see fit to ring the bell on me. I'll do one of two things. I'll have a bite of lunch and then drive up there, unaccompanied, or I'll make it as hard as I possibly can for this man you sent to get me outside the city limits—whichever you prefer. Here he comes now."

"Here who comes?"

"Your man. Coming in the door. If you decide you want to see me today, tell him not to trail along behind me. It makes me self-conscious."

A silence. Then, "You were told not to leave the county."

"I was not. By no one."

"Neither you nor Wolfe was at home at eleven o'clock—or if you were you wouldn't see my man."

"I was in the Easter parade."

Another silence, longer. "What time will you be here? At Birchvale."

"I can make it by two o'clock."

"My man is there?"

"Yes."

"Let me talk to him."

That was satisfactory. I liked that all right, except for one thing. After the Westchester dick was finished on the phone and it was settled that I would roll my own, and the sergeant had generously said that the Police Department would contribute the phone call, I asked the dick if he understood that I didn't care to be tailed, and he replied that I needn't worry because he was going back to Thirty-fifth Street to see Nero Wolfe. I didn't care much for that, but said nothing because I hadn't yet decided exactly what to say. So when I found a place on Lexington Avenue for a sandwich and a malted, I went first to a phone booth, called the house, and told Fritz to leave the chain bolt on, tell callers that Wolfe was out of the city and no more, and admit no one.

Being on the move did help. Having decided, while touring the park and avenues, what my immediate trouble was, I now, on my way to Birchvale, got the whole thing into focus. Considering the entire picture, including the detail of putting the house up for sale and the lack of even one little hint for me, let alone a blueprint, it was by no means a bet that Wolfe had merely dived into a foxhole. Look how free Marko had been with his poor-young-friending. It was not inconceivable that Wolfe had decided to chuck it for good. A hundred times and more, when things or people—frequently me—didn't suit him, he had told me about the house he owned in Egypt and how pleasant it would be to live there. I had always brushed it off. I now realized that a man who is eccentric enough to threaten to go and live in Egypt is eccentric enough to do it, especially when it gets to a point where he opens a package of sausage and has to run for his life.

Therefore I would be a dimwit to assume that this was merely time out to gather ammunition and make plans. Nor could I assume that it wasn't. I couldn't assume anything. Was he gone for good, or was he putting on a charade that would make all his other performances look like piker stuff in comparison? Presumably I was to answer that question, along with others, by the light of experience guided by intelligence, and I did not appreciate the compliment. If I was finally and permanently on my own, very well; I would make out. But apparently I was still drawing pay, so what? The result of my getting the whole picture into focus was that as I turned in at the entrance to Birchvale I was sorer than ever.

I was stopped at the entrance by one of Noonan's colleagues, there on guard, and was allowed to proceed up the curving drive only after I had shown him four documents. Parking in a space at the side of the house that was bordered by evergreens, I walked around to the front door and was admitted by a maid who looked pale and puffy. She didn't say anything, just held the door open, but a man was there too, one of the county boys whom I knew by sight but not by name. He said, "This way," and led me to the right, to the same small room I had seen before.

Ben Dykes, sitting there at the table with a stack of papers, grunted at me, "So you finally got here."

"I told Archer two o'clock. It's one-fifty-eight."

"Uh-huh. Sit down."

I sat. The door was standing open, but no sound of any kind came to my ears except the rustling of the papers Dykes was going through.

"Is the case solved?" I inquired courteously. "It's so damn quiet. In New York they make more noise. If you—"

I stopped because I was being answered. A typewriter started clicking somewhere. It was faint, from a distance, but unmistakably a typewriter, with a professional at it.

"I suppose Archer knows I'm here," I stated.

"Don't work up a lather," Dykes advised me without looking up.

I shrugged, stretched my legs and crossed my ankles, and tried to see what his papers were. I was too far away to get any words, but from various aspects I finally concluded that they were typewritten signed statements of the family, guests, and servants. Not being otherwise engaged at the moment, I would have been glad to help Dykes with them, but I doubted if it was worth the breath to make an offer. After the strain of trying to identify the papers, my eyes went shut, and for the first time I was aware how sleepy I was. I thought I had better open my eyes, and then decided it would show more strength of will if I kept awake with them shut. . . .

Someone was using my head for a cocktail shaker. Resenting it, I jerked away and made a gesture of protest with my fist closed, following up by opening my eyes and jumping to my feet. Backing away from me was a skinny guy with a long neck. He looked both startled and angry.

"Sorry," I told him. "I guess I dozed off a second."

"You dozed off forty minutes," Dykes declared. He was still at the table with the papers, and standing beside him was District Attorney Archer.

"That leaves me," I said, "still behind seven hours and more."

"We want a statement," Archer said impatiently.

"The sooner the better," I agreed, and pulled my chair up. Archer sat at the end of the table at my left, Dykes across from me, and the skinny guy, with a notebook and pen, at the other end.

"First," Archer said, "repeat what you told us last night about Mrs. Rackham's visit to Wolfe's office with Leeds."

"But," I objected, "that'll take half an hour, and you're busy. That's routine. I assure you it won't vary."

"Go ahead. I want to hear it, and I have questions."

I yawned thoroughly, rubbed my eyes with the heels of my palms, and started. At first it was fuzzy, but it flowed easy after a minute or two, and it would have been a pleasure to have them compare it with a record from the previous recital if there had been one.

Archer had some questions, and Dykes one or two. At the end Archer asked me, "Will you swear to that, Goodwin?"

"Sure, glad to. If you'll pay the notary fee."

"Go and type it, Cheney."

The skinny guy got up, with his notebook, and left. After the door was closed Archer spoke.

"You might as well know it, Goodwin; you've been contradicted. Mr. Rackham says you're lying about his wife's conversation with Wolfe."

"Yeah? How does he know? He wasn't there."

"He says that she couldn't possibly have said what you report because it wasn't true. He says that there was no question or misunderstanding about money between them. He also says that she told him that she suspected her financial affairs were being mishandled by Mr. Hammond of the Metropolitan Trust Company, and that she was going to consult Nero Wolfe about it."

"Well." I yawned. "That's interesting. Leeds is on my side. Who's on his?"

"No one so far."

"Have you tried it out on Leeds?"

"Yes. As you say, he's on your side. He has signed a statement. So has Mr. Rackham."

"What does Hammond say?"

"I haven't—" Archer paused, regarding me. "Perhaps I shouldn't have told you that. You will keep it to yourself. It's a delicate matter, to approach a responsible officer of a reputable bank on a thing like that."

"Right," I agreed. "It's also a delicate matter to call a millionaire a damn liar—that is, delicate for you. Not for me. I hereby call him a damn liar. I suppose he is a millionaire? Now?"

Archer and Dykes exchanged glances.

"Save it if you want to," I said understandingly. "Leeds will tell me. If he knows. Does he?"

"Yes. The will was read to the family today. I was present. There are a number of bequests to servants and distant relatives. Mrs. Frey gets this place and a million dollars. Leeds gets half a million. Lina Darrow gets two hundred thousand. The rest goes to Mr. Rackham."

"I see. Then he's a millionaire, so it's delicate. Even so, he's a damn liar and it's two to one. I'll sign that statement in triplicate if you want it. Beyond that what can I say?"

"I want to make it three to one." Archer leaned to me. "Listen, Goodwin. I have great respect for Nero Wolfe's talents. I have reason to, as you know. But I do not intend to let his whims interfere with the functions of my office. I want a statement from him supporting yours and Leeds', and I mean to have it without delay. I sent a man to get it. This morning at eleven o'clock he was told that Wolfe wasn't available and that you weren't there and your whereabouts were not known. That was when an alarm was spread for you. I had a phone call from my man an hour ago. He had gone back to Wolfe's house and had been told that Wolfe was out of the city, and that was all he could get."

Archer made a hand into a fist, resting on the table. "I won't stand for it, Goodwin. This is the toughest one I've had in my county since I took office, and I won't stand for it. Whatever else he is, he's a fat conceited peacock and it's time somebody called him. There's a phone you can use. Two hours from now, unless he's here and talking to me, there'll be a warrant for his arrest as a material witness. There's the phone."

"I doubt if you could paste material witness on him. He hasn't been anywhere near here."

"Nuts," Ben Dykes growled. "Don't be a sap. She takes troubles to him Friday and gets murdered Saturday."

I decided to take the plunge. The way I felt, it would have been a pleasure to let them go ahead with a warrant, but if I tried to stall I would need a very fancy excuse tomorrow when they saw the ad in the *Gazette*. So I thought what the hell, now is as good a time as any, and told them.

"I can't phone him because I don't know where he is."

"Ha, ha," Dykes said. "Ha ha ha."

"Yes," I admitted, "it could be a gag. But it isn't. I don't know whether he's out of the city or not. All I know is that he left the house last night, while I was up here, and he hasn't come back—no, that isn't true. I also know that he called on a friend of his named Vukcic and arranged for his plants to be moved out and his cook to take another job. And he gave Vukcic a power of attorney. And he sent an ad to the *Gazette* announcing his retirement from the detective business."

Dykes did not ha-ha again. He merely sat and frowned at me. Archer, his lips puckered, had his eyes focused on me, but as if he was trying to see not me but through me. That went on for seconds, and I got uncomfortable. I can meet a pair of eyes all right, but not two pairs at once, one in front and one off to the left.

Finally Dykes turned his head to tell Archer, "This makes it nice."

Archer nodded, not taking his regard from me. "It's hard to believe, Goodwin."

"I'll say it is. For him to—"

"No, no. It's hard to believe that Wolfe and you would try anything as fantastic as this. Obviously he was absolutely compelled to. You phoned him from Leeds' place last night, as soon as you could get to a phone after Mrs. Rackham was murdered. That was—"

"Excuse me," I said firmly. "Not as soon as I could get to a phone after Mrs. Rackham was murdered. As soon as I could get to a phone after I found out she had been murdered."

"Very well. We're not in court." He was leaning at me. "That was shortly after midnight. What did you say to him?"

"I told him what had happened. I reported, as fully as I could in the time I had, everything from my arrival here up to then. If the operator listened in you can check with her. I asked if I should limit my talk with the cops to events here and leave the rest for him to tell, and he said no, I should withhold nothing, including all details of Mrs. Rackham's talk with him. That was all. As you know, I followed instructions."

"Jesus," Dykes said. "Son, it looks like your turn to sweat has come."

Archer ignored him. "And after telling you to withhold nothing from the police, Wolfe suddenly decides, in the middle of the night, that he has had enough of detective work, sends an ad to a newspaper announcing his retirement, calls on a friend to arrange for the care of his orchids—and what did he do then? I was so engrossed I may have missed something."

"I don't know what he did. He walked out. He disappeared."

I was aware, of course, of how it sounded. It was completely cuckoo. It was all rayon and a yard wide. I damn near made it even worse by telling them about the sausage and the tear gas, of course without letting on that we knew who had sent it, but realized in time how that would go over in the circumstances. That *would* have made a hit. But I had to say or do something, and decided to produce evidence, so I reached to my pocket for it.

"He left notes on the table in his bedroom," I said, "for Fritz and Theodore and me. Here's mine."

I handed it to Archer. He read it and passed it to Dykes. Dykes read it twice and returned it to Archer, who stuck it in his pocket.

"Jesus," Dykes said again, looking at me in a way I didn't like. "This is really something. I've always thought Nero Wolfe had a lot on the ball, and you too in a way, but this is about the worst I ever saw. Really." He turned to Archer. "It's plain what happened."

"It certainly is." Archer made a fist. "Goodwin, I don't ask you to tell me. I'll tell you. When you found Mrs. Rackham there dead, you and Leeds agreed on a tale about the visit to Nero Wolfe. Leeds came here to break the news. You went to his place to phone Wolfe and report, both the murder and the tale you and Leeds had agreed on—or maybe Wolfe knew that already, since you had pretended to investigate the dog poisoning. In any case, Wolfe knew something that he didn't dare to try to cover and that, equally, he didn't dare to reveal. What made it unbearably hot was the murder. So he arranged to disappear, and we haven't got him, and it may take a day or a week to find him. But we've got you."

The fist hit the table, not hard. "You know where Wolfe is. You know what he knows that he had to run away from. It is vital information required by me in my investigation of a murder. Surely you must see that your position is untenable, you can't possibly get away with it. Twenty Nero Wolfes couldn't bring you out of this with a whole skin. Even if he's cooking up one of his flashy surprises, even if he walks into my office tomorrow with the murderer and the evidence to convict him, I will not stand for this. There is no written record of what you said last night. I'll get the stenographer back in here and we'll tear up his notebook and what he has typed, and you can start from scratch."

"Better grab it, son," Dykes said, perfectly friendly. "Loyalty to your employer is a fine thing, but not when he's got a screw loose."

I yawned. "My God, I'm sleepy. I wouldn't mind this so much if I was helping out with a fix, good or bad, but it's a shame to get stuck with the truth. Ask me tomorrow, ask me all summer, I refuse to tell a lie. And I do not know where Mr. Wolfe is."

Archer stood up. "Get a material witness warrant and lock him up," he said, almost squeaking, and marched out.

Chapter 8

The jail at White Plains uses a gallon of strong disinfectant, diluting it, of course, every day including Sunday. I can back that statement up with two pieces of evidence: the word of the turnkey on the second-floor cell block, whose name is Wilkes, given to me personally, and my sense of smell, which is above average.

I had no opportunity to make a tour of inspection during the twenty hours I was there, that Easter Sunday and the day following, but except for the smell I found nothing to write to the newspapers about, once you grant that society must protect itself against characters like me. My cell—or rather, our cell, since I had a mate—was as clean as they come. There was something about the blankets that made you keep them away from your chin, but that could have been just prejudice. The light was nothing wonderful, but good enough to read by for thirty days.

I didn't really get acquainted with my surroundings or my mate until Monday, I was so darned sleepy when they finally finished with me down below and showed me up to my room. They had been insistent but not ferocious. I had been allowed to phone Fritz that I wouldn't be home, which was a good thing, as there was no telling what he would have done with no word from me coming on top of Wolfe's fadeout, and also to try to call Nathaniel Parker, the only lawyer Wolfe has ever been willing to invite to dinner; but that was no go because he was away for the weekend. When at last I stretched out on the cot, I was dead to the world ten seconds after my head hit the pillow, consisting of my pants wrapped in my shirt.

It was the pants, or rather the coat and vest that went with them, that made my stay pleasanter than it might have been right from the start. I had had perhaps half as much sleep as I could have used when a hell of a noise banged at me and I lifted my head and opened my eyes. Across the cell on another cot, so far away that I would have had to stretch my arm full length to touch him, was my cellmate—a broad-shouldered guy about my age, maybe a little older, with a mop of tousled black hair. He was sitting up, yawning.

"What's all the racket?" I asked. "Jail break?"

"Breakfast and check-up in ten minutes," he replied, getting to his feet, with socks on, to the floor. "Stupid custom."

"Boneheads," I agreed, twisting up to sit on the edge of the cot.

Going to the chair where his wardrobe was, his eye fell on my chair, and he stepped to it for a look at the coat and vest. He fingered the lapel, looked inside at the lining, and inspected a buttonhole. Then, without comment, he returned to his side, two whole steps, and started to dress. I followed suit.

"Where do we wash?" I inquired.

"After breakfast," he replied, "if you insist."

A man in uniform appeared on the other side of the bars and used his hands, and the cell door swung open.

"Wait a minute, Wilkes," my mate told him, and then asked me, "You cleaned out?"

"Naturally. This is a modern jail."

"Would bacon and eggs suit you?"

"Just right."

"Toast white or rye?"

"White."

"Our tastes are similar. Make it two, Wilkes. Two of everything."

"As you say," the turnkey said distinctly, and went. My mate, getting his necktie under his shirt collar, told me, "They won't allow exceptions to the turnout and check-up, but you can pass up the garbage. We'll eat here in privacy."

"This," I said earnestly, "is the brotherhood of man. I would like this breakfast to be on me when I get my wallet back."

He waved it away. "Forget it."

The turnout and check-up, I discovered, were not to be taken as opportunities for conversation. There were around forty of us, all shapes and sizes, and on the whole we were frankly not a blue-ribbon outfit. The smell of the breakfast added to the disinfectant was enough to account for the expressions on the faces, not counting whatever it was that had got them there, and it was a relief to get back to my cozy cell with my mate.

We had our hands and faces washed, and he had his teeth brushed, when the breakfast came on a big clean aluminum tray. The eats were barely usable if you took Fritz's productions as a standard, but compared with the community meal which I had seen and smelled they were a handsome feast. My mate having ordered two of everything, there were two morning *Gazettes*, and before he even touched his orange juice he took his paper and, with no glance at the front page, turned to sports. Finishing his survey of the day's prospects, he drank some orange juice and inquired, "Are you interested in the rapidity of horses?"

"In a way." I added earnestly, "I like the way you talk. I enjoy being with cultured people."

He gave me a suspicious look, saw my honest candid countenance, and relaxed. "That's natural. Look at your clothes."

We were on the chairs, with the little wooden table between us. It was comfortable enough except that there was no room to prop up our morning papers. He flattened his out, still open at sports, on the end of the cot, and turned to it while disposing of a bite of food. I arranged mine, front page, on my knee. In the picture of Mrs. Rackham the poor woman looked homelier than she had actually been, which was a darned shame even though she wasn't alive to see it. Wolfe's name and mine both appeared in the subheads under the three-column spread about the murder. I glanced at the bottom, followed the instruction to turn to page four, and there saw more pictures. The one of Wolfe was only fair, making him look almost bloated, but the one of me was excellent. There was one of a Doberman pinscher standing at attention. It was captioned Hebe, which I doubted. The play in the text on Wolfe and me was on his sudden retirement from business and absence from the city, and on my presence at the scene of the murder and arrest as a material witness. There was also a report of an interview with Marko Vukcic, a *Ga-*

zette exclusive, with Lon Cohen's by-line. I would have given at least ten to one that Lon had used my name in getting to Marko.

With the breakfast all down, including the coffee, which was pretty good, I was so interested in my reading that I didn't notice that my mate had finished with sports and proceeded to other current events. What got my attention was the feeling that I was being scrutinized, and sure enough I was. He was looking at me, and then at his page four, and back at me again.

I grinned at him. "Pretty good likeness, huh? But I don't think that's the right dog. I'm no expert, but Hebe isn't quite as slim as that."

He was regarding me with a new expression, not particularly matey. "So you're Nero Wolfe's little Archie."

"I was." I gestured. "Read the paper. Apparently I am now my own little Archie."

"So I bought a meal for a shamus."

"Not at all. Didn't I say it was on me when I get my wallet back?"

He shook his head. "I wouldn't have believed it. With them clothes? I supposed you had got snagged in the raid on the Covered Porch. It gets worse all the time, the dicks. Look at this, even here in the can I meet a guy with a suit of clothes like that, and he's a dick!"

"I am not a dick, strictly speaking." I was hurt. "I am a private eye. I said I liked the way you talk, but you're getting careless. I also noticed you were cultured, and that should have put me on my guard. Cultured people are not often found in the coop. But nowadays dicks are frequently cultured. They tossed me in here because they think I'm holding out on a murder, which I'm not, and the fact that it has been tried before doesn't mean they wouldn't try it again. Putting you in here with me wasn't so dumb, but you overplayed it, buying me a breakfast first pop. That started me wondering."

He was on his feet, glaring down at me. "Watch it, loose-lip. I'm going to clip you."

"What for?"

"You need a lesson. I'm a plant, am I?"

"Nuts. Who's insulted now?" I gestured. "You call me a name, I call you a name. I take it, you take it. Let's start over."

But he was too sensitive to make up as quick as all that. He undid his fist, glared at me some more, sidled between his chair and his cot, and got comfortable on the cot with his *Gazette*. With his head toward the corridor he was getting as good light as there was, and I followed his example, folding one of the blankets for a pillow and spreading my handkerchief on it. Two hours and ten minutes passed without a word from either cot. I happen to know because as I stretched out I glanced at my watch, wondering how soon I could reasonably expect Parker to show up with a crowbar to pry me loose, and it was twenty past nine; and, after giving that *Gazette* as good a play as a newspaper ever got, I had just looked at my watch for the twentieth time and seen 11:30 when he suddenly spoke.

"Look, Goodwin, what are you going to do now?"

I let the paper slide to the floor. "I don't know, take a nap, I guess."

"I don't mean now, this minute. Is anyone looking after you?"

"If he isn't he'd better be. A high-priced lawyer named Parker."

"Then what?"

"I'll go home and take a bath."

"Then what?"

"I'll brush my teeth and shave."

"Then what?"

I swiveled my head to glance at him. "You're pretty damn persistent. Where do you want us to get to?"

"Nowhere in particular." He stayed supine, and I noticed that in profile he looked a little like John L. Lewis, only a lot younger. He went on, "I was just thinking, with Nero Wolfe gone I suppose your job's gone. Can't I think?"

"Sure. If it doesn't hurt."

A brief silence. He spoke again. "I've heard about you a little. What kind of a guy are you?"

"Oh—I'm a thinker too, and I'm cultured. I got good marks in algebra. I sleep well. I'm honest and ambitious, with a good personality."

"You know your way around."

"In certain circles, yes. It would be hard to lose me within ten miles of Times Square unless I was blindfolded. What are the requirements of the position you are about to offer?"

He ignored that and took another angle. "My name is Christy—Max Christy. Ever hear of me?"

If I had it was vague, but I saw no point in hurting his feelings. "Max Christy?" I snorted. "Don't be silly."

"I thought you might have. I've only been around the big town a couple of years, and I don't toot a horn, but some people get talked about. How much has Wolfe been paying you?"

"That's asking," I objected mildly. "I wouldn't

want it to get in the papers. I've been eating all right and I've got a government bond. Anything over—"

Footsteps in the corridor stopped at our door, and the turnkey's voice came. "Mr. Christy! They want you down in the office."

My mate stayed flat. "Come back in ten minutes, Wilkes," he called. "I'm busy."

I confirmed it. "We're in conference, Wilkes," I snapped.

"But I think it's your out."

"I suppose so. Come back in ten minutes."

Wilkes, mumbling something, went away. Christy resumed. "You were saying . . ."

"Yeah. That anything over fifty grand a year would find me a good listener."

"I'm being serious, Goodwin."

"So am I."

"You are not. You never got within a mile of fifty grand a year." His head was turned to face me now. "Anyway, it's not a question of so many grand a year —not in this business."

"In what business?"

"The business I'm in. What did I say my name is?"

"Max Christy."

"Then what more do you want? Take my being here now, for example. I got raked in at the Covered Porch yesterday by mistake, but I would have been loose in an hour if it hadn't been Sunday—and Easter too. Here it is"—he looked at his wrist—"not quite noon, and I'm walking out. There has never been an organization to compare with it. For a man like you there would be special jobs and special opportunities if you once got taken in. With your record, which is bad as far as I know it, that would take a while. You would have to show, and show good. Your idea about so many grand a year just isn't realistic, certainly not while you're being tried, but after that it would depend on you. If you've got it in you there's practically no limit. Another thing is income tax."

"Yeah, what about income tax?"

"You simply use your judgment. Say Wolfe paid you thirty grand a year, which he didn't, nothing like it, what did you have to say about income tax? Nothing. It was taken out before you got paid. You never even saw it. In this business you make your own decisions about it. You want to be fair, and you want to be in the clear, but you don't want to get gypped, and on that basis you use your judgment."

Christy raised his torso and sat on the edge of the cot. "You know, Goodwin, I'm just tossing this at you on the spur of the moment. I laid here reading about you, and I thought to myself, here's a man the right age and experience, not married, the right personality, he knows people, he knows lots of cops, he has been a private eye for years and so he would be open to anything that sounds good enough; he is just out of a job, he's got himself tangled in a hot homicide here in Westchester, and he may need help right now. That's what I was thinking, and I thought why not ask him? I can't guarantee anything, especially if you're headed for a murder rap, but if you need help now and then later on you would like a chance at something, I'm Max Christy and I could pass the word along. If you—"

He paused at the sound of footsteps. Wilkes' voice came from the door. "They want you down there, Mr. Christy. I told them you was busy personally, but they're sending up."

"All right, Wilkes. Coming." My mate stood up. "What about it, Goodwin?"

"I appreciate it," I said warmly. Wilkes, having unlocked the door, was standing there, and, using my judgment, I kept it discreet. "When I get out and look around a little I'll know better how things stand." I had got to my feet. "How do I get in touch with you?"

"Phone is best. Churchill five, three two three two. I'm not there much, but a message will reach me promptly. Better write it down."

"I'll remember it." I took his offered hand and we shook. "It's been a pleasure. Where can I mail a check for the breakfast?"

"Forget it. It was a privilege. Be seeing you, I hope." He strode out like an executive going to greet a welcome caller, Wilkes holding the door for him.

I sat down on the cot, thinking it was a hell of a note for a Max Christy to get sprung before an Archie Goodwin. What was keeping Parker? In jail a man gets impatient.

Chapter 9

It was seven o'clock that evening, just getting dark, when I left the car at the curb on West Thirty-fifth Street in front of Wolfe's house and climbed the seven steps to the stoop. Parker, armed with papers which stated, among other things, that my continued availability to the People of the State of New York was worth ten thousand dollars, had arrived at the jail shortly after two, and in another ten minutes I had been unleashed on society again, but District Attorney Archer had requested another session with me in the presence of my attorney, and Parker and I had obliged. It had dragged on and on, and was really a bore, because there was nothing for me to try to be witty about. Unlike some other occasions when I had been in conference with the law, there was nothing to stimulate me because all I had to do was tell the truth, and all of it—except the sausage part and the phone call from Arnold Zeck.

When they had finally called it a day and Parker and I were standing on the sidewalk in front of the courthouse, he asked me, "Am I to know where Wolfe is?"

"I doubt it. He told me not to look for him."

"I see."

His tone of voice irritated me. "Every word you heard me say in there," I asserted, "was the truth, I haven't the thinnest idea where he is or what he's doing."

He shrugged. "I'm not complaining. I only hope he hasn't tumbled in where it's too deep this time—and you too."

"Go to hell," I advised him, and marched off. I couldn't really blame the Westchester bunch, but Parker should have known me well enough to tell which side of my mouth I was talking out of. It's damn discouraging, when you do tell the truth, not to have it recognized.

Also discouraging was the welcome I got on entering Wolfe's house that evening. It was in the form of a note stuck in the corner of my desk blotter, unfolded.

Dear Archie—

I am sorry you are in jail and hope it will not last long. Mr. Vukcic has been to see me and I am leaving now to go to work for him $1500. There has been no word from Mr. Wolfe. God grant he is safe and well and I think you should find him no matter what he wrote. I threw out the jar of sardines and stopped the milk. My very best regards and wishes,

Fritz
1:35 P.M.

I was pleased to observe that he stuck to routine to the end, putting the time down. Also it was nice of him to end his note to me the same as Wolfe had ended his. Nevertheless, it was a discouraging welcome home after a night in the hoosegow. And there had been a period of more than five hours when any phone calls that might have come would not have been answered, something that had never happened before in all the years I had worked and lived there. Unless Theodore . . .

I beat it to the stairs and up the three flights, and entered the plant rooms. One step inside the first room, the warm one, I stopped and surveyed. It was more of a shock, somehow, than it had been a year ago when it had been used as a target for tommy guns from across the street. Then they had at least left a mess; now there was nothing but the benches and stands. It really got me for a minute. I moved on through: medium room, cool room, potting room, spray chamber, Theodore's room—all empty. Hewitt must have sent an army to clean all that out in one day, I thought, heading back downstairs.

In the kitchen was another longer note from Fritz, reporting phone calls that had come before he left and various minor matters. I opened the refrigerator and poked around, and settled for a jar of home-made pâté, a hunk of Italian bread, Vermont cheese, and milk. As I sat working at it with an evening paper propped up before me, I kept listening for something—nothing in particular, just something. It had never been a noisy house, but I had never known it anything like that quiet. Almost no cars went by, and the few that did must have been coasting in neutral.

My meal finished and things put away, I wandered into the dining room, office, front room, down to the basement to Fritz's room, up one flight to Wolfe's room, up another to my room. As I undressed for my post-jail bath, I thought that the hell of it wasn't how I felt, but that I didn't know how to feel. If I had actually seen the last of Nero Wolfe, it was a damn sad day for me, there were no two ways about that, and if I got a lump in my throat and somebody walked in I would just as soon show him the lump as not. But what if it was Wolfe himself who walked in? That was the trouble. Damned if I was going to work up a fancy lump and then have him suddenly appear and start crabbing about something.

After I had bathed and shaved and got into clean pajamas, and answered a couple of phone calls from journalists, and moseyed down to the office and fooled around a while, someone did walk in. When I heard the front door open I made for the hall as if I had been expecting another package of sausage, and there was Fritz. He turned from closing the door, saw me, and beamed.

"Ah! Archie! You escaped?"

"I'm out on bail." He seemed to want to shake hands, and I was willing. "Thanks for your note. How's the new job?"

"Terrible. I'm played up. Mr. Wolfe?"

"I know nothing about Mr. Wolfe. I ate half a jar of pâté."

He stopped beaming. "Mr. Vukcic is going to sell this house."

"He's going to offer it for sale, which is not the same thing."

"Perhaps not." He sighed. "I'm tired. Mr. Vukcic said there is no reason why I should not sleep here but I should ask you. It would be good for me—I am so used to that room . . ."

"Certainly. I'm used to mine too. I'm going to sleep here until further notice."

"Good." He started for the kitchen, stopped, and turned. "Are you going to look for him?"

"No!" Hearing myself shout, it seemed a relief and I did it again. "I am not!" I went to the stairs and started up. "Good night."

"Good night, Archie."

I was on the first landing when his voice came. "I'll get your breakfast! I don't have to leave until ten!"

"Swell!" I called back. "We'll never miss him!"

The next day, Tuesday, I had no time to raise a lump. There were dozens of phone calls, from newspapers, former clients, friends, and miscellaneous. One was from Calvin Leeds, asking me to go up there to see him, and I told him I had had enough of Westchester for a while. When he insisted, I agreed to receive him at the office at two o'clock. I took advantage of another call, from Lon Cohen at the *Gazette*, to ask about my recent cellmate, Max Christy. Lon asked why I wanted to know. Lon is a good guy, but no newspaperman on earth can answer the simplest question without asking you one first, and more if possible.

"Just curious," I told him. "I met him in jail over the weekend, and thought he was charming. I don't want a biography, just a line or two."

"For quotation?"

"No."

"Right. He's comparatively new to this section, but he's a fast mover. Not really big yet. As far as I know, the only thing he's close to right in town is a string of rooms for transients. He seems to be specializing on little weekend roundups in the suburbs."

"Just games, or women, or what?"

"Anything men risk money for. Or pay it for. I

have heard that he is seen around sometimes with
Brownie Costigan. How curious are you? Is it worth
a steak? Or is it worth a phone number or address
where I can reach Nero Wolfe?"

By that time I had abandoned the idea of selling
anyone, even Lon Cohen, the idea that I ever told
the truth, so I thanked him and hung up.

A couple of checks in the morning mail, one from
a man who was paying in installments for having a
blackmailer removed from his throat, were no problem, since there was a rubber stamp for endorsing
them, but in order to pay three bills that came in I
had to make a trip to Fifty-fourth Street to see if the
formalities about Marko's power of attorney had
been attended to. They had, by Parker, and I was
glad to see that Marko signed the checks on my say-
so, without looking at the bills. If he had started au-
diting on me I swear to God I would have moved out
and got a hotel room.

There were other chores, such as phoning Hewitt's place on Long Island to ask if the plants and
Theodore had arrived safely, making arrangements
with a phone-answering service, handling a report
from Fred Durkin on a poison-letter job that was the
main item of unfinished business, and so on, but I
managed to have them all under control when two
o'clock came and brought Calvin Leeds.

When I went to let him in and took him to the
office, there was a problem. Should I sit at my desk
or at Wolfe's? On the one hand, I was not Wolfe and
had no intention of trying to be. On the other hand,
when a pinch-hitter is called on he stands at the plate
to bat, not off to one side. Also it would be interesting to see, from Wolfe's position, what the light was
like on the face of a man sitting in the red leather

chair. So again, this time intentionally, I sat behind Wolfe's desk.

"I came here to get an explanation," Leeds said, "and I'm going to get it."

He looked as if he could stand a dose of something —if not an explanation, then maybe castor oil. The hide of his face still looked tough and weathered, or rather as if it had been but someone had soaked it in something to make it stretch and get saggy. His eyes looked determined, but not clear and alert as before. No one would have guessed that he had just inherited half a million bucks, and not from a dearly beloved wife or sister but merely a cousin.

Something like a million times I had seen Wolfe, faced with a belligerent statement from a caller, lean back and close his eyes. I thought I might as well try it, and did so. But the springs which let the chair's back slant to the rear were carefully adjusted to the pressure of Wolfe's poundage, not mine, and I had to keep pushing to maintain the damn thing in the leaning position.

"A man who comes forty miles for an explanation," I said, with my eyes closed, "is entitled to one. What needs explaining?"

"Nero Wolfe's behavior does."

"That's nothing new." It was too much of a strain keeping the chair back in a leaning position, and I straightened up. "It often has. But that's not my department."

"I want to see him."

"So do I."

"You're a liar, Goodwin."

I shook my head, my lips tight. "You know," I said, "I have probably told as many lies as any man my age except psychos. But I have never been called a liar as frequently as in the past twenty-four hours, and I have never stuck so close to the truth. To hell with it. Mr. Wolfe has gone south to train with the Dodgers. He will play shortstop."

"That won't help any," Leeds said, patient but determined, "that kind of talk. If you don't like being called a liar, neither do I, and the difference is that I'm not. The district attorney says I'm lying, because Nero Wolfe has suddenly disappeared, and he disappeared because he doesn't dare answer questions about my cousin Sarah's visit to him here, and that proves that your report of that visit is false, and since my report is the same as yours mine is false too. Now that sounds logical, but there's a flaw in it. The flaw is their assumption that his disappearance was connected with my cousin's visit. I know it couldn't have been, because there was nothing about our talk that day that could possibly have had such a result. I have told them that, and they think I'm lying. As long as they think I'm lying, and you too, they'll have their minds on that and they won't find out who killed my cousin and why—and anyway, I don't want to be suspected of lying when I'm not, especially not in connection with the murder of my cousin."

Leeds paused for breath and went on, "There's only one way out that I can see, and that's for you to tell them the real reason for Wolfe's disappearance—or, better still, he ought to tell them himself. I want you to put this up to him. Even if his own safety is involved, he ought to manage somehow. If it was something about some client that made him disappear, in the interest of some client, then you can tell him from me that I saw him take a check from my cousin for ten thousand dollars and it seems to me he's under obligation to her as much as any other client, to protect her interests, and it surely isn't in her interest to have suspicion centered in the wrong place about who killed her—and killed her dog too." His jaw quivered a little, and he clamped it tight.

"Do you mean," I inquired, "that suspicion is centered on you? How come?"

"Not on me as—as a murderer, I don't suppose so, but on me as a liar, and you and Wolfe. Even though she left me a great deal of money—I'm not thinking about being arrested for murder."

"Who do you think ought to be?"

"I don't know." He gestured. "You're trying to change the subject. It's not a question of me and what I think, it's you and what you're going to do. From what I've heard of Wolfe, I doubt if it would help for you to tell him what I've said; I've got to see him and tell him myself. If he has really got to hide from somebody or something, do it however you want to. Blindfold me and put me face down in your car. I've got to see him. My cousin would have wanted me to, and he took her money."

I was half glad there for a moment that I did not know where Wolfe was. I had no admiration for Leeds' preference in pets, since I would put a woman ahead of a Doberman pinscher any day, and there was room for improvement in him in a few other respects, but I couldn't help but admit he had a point and was not being at all unreasonable. So if I had known where Wolfe was I would have had to harden my heart, and as it was all I had to harden was my voice. It struck me then, for the first time, that maybe I shouldn't be so sore at Wolfe after all.

Leeds hung on for another quarter of an hour, and I prolonged it a little myself by trying to get something out of him about the progress the cops had made, without success. He went away mad, still calling me a liar, which kept it unanimous. What he got from me was nothing. What I got from him was that Mrs. Rackham's funeral would be the next morning, Wednesday. Not a profitable way to spend most of an hour, for either of us.

I spent what was left of the afternoon looking into the matter of sausage. Within ten minutes after the package had been opened that day, Wolfe had phoned both Mummiani and the Fleet Messenger Service and got a blank as expected; but on the outside chance that I might at least get a bone for my curiosity to gnaw on I made a trip to Fulton Street and one uptown. At Mummiani's no one knew anything. Since Wolfe had been getting Darst's sausage from them for years, and in that time their personnel had come and gone, any number of outsiders could know about it. At the Fleet Messenger Service they were willing to help but couldn't. They remembered the package because Wolfe had phoned about it, but all I learned was that it had been left there by a youth who might have been playing hookey from the eighth grade, and I didn't even bother to listen to the description, such as it was.

Fed up with an empty house and the phone ringing and being called a liar, I put in a call myself from a drugstore booth, and made personal arrangements for dinner and a show.

Wednesday morning a visitor came that I let in. I had formed the habit, since returning from jail, of hearing the doorbell ring, going to the hall, observing through the one-way glass panel who it was out on the stoop, making a face, and returning to the office. If the bell kept ringing long enough to be a nuisance

I flipped the switch that turned it off. This time, around eleven Wednesday morning, instead of making a face I went and opened the door and said, "Well, hello! Coming in?"

A chunky specimen about my height, with wrinkled pink skin and gray hair and sharp gray-blue eyes, grunted a greeting and stepped over the sill. I said it was cold for April, and he agreed. As I hung his topcoat on the rack I told myself that I must be more restrained. The fact that I was alone in the house was no reason to give Inspector Cramer of Manhattan Homicide the impression that I was glad to see him. Wolfe or no Wolfe, I could keep up appearances.

I let him lead the way to the office. This time I sat at my own desk. I was tempted to take Wolfe's chair again just to see how he would react, but it would have put me at a disadvantage, I was so used to dealing with him, in the red leather chair, from my own angle.

He eyed me. "So you're holding the fort," he growled.

"Not exactly," I objected. "I'm only the caretaker. Or maybe I'm going down with the ship. Not that those who have left are rats."

"Where's Wolfe?"

"I don't know. Next, you call me a liar. Then I say I have been, but not now. Then you—"

"Nuts. Where is he, Archie?"

That cleared the atmosphere. Over the years he had called me Goodwin fifty times to one Archie. He called me Archie only when he wanted something awful bad or when he had something wrapped up that Wolfe had given him and his humanity overcame him. So we were to be mellow.

"Listen," I said, friendly but firm. "That routine is all right for people like district attorneys and state cops and the representatives of the press, but you're above it. Either I don't know where he is, or I do know but I'm sitting on it. What's the difference? Next question."

He took a cigar from his pocket, inspected it, rubbed it between his palms, and inspected it again. "It must be quite a thing," he remarked, not growling. "That ad in the paper. The plants gone. Fritz and Theodore gone. Vukcic listing the house for sale. I'm going to miss it, I am, never dropping in to see him sitting here thinking he's smarter than God and all His angels. Quite a thing, it must be. What is it?"

I said slowly and wearily, "Either I don't know what it is, or I do know but—"

"What about the sausage that turned into tear gas? Any connection?"

I am always ready for Inspector Cramer, in the light of experience guided by intelligence, and therefore didn't bat an eye. I merely cocked my head a little, met his gaze, and considered the matter until I was satisfied. "I doubt if it was Fritz," I stated. "Mr. Wolfe has him too well trained. But in the excitement Sunday morning, Mr. Wolfe being gone, Fritz told Theodore, and you got it out of Theodore." I nodded. "That must be it."

"Did the tear gas scare him out of his skin? Or out of his house, which is the same thing. Was that it?"

"It might have, mightn't it? A coward like him?"

"No." Cramer put the cigar between his teeth, tilted up. "No, there are plenty of things about Wolfe I can and do object to, but he's not a coward. There might have been something about that tear gas that would have scared anybody. Was there?"

"As far as I know, it was just plain tear gas, nothing fancy." I decided to shove a little. "You know, it's nice to have you here any time, just for company, but aren't you spreading out some? Your job is homicide, and the tear gas didn't even make us sick, let alone kill us. Also your job is in the County of New York, and Mrs. Rackham died in Westchester. I enjoy talking with you, but have you got credentials?"

He made a noise that could have been a chuckle. "That's more like it," he said, not sarcastically. "You're beginning to sound natural. I'll tell you. I'm here at the request of Ben Dykes, who would give all his teeth and one ear to clear up the Rackham case ahead of the state boys. He thinks that Archer, the DA, may have swallowed the idea that you and Leeds are lying too deep, and he came to me as an expert on Nero Wolfe, which God knows I am. He laid it all out for me and wanted my opinion."

He shifted the cigar to a new angle. "The way it looked to me, there were three possibilities. First, the one that Archer has sold himself on, that you and Leeds are lying, and that what Mrs. Rackham really told Wolfe when she came here, together with her getting murdered the next day, somehow put Wolfe on a spot that was too hot for him, and he scooted, after fixing with you to cover as well as you could. I told Dykes I would rule that out, for various reasons —chiefly because neither you nor Wolfe would risk that much on a setup that depended on a stranger like Leeds sticking to a lie. Shall I analyze it more?"

"No, thanks, that'll do."

"I thought so. Next, the possibility that when you phoned Wolfe right after the body was found you told him something that gave him a line on the murderer, but it's tricky and he had to go outdoors to get his evidence, preparing to grandstand it for the front page. I told Dykes I would rule that out too. Wolfe is quite capable of a play like that, sure he is, but if that's all it amounted to, why move the plants out and put Fritz to work in a restaurant and list the house for sale? He's colorful, but not that colorful. Mrs. Rackham only paid him ten thousand, about what I make a year. Why should he spend it having his orchids carted around?"

Cramer shook his head. "Not for my money. That leaves the third possibility: that something really did scare him. That there was something about Mrs. Rackham's murder, or anyhow connected with it, that he knew he couldn't handle sitting there in that chair, but for some reason he had to handle it. So he scooted. As you say, you either don't know where he is or you know and won't tell—and that's no help either way. Now I've got a lot to say about this possibility. You got time to listen?"

"I've got all day, but Fritz isn't here to get our lunch."

"We'll go without." He clasped his hands behind his head and shifted his center of gravity. "You know, Archie, sometimes I'm not as far behind as you think I am."

"Also sometimes I don't think you're as far behind as you think I do."

"That's possible. Anyhow, I can add. I think he got word direct from Arnold Zeck. Did he?"

"Huh? Who's Arnold Zeck? Did you just make it up?"

I knew that was a mistake the instant it was out of my mouth. Then I had to try to keep it from showing on my face, the realization that I had fumbled it, but whether that was a success or not—and I couldn't very well look in a mirror to find out—it was too late.

Cramer looked pleased. "So you've been around all these years, a working detective, meeting the people you do, and you've never heard of Arnold Zeck. Either I've got to believe that, or I touched a tender spot."

"Sure I've heard of him. It just didn't click for a second."

"Oh, for God's sake. It's affecting you already, having Wolfe gone. That wasn't just a shot in the dark. One day two years ago I sat here in this chair. Wolfe sat there." He nodded at Wolfe's chair. "You were where you are now. A man named Orchard had been murdered, and so had a woman named Poole. In the course of our long talk Wolfe explained in detail how an ingenious and ruthless man could operate a blackmail scheme, good for at least a million a year, without sticking his neck out. Not only could; it was being done. Wolfe refused to name him, and since he wasn't behind the murders it was out of my territory, but a thing or two I heard and a couple of things that happened gave me a pretty clear idea. Not only me—it was whispered around: Arnold Zeck. You may perhaps remember it."

"I remember the Orchard case, certainly," I conceded. "I didn't hear the whispering."

"I did. You may also remember that a year later, last summer, Wolfe's plant rooms got shot up from a roof across the street."

"Yes. I was sitting right here and heard it."

"So I understand. Since no one was killed that never got to me officially, but naturally I heard things. Wolfe had started to investigate a man named Rony, and Rony's activities were the kind that might lead a first-class investigator like Wolfe in the direction of Arnold Zeck, maybe up close to Zeck, possibly even clear to him. I thought then that Wolfe had got warned off, by Zeck himself or someone near him, and he had disregarded it, and for a second warning they messed up his orchids. Then Rony got killed, and that was a break for Wolfe because it put him and Zeck on the same side."

"Gosh," I remarked, "it sounds awful complicated to me."

"I'll bet it does." Cramer moved the cigar—getting shorter now, although he never lit one—to the other side of his mouth. "All I'm doing is showing you that I'm not just hoping for a bite, and I don't want to string it out. It was a good guess that Wolfe had jostled up against Arnold Zeck in both the Orchard case and the Rony case, and now what happens? Not long after Mrs. Rackham calls on him and hires him to check on her husband's income, someone sends him a cylinder of tear gas—not a bomb to blow out his guts, which it could have been, just tear gas, so of course it was for a warning. And that night Mrs. Rackham gets murdered. You tell him about it on the phone, and when you get home he's gone."

Cramer took the cigar from his mouth and pointed it at me. "I'll tell you what I believe, Archie. I believe that if Wolfe had stayed and helped, the murderer of Mrs. Rackham would be locked up by now. I believe that he had reason to think that if he did that, helped to catch the murderer, he would have to spend the rest of his life trying to keep Arnold Zeck from getting him. I believe that he decided that the only way out was for him to get Zeck. How's that?"

"No comment," I said politely. "If you're right

you're right, and if you're wrong I wouldn't want to hurt your feelings."

"Much obliged. But he did get a warning from Zeck—the tear gas."

"No comment."

"I wouldn't expect any. Now here's what I came for. I want you to give Wolfe a personal message from me, not as a police officer but as a friend. This is between you and me—and him. Zeck is out of his reach. He is out of anybody's reach. It's a goddam crime for an officer of the law to have to say a thing like that, even privately, but it's true. Here's a murder case, and thank God it's not mine. I'm not pointing at Ben Dykes or the DA up there, I'm not pointing at any person or persons, but if the setup is that Barry Rackham is tied in with one or more of Zeck's operations, and if Rackham killed his wife, I say he will never burn. I don't say at what point Zeck will get his hand in, or who or what he will use, but Rackham will never burn."

Cramer hurled his cigar at my wastebasket and missed it by a foot. Since it wasn't lit I ignored it. "Hooray for justice," I cheered.

He snarled, but apparently not at me. "I want you to tell Wolfe that. Zeck is out of his reach. He can't get him."

"But," I objected, "granting that you've got it all straight, which I haven't, that's a hell of a message. Look at it from the other end. He is not out of Zeck's reach, not if he comes home. I know he doesn't go out much, but even if he never did people have to come in—and things, like packages of sausage. Not to mention that the damage they did to the plants and equipment last year came to thirty-eight thousand bucks. I get the idea that he is to lay off of Zeck, but that's only what he doesn't do. What does he do?"

Cramer nodded. "I know. That's it. He's so damn bullheaded. I want you to understand, Archie, why I came here. Wolfe is too cocky to live. He has enough brass and bluster to outfit a thousand sergeants. Sure, I know him; I ought to. I would love to bloody his nose for him. I've tried to often enough, and someday I will and enjoy it. But I would hate to see him break his neck on a deal like this where he hasn't got a chance. It's a good guess that in the past ten years there have been over a hundred homicides in this town that were connected in one way or another with one of the operations Arnold Zeck has a hand in. But not in a single case was there the remotest hope of tying Zeck up with it. We couldn't possibly have touched him."

"You're back where you started," I complained. "He can't be reached. So what?"

"So Wolfe should come back where he belongs, return what Mrs. Rackham paid him to her estate, let the Westchester people take care of the murder, which is their job anyhow, and go on as before. You can tell him I said that, but by God don't quote me around. I'm not responsible for a man like Zeck being out of reach."

"But you never strained a muscle stretching for him."

"Nuts. Facts are facts."

"Yeah, like sausage is tear gas." I stood up so as to look down my nose at him. "There are two reasons why your message will not get to Mr. Wolfe. First, he is to me as Zeck is to him. He's out of my reach. I don't know where he is."

"Oh, keep it up."

"I will. Second, I don't like the message. I admit that I have known Mr. Wolfe to discuss Arnold Zeck. I once heard him tell a whole family about him, only he was calling him X. He was describing the difficulties he would be in if he ever found himself tangled with X for a showdown, and he told them that he was acquainted, more or less, with some three thousand people living or working in New York, and there weren't more than five of them of whom he could say with certainty that they were in no way involved in X's activities. He said that none might be or that any might be. On another occasion I happened to be inquiring about Zeck of a newspaperman, and he had extravagant notions about Zeck's payroll. He mentioned, not by name, politicians, barflies, cops, chambermaids, lawyers, private cops, crooks of all types, including gunmen—maybe housewives, I forget. He did not specifically mention police inspectors."

"Just forgot, perhaps."

"I suppose so. Another thing, those five exceptions that Mr. Wolfe made out of his three thousand acquaintances, he didn't say who they were, but I was pretty sure I could name three of them. I thought probably one of the other two was you, but I could have been wrong. You have made a point of how you would hate to see him break his neck where he hasn't got a chance. You took the trouble to come here with a personal message but don't want to be quoted, which means that if I mention this conversation to anyone but Mr. Wolfe you'll call me a liar. And what's the message? That he should lay off Zeck, that's what it amounts to. If in earning the fee Mrs. Rackham paid him he is liable to hurt somebody Zeck doesn't want hurt, he should return the fee. The way it looks from here, sending a message like that to the best and toughest detective on earth is exactly the kind of service Zeck would pay good money for. I wouldn't say—"

I didn't get to say what I wouldn't say. Cramer, out of his chair and coming, had a look on his face that I had never seen before. Time and again I had seen him mad at Wolfe, and me too, but never to the point where the pink left his cheeks completely and his eyes looked absolutely mean.

He swung with his right. I ducked. He came up from beneath with his left, and I stopped it with my forearm. He tried with the right again, and I jerked back, stepped aside, and dived around the corner of Wolfe's desk.

I spoke. "You couldn't hit me in a year and I'm not going to plug you. I'm twenty years younger, and you're an inspector. If I'm wrong, someday I'll apologize. If I'm wrong."

He turned and marched out. I didn't go to the hall to help him on with his coat and open the door.

Chapter 10

Three weeks went by.

At first, that first night, I was thinking that word might come from Wolfe in the next hour. Then I started thinking it might come the next day. As the days kept creeping along they changed my whole attitude, and before the end of April I was thinking it might come next week. By the time May had passed, and most of June, and the calendar and the heat both said summer, I was beginning to think it might never come.

But first to finish with April. The Rackham case followed the routine of spectacular murders when they never quite get to the point of a first-degree charge against anyone. For a week, the front page by unanimous consent; then, for a week or ten days, the front page only by cooking up an angle; and then back to the minors. None of the papers happened to feel like using it to start a crusade in the name of justice, so it took a normal course. It did not roll over and die, not with that all-star cast, including Nobby and Hebe; even months later a really new development would have got a three-column spread; but the development didn't come.

I made three more trips, by official request, to White Plains, with no profit to anyone, including me. All I could do was repeat myself, and all they could do was think up new ways to ask the same questions. For mental exercise I tried to get a line on whether Cramer's notions about Arnold Zeck had been passed on to Archer and Ben Dykes, but if so they never let on.

All I knew was what I read in the papers, until one evening I ran into Sergeant Purley Stebbins at Jake's and bought him a lobster. From him I got two little unpublished items: two FBI men had been called in to settle an argument about the legibility of fingerprints on the crinkly silver handle of the knife, and had voted no; and at one point Barry Rackham had been held at White Plains for twenty straight hours while the battle raged over whether they had enough to charge him. The noes won that time too.

The passing days got very little help from me. I had decided not to start pawing the ground or rearing up until Wolfe had been gone a full month, which would be May ninth, and I caught up on a lot of personal things, including baseball games, which don't need to be itemized. Also, with Fred Durkin, I finished up the poison-pen case and other loose ends that Wolfe had left dangling—nothing important—drove out to Long Island to see if Theodore and the plants had got settled in their new home, and put one of the cars, the big sedan, in dead storage.

One afternoon when I went to Rusterman's Restaurant to see Marko Vukcic he signed the checks I had brought, for telephone and electricity bills and my weekly salary, and then asked me what the bank balance was. I told him a little over twenty-nine thousand dollars, but I sort of regarded Mrs. Rackham's ten grand as being in escrow, so I would rather call it nineteen.

"Could you bring me a check for five thousand tomorrow? Drawn to cash."

"Glad to. But speaking as the bookkeeper, what do I charge it to?"

"Why—expense."

"Speaking as a man who may someday have to answer questions from an internal revenue snoop, whose expense and what kind?"

"Call it travel expense."

"Travel by whom and to where?"

Marko made some kind of a French noise, or foreign at least, indicating impatience, I think. "Listen, Archie, I have a power of attorney without limit. Bring me a check for five thousand dollars at your convenience. I am stealing it from my old friend Nero to spend on beautiful women or olive oil."

So I was not entirely correct when I said that I got no word at all from Wolfe during those weeks and months, but you must admit it was pretty vague. How far a man gets on five grand, and where he goes, depends on so many things.

When I returned to the office from a morning walk on the third day of May, a Wednesday, and called the phone-answering service as usual, I was told there had been three calls but only one message —to ring a Mount Kisco number and ask for Mrs. Frey. I considered the situation, told myself the thing to do was skip it, and decided that I must be hard of hearing when I became aware that I had dialed the operator and asked for the number. Then, after I had got it and spelled my name and waited a minute, Annabel Frey's voice was in my ear. At least the voice said it was her, but I wouldn't have recognized it. It was sort of tired and hopeless.

"You don't sound like you," I told her.

"I suppose not," she conceded. "It seems like a million years since you came that day and we watched you being a detective. You never found out who poisoned the dog, did you?"

"No, but don't hold it against me. I wasn't expected to. You may have heard that that was just a blind."

"Yes, of course. I don't suppose Nero Wolfe is back?"

"Nope."

"You're running his office for him?"

"Well, I wouldn't call it running. I'm here."

"I want to see you."

"Excuse me for staring, but do you mean on business?"

"Yes." A pause, then her voice got more energetic. "I want you to come up here and talk with us. I don't want to go on like this, and I'm not going to. When people look at me I can see it in their eyes—was it me that killed my mother-in-law?—or in some of them I can see it, and that makes me think it's there with all of them. It's been nearly a month now, and all the police are doing—but you read the papers. She left me this place and a lot of money, and I wish I could hire Nero Wolfe. You must know where he is."

"Sorry. I don't."

"Then I want to hire you. You're a good detective, aren't you?"

"Opinions vary. I rate myself close to the top, but you have to discount that for my bias."

"Could you come up here today? This evening?"

"I couldn't make it today." My brain was having some exercise for the first time in weeks. "Look, Mrs. Frey, I wouldn't be in a hurry about this. There's—"

"A hurry?" She sounded bitter. "It's been nearly a month!"

"I know, and that's why another few days won't matter. There's nothing fresh about it, to get stale. Why don't you do this, let me do a little looking around, just on my own, and then you'll hear from me. After that you can decide whether you want to hire me or not."

"I've already decided."

"I haven't. I don't want your dough if there's no chance of earning it."

Since her mind had been made up before she called me, she didn't like it my way but finally settled for it.

I discovered when I hung up that my mind was made up too. It had made itself up while I was talking to her. I couldn't go on like this forever, nothing but a damn caretaker with no telling from day to day how long it might last. Nor could I, while drawing pay as Wolfe's assistant, take a boat for Europe or run for Mayor of New York or buy an island and build up a harem, or any of the other things on my deferred list; and certainly, while taking his pay, I couldn't personally butt into a case that he had run away from.

But there was nothing to prevent me from taking advantage of the gratitude that was still felt, even after paying the fee, by certain former clients of ours, and I took up the phone again and got the president of one of the big realty outfits, and was glad to learn that I hadn't overestimated his gratitude.

When I had explained my problem he said he would do all he could to help, starting right then.

So I spent the afternoon looking at offices in the midtown section. All I wanted was one little room with a light that worked, but the man that the realty president sent to go around with me was more particular than I was, and he turned his nose up at two or three that I would have bought. We finally got to one on Madison Avenue, tenth floor, in the forties, which he admitted might do. It wouldn't be vacated until the next day, but that didn't matter much because I still had to buy furniture. I was allowed to sign for it on a month-to-month basis.

The next couple of days I had to keep myself under control. I had never been aware of any secret longing to have my own agency, but I had to choke off an impulse to drop in at Macgruder's Thursday morning and blow a couple of thousand of my own jack on office equipment. Instead, I went to Second Avenue and found bargains. Having decided not to take anything from Thirty-fifth Street, I made up a shopping list of about forty items, from ash trays to a Moorhead's Dictionary, and shot the works.

Late Saturday afternoon, with a package under my arm, I emerged from the elevator, went down the hall to the door of 1019, and backed off to give it a look.

ARCHIE GOODWIN
Private Detective

Not bad at all, I thought, unlocking the door and entering. I had considered having the painter put beneath it "By Appointment Only" to keep the crowd down, but decided to save the extra three bucks. I put my package on the desk, unwrapped it, and inspected my new letterheads and envelopes. The type of my name was a little too bold, maybe, but otherwise it was pretty neat. I uncovered the typewriter, a rebuilt Underwood that had set me back $62.75, inserted one of the letterheads, and wrote:

Dear Mrs. Frey:

If you still feel as you did when you phoned me on Wednesday, I would be glad to call on you to discuss the situation, with the understanding that I shall be representing no one but myself.

My new business address and phone number are above. Ring me or write me if you wish me to come.

Sincerely,

AG:hs

I read it over and signed it. It looked businesslike, I thought, with the regulation initialing at the bottom, the "hs" being for "himself." When I left, after putting the stationery in a drawer and getting things in order for the rush of business on Monday morning, I dropped the envelope in the mail chute. I was doing it that way, instead of phoning her, for three reasons: if she had changed her mind she could just ignore it; I had a date, purely personal, for the weekend; and I had drawn myself a salary check, the last one, for that week. On my way home I made a detour to Fifty-fourth Street, to tell Marko Vukcic what I had done, because I thought he should be the first to know.

He made it not only plain but emphatic that he disapproved. I told him, "Experience tells me that pants wear out quicker sitting down than moving around. Intelligence tells me that it's better to wait till you die to start to rot. I would appreciate it if you will convey that to him next time you write him or phone him."

"You know perfectly good, Archie, that—"

"Not perfectly good. Perfectly well."

"You know that I have said nothing, but nothing, that might make you think I can write him or phone him."

"You didn't need to. I know it's not your fault, but where does it leave me? Let me know any time you get a buyer for the house, and I'll move out."

I left him still wanting to argue.

I was not kidding myself that I had really cut loose, since I hadn't moved my bed out, but the way I figured it a caretaker who is drawing no pay has a right to a room; and besides, Fritz was still sleeping there and we were splitting on the groceries for breakfast, and I didn't want to insult either him or my stomach by breaking that up.

I shall now have to specify when I say office—or, better, I'll say office when I mean Wolfe's office, and when I mean my Madison Avenue suite I'll say 1019. Monday morning, arriving at 1019 a little after ten, I rang the phone-answering service and was told that there had been no calls, and then dug into the morning mail, which consisted of a folder from a window-cleaning outfit. After giving it full consideration, I typed notes on my new stationery to some personal friends, and an official letter to the City of New York giving notice of my change of address as a licensed detective. I was sitting trying to think who else I might write to when the phone rang—my first incoming call.

I picked it up and told the transmitter plainly, "Archie Goodwin's office."

"May I speak to Mr. Goodwin, please?"

"I'll see if he's in. Who is calling, please?"

"Mrs. Frey."

"Yes, he's in. This is me. You got my note?"

"It came this morning. I don't know what you mean about representing no one but yourself."

"I guess I didn't make it very clear. I only meant I wouldn't be acting as Nero Wolfe's assistant. I'm just myself now."

"Oh. Well—naturally, if you don't even know where he is. Can you come this evening?"

"To Birchvale?"

"Yes."

"What time?"

"Say eight-thirty?"

"I'll be there."

You can't beat that, I thought to myself as I hung up, for the first incoming call to a new office—making a deal with a client who has just inherited a country estate and a million monetary units. Then, fearing that if it kept up like that I might get swamped, I closed the office for the day and headed for Sulka's to buy a tie.

Chapter 11

On my previous visit to Birchvale I had got the impression that Annabel Frey had her head on right side up, and her conduct that Monday evening strengthened it. For one thing, she had had sense enough not to gather that bunch around a dining table but invite them for half-past eight. With the kind of attitudes and emotions that were crisscrossing among those six people, an attempt to feed them at the same trough would have resulted in an acidosis epidemic.

In her first phone call, Wednesday, she had indicated that it was not a tête-à-tête she had in mind, so I was expecting to find company, probably the widower and the cousin, but to my surprise it was a full house. They were all there when I was shown into the big living room. Annabel Frey, as hostess there now, came to meet me and gave me her hand. The other five gave me nothing but dirty looks. I saw right off that my popularity index was way down, so I merely stood, gave them a cool collective greeting, and lifted a brow at my hostess.

"It's not you, Goodwin," the politician Pierce assured me, but in a raspy tone. "It's simply the strain of this unbearable situation. We haven't been all together like this since that terrible night." He glared at Annabel. "It was a mistake to get us here."

"Then why did you come?" Barry Rackham demanded, really nasty. "Because you were afraid not to, like the rest of us. We all hated to come, but we were all afraid to stay away. A bunch of cowards—except one, of course. You can't blame *that* one for coming."

"Nonsense," said Dana Hammond, the banker. The look he was giving Rackham was just the opposite of the kind of look a banker is supposed to give a millionaire. "It has nothing to do with cowardice. Not with me. By circumstances beyond my control I am forced into an association that is hateful to me."

"Have they," Lina Darrow asked him sweetly, "finished with the audit of your department?"

"They haven't finished anything," Calvin Leeds growled, and I didn't know he was aiming at her until he went on. "Not even with wondering what you see in Barry Rackham all of a sudden—if it is sudden."

Rackham was out of his chair, moving toward Leeds, snarling, "You can eat that, Cal, or—"

"Oh, stop it!" Annabel stepped to head Rackham off. She whirled, taking them in. "My God, isn't it bad enough without this?" She appealed to me. "I didn't know this was how it would be!" To Rackham, "Sit down, Barry!"

Rackham backed up and sat. Lina Darrow, who had been standing, went and stretched out on a couch, detaching herself. The others stayed put, with Annabel and me on our feet. I have had plenty of contacts with groups of people, all kinds, who have suddenly had a murder explode among them, but I don't think I have ever seen a bunch blown quite so high.

Annabel said, "I didn't want to have Mr. Goodwin come and discuss it just with me. I didn't want any of you to think—I mean, all I wanted was to find out, for all of us. I thought it would be best for all of us to be here."

"All of us?" Pierce asked pointedly. "Or all but one?"

"It was a mistake, Annabel," Hammond told her. "You can see it was."

"Exactly what," Rackham inquired, "was your idea in sending for Goodwin?"

"I want him to work for us. We can't let it go on this way, you all know we can't. I'll pay him, but he'll be working for all of us."

"All but one," Pierce persisted.

"Very well, all but one! As it is now, it isn't all but one, it's all of us!"

Lina Darrow sang out from the couch, "Is Mr. Goodwin giving a guarantee?"

I had taken a chair. Annabel dropped into one facing me and put it to me. "What about it? Can you do anything?"

"I can't give a guarantee," I told her.

"Of course not. Can you do anything?"

"I don't know. I don't know how it stands. Shall I try sketching it?"

"Yes."

"Stop me if I go wrong. It's true I was here when it happened, but that's no help except what I actually saw and heard. Does everyone know what I was here for?"

"Yes."

"Then they understand why I wasn't much inter-

ested in anyone but Rackham. And you and Miss
Darrow, of course, but that interest wasn't professional. It looks to me like a case that will probably
never be solved by exhibits or testimony on facts.
The cops have had plenty of good men on it, and if
they had got anything usable on footprints or fingerprints, or getting the steak knife from the drawer, or
alibis or timetables, or something like shoes that had
been worn in the woods, someone would have been
arrested long ago. And they've had it for a month, so
no kind of routine would be any good now, and that's
all most detective work amounts to. Motive is no
help, with four of you inheriting piles from two hundred grand up, and the other two possibly counting
on marrying one of the piles. Only I must say, in the
atmosphere here tonight, courtship doesn't seem to
be on the program."

"It isn't," Annabel asserted.

I glanced at Hammond and Pierce, but neither of
them seemed to want the floor.

"So," I continued, "unless the cops have got a
trap set that you don't know about, it's one of those
things. You never can tell. It would be a waste of
money to pay me to go over the ground the cops
have covered—or any other detective except Nero
Wolfe, and he's not around. There's only one way to
use me, or anyhow only one way to start, and stand a
chance of getting your money's worth, and that
would be to give me a good eight or ten hours with
each of you six people, each one separately. I have
watched and listened to Nero Wolfe a good many
years and I can now do a fair imitation. It might possibly turn out to be worth it to all of you—except
one, as Mr. Pierce would say."

I flipped a hand. "That's the best suggestion I can offer. With nothing like a guarantee."

Annabel said, "No one would tell you everything you asked. I haven't myself, to the police."

"Sure. I understand that. That's part of it."

"You would be working for me—for us. It would be confidential."

"Things that weren't used would be confidential. Nothing that was evidence would be."

Annabel sat and regarded me. She had had her fingers twisted tight together, and now she loosened them and then they twisted again. "I want to ask you something, Mr. Goodwin. Do you think one of us killed Mrs. Rackham?"

"I do now. I don't know what I would think after I had worked at it."

"Do you think you know which one?"

"Nope. I'm impartial."

"All right. You can start with me." She turned her head. "Unless one of you would rather be first?"

No one moved or spoke. Then Calvin Leeds: "Count me out, Annabel. Not with Goodwin. Let him tell us first where Nero Wolfe is and why."

"But Cal—you won't?"

"Not with him I won't."

"Dana?"

Hammond looked unhappy. He got up and went to her. "Annabel, this was a mistake. The whole idea was no good. What can Goodwin do that the police couldn't do? I doubt if you have any conception of how a private detective works."

"He can try. Will you help, Dana?"

"No. I hate to refuse, but I must."

"Oliver, will you?"

"Well." The statesman was frowning, not at her,

at me. "This seems to me to be a case of all or none. I
don't see how anything could be accomplished—"

"Then you refuse me too?"

"Under the circumstances I have no other
course."

"I see. You won't even give me a straight no.
Barry?"

"Certainly not. Goodwin has lied to the police
about my wife's visit to Wolfe. I wouldn't give him
eight seconds, let alone eight hours."

Annabel left her chair and went toward the
couch. "Lina, I guess it's up to the women. You and
me. She was darned good to us, Lina—both of us.
What about it?"

"Darling," Lina Darrow said. She sat up. "Darling
Annabel. You know you don't like me."

"That isn't true," Annabel protested. "Just because—"

"Of course it's true. You thought I was trying to
squeeze you out. You thought I was making a play
for Barry merely because I was willing to admit he
might be human, so wait and see. You thought I was
trying to snatch Ollie from you, when as a matter of
fact—"

"Lina, for God's sake," Pierce implored her.

Her fine dark eyes flashed at him. "She did, Ollie!
When as a matter of fact she got bored with you, and
I happened to be near." The eyes darted right to left,
sweeping them. "And look at you now, all of you, and
listen to you! You all think Barry killed her—all except one, you would say, Ollie. But you haven't got
the guts to say so. And this Mr. Goodwin of yours,
darling Annabel, have you told him that what you
really want him for is to find some kind of proof that

Barry did it? No, I suppose you're saving that for later."

Lina arose, in no hurry, and confronted Annabel from springing distance. "I thought it would be something like this," she said, and left us, detouring around Leeds' chair and heading for the door to the reception hall. Eyes followed her, but no one said anything; then, as she passed out of sight, Barry Rackham got up and, without a glance for any of us, including his hostess, tramped from the room.

The remaining three guests exchanged looks. Leeds and Pierce left their chairs.

"I'm sorry, Annabel," Leeds said gruffly. "But didn't I tell you about Goodwin?"

She didn't reply. She only stood and breathed. Leeds went, with not as much spring to his step as I had seen, and Pierce, mumbling a good night, followed. Dana Hammond went to Annabel, had a hand out to touch her arm, and then let it drop.

"My dear," he said, appealing to her, "it was no good. It couldn't be. If you had consulted me—"

"I'll remember next time, Dana. Good night."

"I want to talk with you, Annabel. I want to—"

"For God's sake, let me alone! Go!"

He backed up a step and scowled at me, as if I were to blame for everything. I lifted my right brow at him. It's one of my few outstanding talents, lifting one brow, and I save it for occasions when nothing else would quite serve the purpose.

He walked out of the room without another word.

Annabel dropped onto the nearest chair, put her elbows on her knees, and buried her face in her hands.

I stood looking down at her. "It was not," I told her sympathetically, "what I would call a success, but anyhow you tried. Not to try to make you feel better, but for future guidance, it might have been wiser, instead of calling a convention, to tackle them one at a time. And it was too bad you picked Leeds to sell first, since he has a grudge against me. But the truth is you were licked before you started. The shape their nerves are in, touching them with a feather wouldn't tickle them, it would give them a stroke. Thanks all the same for asking me."

I left her. By the time I got out to the parking space the cars of the other guests were gone. Rolling down the curving driveway, I was thinking that my first incoming phone call hadn't been so damned magnificent after all.

Chapter 12

One or two of my friends have tried to tell me that some of my experiences that summer are worth telling about, but even taking them at their word, I'm not going to drag it in here. However, it is true that after I ran an ad in the *Gazette* and word got around I soon quit keeping count of the incoming calls. All I'll do here is summarize it by months:

May. Woman with pet cat stolen. Got it back; fifty dollars and expenses. Guy who got rolled in a joint on Eighth Avenue and didn't want to call the cops. Found her and scared most of it out of her. Two Cs for me. Man who wanted his son pried loose from a blond sharpie. Shouldn't have tried; fell on my nose; took a C above expenses anyhow. Restaurant with a dumb cashier with sticky fingers; took only one afternoon to hook her; client beefed about my request for sixty-five dollars but paid it.

June. Spent two full weeks handling a hot insurance case for Del Bascom and damn near got my skull cracked for good. Cleaned it up. Del had the nerve to offer me 3 Cs; demanded a grand and got it. My idea was to net more per week than I had been getting from Wolfe, not that I cared for the money, but as a matter of principle. Found a crooked bookie for a man from Meadville, Pa. A hundred and fifty dollars. Man wanted me to find his vanished wife, but it looked dim and he could pay only twenty bucks a day, so I passed it. Girl unjustly accused, she said, of giving secret business dope to a rival firm, and fired from her job, pestered me into tackling it. Proved she was right and got her job back, doing five hundred dollars' worth of work for a measly hundred and twenty, paid in installments. Her face wasn't much, but she had a nice voice and good legs. Got an offer of a job from the FBI, my ninth offer from various sources in six weeks, and turned it down.

July. Took a whirl at supervising ten men for a bunch of concessionaires at Coney Island; caught one of them taking a cut from doobey stands; he jumped me with a cooler and I broke his arm. Got tired of looking at a thousand acres of bare skin, mostly peeling, practically all nonseductive, and quit. Eight fifty for seventeen days. Had passed up at least two thousand worth of little chores. Screwball woman on Long Island had had jewelry stolen, uninsured, thought cops were in on it and stalling. Two things happened: I got some breaks, and I did a damn good piece of work. It took me into August. I got all the jewelry back, hung it on an interior decorator's assistant with proof, billed her for thirty-five hundred gross, and collected.

August. I had drawn no pay from Wolfe's checkbook since May sixth, I had not gone near my personal safe deposit box, and my personal bank balance had not only not sunk, it had lifted. I decided I had a vacation coming. The most I had ever been able to talk Wolfe out of was two weeks, and I thought I should double that at least. A friend of mine, whose name has appeared in print in connection with one of Wolfe's cases, had the idea that we should take a look at Norway, and her point of view seemed sound.

Slow but sure, I was working myself around to an attitude toward life without Nero Wolfe on a permanent basis. One thing that kept it slow was the fact that early in July Marko Vukcic had asked me to bring him another check for five grand drawn to cash. Since if you wanted to eat in his restaurant you had to reserve a table a day in advance, and then pay six bucks for one helping of guinea hen, I knew he wasn't using it himself, so who was? Another thing, the house hadn't been sold, and, doing a little snooping on my own account, I had learned that the asking price was a hundred and twenty thousand, which was plain silly. On the other hand, if Marko was getting money to Wolfe, that didn't prove that I was ever going to see him again, and there was no hurry about selling the house until the bank balance began to sag; and also there was Wolfe's safe deposit box. Visiting his safe deposit box was one item on the select list of purposes for which Wolfe had been willing to leave his house.

I did not really want to leave New York, especially to go as far as Norway. I had a feeling that I would about be passing Sandy Hook when word would come somehow, wire or phone or letter or messenger, to Thirty-fifth Street or 1019, in a code that I would understand—if I was there to get it. And if it did come I wanted to be there, or I might be left out of the biggest charade Wolfe had ever staged. But it hadn't been days or weeks, it had been months, and my friend was pretty good at several things, including riding me about hanging on forever to the short end of the stick, so we had reservations on a ship that sailed August twenty-sixth.

Four days before that, August twenty-second, a Tuesday afternoon, I was sitting at my desk at 1019, to keep an appointment with a man who had phoned. I had told him I was soon leaving for a month's vacation, and he hadn't felt like giving a name, but I thought I recognized the voice and had agreed to see him. When he walked in on the dot, at 3:15, I was glad to know that my memory for voices was holding up. It was my old cellmate, Max Christy.

I got up and we shook. He put his panama on the desk and glanced around. His black mop was cut a little shorter than it had been in April, but the jungle of his eyebrows hadn't been touched, and his shoulders looked just as broad in gray tropical worsted. I invited him to sit and he did.

"I must apologize," I said, "for never settling for that breakfast. It was a life-saver."

He waved it away. "The pleasure was mine. How's it going?"

"Oh—no complaints. You?"

"I've been extremely busy." He got out a handkerchief and dabbed at his face and neck. "I certainly sweat. Sometimes I think it's stupid, this constant back and forth, push and shove."

"I hear you mentioned around."

"Yes, I suppose so. You never phoned me. Did you?"

"The number," I said, "is Churchill five, three two three two."

"But you never called it."

"No, sir," I admitted, "I didn't. One thing and another kept coming up, and then I didn't care much for your line about if I got taken in and my being given a trial. I am by no means a punk, and the ink on my license dried long ago. Here, look behind my ears."

He threw back his head and haw-hawed, then shut it off and told me soberly, "You got me wrong, Goodwin. I only meant we'd have to go slow on account of your record." He used the handkerchief on his forehead. "I certainly do sweat. Since then your name has been discussed a little, and I assure you, you are not regarded as a punk. We have noticed that you seem to have plenty of jobs since you opened this office, but so trivial for a man like you. Why did you turn down the offer from the Feds?"

"Oh, they keep such long hours."

He nodded. "And you don't like harness, do you?"

"I never tried it and don't intend to."

"What have you got on hand now? Anything important?"

"Nothing whatever, important or otherwise. I told you on the phone, I'm taking a vacation. Sailing Saturday."

He regarded me disapprovingly. "You don't need a vacation. If anybody needs a vacation it's me, but I don't get one. I've got a job for you."

I shook my head. "Not right now. When I get back maybe."

"It won't wait till you get back. There's a man we want tailed and we're short of personnel, and he's tough. We had two good men on him, and he spotted both of them. You would need at least two helpers; three would be better. You use men you know, handle that yourself, and pay them and expenses out of the five hundred a day you'll get."

I whistled. "What's so hot about it?"

"Nothing. It's not hot."

"Then who's the subject, the Mayor?"

"I'm not naming him. Perhaps I don't even know. It's merely a straight tailing job, but it has to be watertight and no leaks. You can net three hundred a day easy."

"Not without a hint who he is or what he looks like." I waved it away. "Forget it. I'd like to oblige an old cellmate, but my vacation starts Saturday."

"Your vacation can wait. This can't. At ten o'clock tonight you'll be walking west on Sixty-seventh Street halfway between First and Second Avenues. A car will pick you up, with a man in it that wants to ask you some questions. If your answers suit him he'll tell you about the job—and it's your big chance, Goodwin. It's your chance for your first dip into the biggest river of fast dough that ever flowed."

"What the hell," I protested, "you're not offering me a job, you're just giving me a chance to apply for one I don't want."

It was perfectly true at that point, and it was still true ten minutes later, when Max Christy left, that I didn't want the job, but I did want to apply for it. It wasn't that I had a hunch that the man in the car who wanted to ask me some questions would be Arnold Zeck, but the way it had been staged gave me the notion that it was just barely possible; and the opportunity, slim as it was, was too good to miss. It would be interesting to have a chat with Zeck; besides, he might give me an excuse to take a poke at him and I might happen to inadvertently break his neck. So I told Christy that I would be walking on Sixty-seventh Street at ten that evening as suggested. I had to break a date to do it, but even if the chance was only one in a million I wanted it.

To get that point settled and out of the way, the

man who wanted to quiz me was not Arnold Zeck. It was not even a long black Cadillac; it was only a '48 Chevy two-door sedan.

It was a hot August night, and as I walked along that block I was sweating a little myself, especially my left armpit under the holster. There was a solid string of parked cars at the curb, and when the Chevy stopped and its door opened and my name was called, not loud, I had to squeeze between bumpers to get to it. As I climbed in and pulled the door shut the man in the front seat, behind the wheel, swiveled his head for a look at me and then, with no greeting, went back to his chauffeuring, and the car started forward.

My companion on the back seat muttered at me, "Maybe you ought to show me something."

I got out my display case and handed it to him with the license—detective, not driver's—uppermost. When we stopped for a light at Second Avenue he inspected it with the help of a street lamp, and returned it. I was already sorry I had wasted an evening. Not only was he not Zeck; he was no one I had ever seen or heard of, though I was fairly well acquainted, at least by sight, with the high brass in the circles that Max Christy moved in. This bird was a complete stranger. With more skin supplied for his face than was needed, it had taken up the slack in pleats and wrinkles, and that may have accounted for his sporting a pointed brown beard, since it must be hard to shave pleats.

As the car crossed the avenue and continued west, I told him, "I came to oblige Max Christy—if suggestions might help any. I'll only be around till Saturday."

He said, "My name's Roeder," and spelled it.

I thanked him for the confidence. He broadened it. "I'm from the West Coast, in case you wonder how I rate. I followed something here and found it was tied in with certain operations. I'd just as soon leave it to local talent and go back home, but I'm hooked and I have to stick." Either he preferred talking through his nose or that was the only way he knew. "Christy told you we want a man tailed?"

"Yes. I explained that I'm not available."

"You have got to be available. There's too much involved." He twisted around to face me. "It'll be harder than ever now, because he's on guard. It's been messed up. They say if anyone can do it you can, especially with the help of a couple of men that Nero Wolfe used. You can get them, can't you?"

"Yeah, I can get them, but I can't get me. I won't be here."

"You're here now. You can start tomorrow. As Christy told you, five Cs a day. It's a straight tailing job, where you're working for a man named Roeder from Los Angeles. The cops might not like it too well if you tied in with a local like Wilts or Brownie Costigan, but what's wrong with me? You never heard of me before. You're in business as a private detective. I want to hire you, at a good price, to keep a tail on a man named Rackham and report to me on his movements. That's all, a perfectly legitimate job."

We had crossed Park Avenue. The light was dim enough that I didn't have to be concerned about my face showing a reaction to the name Rackham. The reaction inside me was my affair.

"How long would it last?" I inquired.

"I don't know. A day, a week, possibly two."

"What if something hot develops? A detective doesn't take a tailing job sight unseen. You must have told me why you were curious about Rackham. What did you tell me?"

Roeder smiled. I could just see the pleats tightening. "That I suspected my business partner had come east to make a deal with him, freezing me out."

"That could be all right if you'll fill it in. But why all the mystery? Why didn't you come to my office instead of fixing it to pick me off the street at night?"

"I don't want to show in the daytime. I don't want my partner to know I'm here." Roeder smiled again. "Incidentally, that's quite true, that I don't want to show in the daytime—not any more than I can help."

"That I believe. Skipping the comedy, there aren't many Rackhams. There are none in the Manhattan phone book. Is this the Barry Rackham whose wife got killed last spring?"

"Yes."

I grunted. "Quite a coincidence. I was there when she was murdered, and now I'm offered the job of tailing him. If he gets murdered too that *would* be a coincidence. I wouldn't like it. I had a hell of a time getting out from under a bond as a material witness so I could take a vacation. If he got killed while I was on his tail—"

"Why should he?"

"I don't know. I didn't know why she should either. But it was Max Christy who arranged this date, and while he is not himself a marksman as far as I know, he moves in circles that like direct action." I waved a hand. "Forget it. If that's the kind of interest you've got in Rackham you wouldn't tell me anyhow. But another thing: Rackham knows me. It's twice as hard to tail a guy that knows you. Why hire a man that's handicapped to begin with? Why not—"

I held it because we had stopped for a red light,

on Fifth Avenue in the Seventies, and our windows were open, and the open window of a car alongside was only arm's distance away.

When the light changed and we rolled again Roeder spoke. "I'll tell you, Goodwin, this thing's touchy. There'll be some people scattered around that are in on things together, and they trust each other up to a point. As long as their interests all run the same way they can trust each other pretty well. But when something comes up that might help some and hurt others, then it gets touchy. Then each man looks out for himself, or he decides where the strength is and lines up there. That's where I am, where the strength is. But I'm not trying to line you up; we wouldn't want to even if we could; how could we trust you? You're an outsider. All we want you for is an expert tailing job, and you report to me and me only. Where are you going, Bill?"

The driver half-turned his head to answer, "Here in the park it might be cooler."

"It's no cooler anywhere. I like straight streets. Get out again, will you?"

The driver said he would, in a hurt tone. Roeder returned to me. "There are three men named Panzer, Cather, and Durkin who worked for Nero Wolfe off and on. That right?"

I said it was.

"They'll work for you, won't they?"

I said I thought they would.

"Then you can use them, and you won't have to show much. I'm told they're exceptionally good men."

"Saul Panzer is the best man alive. Cather and Durkin are way above average."

"That's all you'll need. Now I want to ask you

something, but first here's a remark. It's a bad thing
to mislead a client, I'm sure you realize that, but in
this case it would be worse than bad. I don't have to
go into details, do I?"

"No, but you're going too fast. I haven't got a client."

"Oh, yes, you have." Roeder smiled. "Would I
waste my time like this? You were there when Mrs.
Rackham was killed, you phoned Nero Wolfe and in
six hours he was gone, and you were held as a material witness. Now here I want to hire you to tail
Rackham, and you don't know why. Can you say no?
Impossible."

"It could be," I suggested, "that I've had all I
want."

"Not you, from what I've heard. That's all right,
not being able to let go is a good thing in a man, but
it brings up this question I mentioned. You're on
your own now apparently, but you were with Nero
Wolfe a long time. You're still living in his house. Of
course you're in touch with him—don't bother to
deny it—but that's no concern of ours as long as he
doesn't get in the way. Only on this job it has to be
extra plain that you're working for the man who
pays you. If you get facts about Rackham and peddle
them elsewhere, to Nero Wolfe for example, you
would be in a very bad situation. Perhaps you know
how bad?"

"Sure, I know. If I were standing up my knees
would give. Just for the record, I don't know where
Mr. Wolfe is, I'm not in touch with him, and I'm in no
frame of mind to peddle him anything. If I take this
on, tailing Rackham, it will be chiefly because I've
got my share of monkey in me. I doubt if Mr. Wolfe,

wherever he is, would recognize the name Rackham if he heard it."

The brown pointed beard waggled as Roeder shook his head. "Don't overplay it, Goodwin."

"I'm not. I won't."

"You are still attached to Wolfe."

"Like hell I am."

"I couldn't pay you enough to tell me where he is —assuming you know."

"Maybe not," I conceded. "But not selling him is one thing, and carrying his picture around is another. I freely admit he had his good points, I have often mentioned them and appreciated them, but as the months go by one fact about him stands out clearer than anything else. He was a pain in the ass."

The driver's head jerked around for a darting glance at me. We had left the park and were back on Fifth Avenue, headed uptown in the Eighties. My remarks about Wolfe were merely casual, because my mind was on something else. Who was after Rackham and why? If it was Zeck, or someone in one of Zeck's lines of command, then something drastic had happened since the April day when Zeck had sent Wolfe a package of sausage and phoned him to let Rackham alone. If it wasn't Zeck, then Max Christy and this Roeder were lined up against Zeck, which made them about as safe to play with as an atomic stockpile. Either way, how could I resist it? Besides, I liked the logic of it. Nearly five months ago Mrs. Rackham had hired us to do a survey on her husband, and paid in advance, and we had let it slide. Now I could take up where we had left off. If Roeder and his colleagues, whoever they were, wanted to pay me for it, there was no use offending them by refusing.

So, rolling north on the avenue, Roeder and I agreed that we agreed in principle and got down to brass tacks. Since Rackham was on guard it couldn't be an around-the-clock operation with less than a dozen men, and I had three at the most. Or did I? Saul and Fred and Orrie might not be immediately available. There was no use discussing an operation until I found out if I had any operators. Having their phone numbers in my head, I suggested that we stop at a drugstore and use a booth, but Roeder didn't like that. He thought it would be better to go to my office and phone from there, and I had no objection, so he told the driver to go over to Madison and downtown.

At that hour, getting on toward eleven, Madison Avenue was wide open, and so was the curb in front of the office building. Roeder told the driver we would be an hour or more, and we left him parked there. In the brighter light of the elevator the pleats of Roeder's face were less noticeable, and he didn't look as old as I would have guessed him in the car, but I could see there was a little gray in his beard. He stood propped in a corner with his shoulder slumped and his eyes closed until the door opened for the tenth floor, and then came to and followed me down the hall to 1019. I unlocked the door and let us in, switched on the light, motioned him to a chair, sat at the desk, pulled the phone to me, and started dialing.

"Wait a minute," he said gruffly.

I put it back on the cradle, looked at him, got a straight clear view of his eyes for the first time, and felt a tingle in the small of my back. But I didn't know why.

"This must not be heard," he said. "I mean you and me. How sure are you?"

"You mean a mike?"

"Yes."

"Oh, pretty sure."

"Better take a look."

I left my chair and did so. The room being small and the walls mostly bare, it wasn't much of a job, and I made it thorough, even pulling the desk out to inspect behind it. As I straightened up from retrieving a pencil that had rolled off the desk when I pushed it back in place, he spoke to my back.

"I see you have my dictionary here."

Not through his nose. I whirled and went rigid, gaping at him. The eyes again—and now other items too, especially the forehead and ears. I had every right to stare, but I also had a right to my own opinion of the fitness of things. So while staring at him I got myself under control, and then circled the end of my desk, sat down and leaned back, and told him, "I knew you all—"

"Don't talk so loud."

"Very well. I knew you all the time, but with that damn driver there I had to—"

"Pfui. You hadn't the slightest inkling."

I shrugged. "That's one we'll never settle. As for the dictionary, it's the one from my room which you gave me for Christmas nineteen thirty-nine. How much do you weigh?"

"I've lost a hundred and seventeen pounds."

"Do you know what you look like?"

He made a face. With the pleats and whiskers, he didn't really have to make one, but of course it was an old habit which had probably been suppressed for months.

"Yes," he said, "I do. I look like a sixteenth-century prince of Savoy named Philibert." He flipped a hand impatiently. "This can wait, surely, until we're home again?"

"I should think so," I conceded. "What's the difference, another year or two? It won't be as much fun, though, because now I'll know what I'm waiting for. What I really enjoyed was the suspense. Were you dead or alive or what? A perfect picnic."

He grunted. "I expected this, of course. It is you, and since I decided long ago to put up with you, I even welcome it. But you, also long ago, decided to put up with me. Are we going to shake hands or not?"

I got up and went halfway. He got up and came halfway. As we shook, our eyes met, and I deliberately focused on his eyes, because otherwise I would have been shaking with a stranger, and one hell of a specimen to boot. We returned to our chairs.

As I sat down I told him courteously, "You'll have to excuse me if I shut my eyes or look away from time to time. It'll take a while to get adjusted."

Chapter 13

No other course," Wolfe said, "was possible. I had accepted money from Mrs. Rackham and she had been murdered. I was committed in her interest, and therefore against Arnold Zeck, and I was no match for him. I had to ambush him. With me gone, how should you act? You should act as if I had disappeared and you knew nothing. Under what circumstances would you do that most convincingly? You are capable of dissimulation, but why try you so severely? Why not merely—"

"Skip it," I told him. "Save it for later. Where do we stand now, and what chance have we got? Any at all?"

"I think so, yes. If the purpose were merely to expose one or more of Zeck's operations, it could be done like that." He snapped his fingers. "But since he must himself be destroyed—all I can say is that I have reached the point where you can help. I have talked with him three times."

"Exactly who and what are you?"

"I come from Los Angeles. When I left here, on April ninth, I went to southern Texas, on the Gulf, and spent there the most painful month in my life—

except one, long ago. At its end I was not recognizable." He shuddered. "I then went to Los Angeles, because a man of importance there considers himself more deeply in my debt even than he is. He is important but not reputable. The terms are not interchangeable."

"I never said they were."

"Through him I met people and I engaged in certain activities. In appearance I was monstrous, but in the circles I frequented my stubble was accepted as a masquerade, which indeed it was, and I displayed myself publicly as little as possible. With my two invaluable assets, my brains and my important debtor, and with a temporary abandonment of scruple, I made a substantial impression in the shortest possible time, especially with a device which I conceived for getting considerable sums of money from ten different people simultaneously, with a minimum of risk. Luck had a hand in it too, but without luck no man can keep himself alive, let alone prevail over an Arnold Zeck."

"So then Los Angeles was too hot for you."

"It was not. But I was ready to return east, both physically and psychologically, and knowing that inquiries sent to Los Angeles would get a satisfactory response, I arrived on July twelfth. You remember that I once spoke of Arnold Zeck, calling him X, to the Sperling family?"

"I do."

"And I described briefly the echelons of crime. First, the criminal himself—or gang. In the problem of disposal of the loot, or of protection against discovery and prosecution, he can seldom avoid dealing with others. He will need a fence, a lawyer, witnesses for an alibi, a channel to police or political influence—no matter what, he nearly always needs someone or something. He goes to one he knows, or knows about, one named A. A, finding a little difficulty, consults B. B may be able to handle it; if not, he takes it on to C. C is usually able to oblige, but when he isn't he communicates with D. Here we are getting close. D has access to Arnold Zeck, not only for the purpose described, but also in connection with one or more of the enterprises which Zeck controls."

Wolfe tapped his chest with a forefinger, a gesture I had never before seen him use, acquired evidently along with his pleats and whiskers. "I am a D, Archie."

"Congratulations."

"Thank you. Having earned them, I accept them. Look at me."

"Yeah, I am. Wait till Fritz sees you."

"If he ever does," Wolfe said grimly. "We have a chance, and that's all. If all we needed were evidence of Zeck's complicity in felonies, there would be no problem; I know where it is and I could get it. But his defenses are everywhere, making him next to invulnerable. It would be fatuous to suppose that he could ever be convicted, and even if he were, he would still be living, so that wouldn't help any. Now that I am committed against him, and he knows it, there are only two possible outcomes—"

"How does he know it?"

"He knows me. Knowing me, he knows that I intend to get the murderer of Mrs. Rackham. He intends to prevent me. Neither—"

"Wait a minute. Admitting he knows that about Nero Wolfe, what about you as Roeder? You say you're a D. Then you're on Zeck's payroll."

"Not on his payroll. I have been placed in charge

of the operation here of the device which I conceived and used in Los Angeles. My handling of it has so impressed him that I am being trusted with other responsibilities."

"And Max Christy and that driver downstairs—they're Zeck men?"

"Yes—at a distance."

"Then how come salting Barry Rackham? Wasn't it Zeck money that Rackham was getting?"

Wolfe sighed. "Archie, if we had more time I would let you go on and on. I could shut my eyes and pretend I'm back home." He shook his head vigorously. "But we must get down to business. I said that driver is a Zeck man at a distance, but that is mere surmise. Being new and by no means firmly established in confidence, I am certainly being watched, and that driver might even report to Zeck himself. That was why I prolonged our talk in the car before suggesting that we come here. We shouldn't be more than an hour, so you'd better let me—"

He stopped as I grasped the knob and pulled the door open. I had tiptoed across to it as he talked. Seeing an empty hall in both directions, I closed the door and went back to my chair.

"I was only asking," I protested, "why the play on Rackham?"

"How long," Wolfe asked, "have you and I spent, there in the office, discussing some simple affair such as the forging of a check?"

"Oh, anywhere from four minutes to four hours."

"Then what should we take for this? By the way, you will resume drawing your pay check this week. How much have you taken from the safe deposit box in New Jersey?"

"Nothing. Not a cent."

"You should have. That was put there for the express purpose of financing this eventuality if it arose. You have been using your personal savings?"

"Only to buy these little items." I waved a hand. "Put it back long ago. I've been taking it easy, so my income from detective work has only been a little more than double what you were paying me."

"I don't believe it."

"I didn't expect you to, so I'll have an audit—" I stopped. "What the hell! My vacation!"

Wolfe grunted. "If we get Zeck you may have a month. If he gets me—" He grunted again. "He will, confound it, if we don't get to work. You asked about Rackham; yes, the source of his income, which his wife asked us to discover, was Zeck. He met him through Calvin Leeds."

I raised the brows. "Leeds?"

"Don't jump to conclusions. Leeds sold dogs to Zeck, two of them, to protect his house, and spent a week there, training them for their job. Zeck does not miss an opportunity. He used Rackham in one of his less offensive activities, gambling arrangements for people with too much money. Then when Rackham inherited more than half of his wife's wealth a new situation developed; it was already developing when I arrived six weeks ago. I managed to get informed about it. Of course I had to be extremely careful, new as I was, but on the other hand my being a newcomer was an advantage. In preparing a list of prospects for the device I had conceived, a man in Rackham's position was an eminently suitable candidate, and naturally I had to know all about him. That placed me favorably for starting, with the greatest caution, certain speculations and suspicions, and I got it to the point where it seemed desirable to put him under surveillance. Luckily I didn't have to introduce your name; your enlistment had previously been considered, on a suggestion by Max Christy. I was ready for you anyhow—I had gone as far as I could without you—and that made it easier. I wouldn't have dared to risk naming you myself, and was planning accordingly, but it's vastly better this way."

"Am I to proceed? Get Saul and Orrie and Fred? Tail Rackham?"

Wolfe looked at his wrist. His charade was certainly teaching him new tricks. In all my years with him he had never sported a watch, and here he was glancing at his wrist as if born to it. The way that wrist had been, normal, it would have required a custom-made strap.

"I told that man an hour or more," he said, "but we shouldn't be that long. A minimum of cause for suspicion and I'm through. Nothing is too fantastic for them; they could even learn if we've been using the phone. Confound it, I must have hours with you."

"Ditch him and we'll meet somewhere."

"Impossible. No place would be safe—except one. There is only one circumstance under which any man is granted the right to an extended period of undisturbed privacy, either by deliberation or on impulse. We need a woman. You know all kinds."

"Not all kinds," I objected. "I do draw the line. What kind do we need?"

"Fairly young, attractive, a little wanton in appearance, utterly devoted to you and utterly trustworthy, and not a fool."

"My God, if I knew where to find one like that I'd have been married long ago. Also I would be bragging—"

"Archie," he snapped. "If after all your promiscuous philandering you can't produce a woman to those specifications, I've misjudged you. It's risky to trust anyone at all, but any other way would be still riskier."

I had my lips puckered. "Ruth Brady?"

"No. She's an operative, and known. Out of the question."

"There's one who might take this as a substitute for a trip to Norway, which is now out. I could ask her."

"What's her name?"

"You know. Lily Rowan."

He made a face. "She is rich, intemperate, and notorious."

"Nuts. She is well-heeled and playful. You remember the time she helped out with an upstate murderer. I have no further suggestions. Do I phone her?"

"Yes."

"And tell her what?"

He explained in some detail. When he had answered my three or four questions, and filed my objection by asking if I had something better to offer, I pulled the phone to me and dialed a number. No answer. I tried the Troubadour Room of the Churchill; she wasn't there. Next in order of priority was the Flamingo Club. That found her. Asked my name, I said to tell her it was Escamillo, though she hadn't called me that for quite a while.

After a wait her voice came. "Archie? Really?"

"I prefer Escamillo," I said firmly. "It's a question of security. How high are you?"

"Come and find out. I'm tired of the people I'm

with anyhow. Listen, I'll wander out and meet you in front and we'll go—"

"We will not. I'm working, and I'm on a spot, and I need help. You're just the type for it, and I pay a dollar an hour if you give satisfaction. I'm offering you a brand new thrill. You have never earned a nickel in your life, and here's your chance. What mood are you in?"

"I'm bored as the devil, but all I need is six dances with you and—"

"Not tonight, my colleen donn. Damn it, I'm working. Will you help?"

"When?"

"Now."

"Is it any fun?"

"So-so. Nothing to brag of."

"Are you coming here for me?"

"No. I'm going—you must get this straight. Now listen."

"That's exactly what I had in mind. I was just telling myself, Lily, my precious, if he starts talking you must listen, because he is very shy and sensitive and therefore—did you say something?"

"I said shut up. I'm at my office. A man is here with me. We'll leave as soon as I hang up. I'll go alone to your place and wait for you outside your door. The man—"

"You won't have to wait. I can make it—"

"Shut up, please. Your first hour has started, so this is on my time. The man with me has a car with a driver parked down in front. He will be driven to the Flamingo Club and stop at the curb, and you will be waiting there in front, and when he opens the door you will climb in, *not* waiting for him to get out like a gentleman, because he won't. You will not speak to the driver, who, when you're inside, will proceed to your address, where you and the man will find me waiting at your door."

"Unless I get in the wrong car, and—"

"I'm telling you. It's a dark gray forty-eight Chevy two-door sedan, New York license OA six, seven, one, one, three. Got that?"

"Yes."

"I'll make it a dollar ten an hour. The man will call you Lily, and you will call him Pete. Joining him in the car and riding up to your place, you need not go to extremes, but it is important for the driver to get the idea that you are mighty glad to see Pete and that you are looking forward with pleasure to the next several hours with him. But—"

"Is it a reunion after a long absence?"

"I'll make it a dollar twenty an hour. I was about to say, you can leave it vague whether you last saw Pete a week ago or two months ago. You're just glad to be with him because you're so fond of him, but don't get thinking you're Paulette Goddard and ham it. Do it right. Pretend it's me. Which brings me to the crux. It's going to be an ordeal for you. Wait till you see Pete."

"What's the matter with him?"

"Everything. He's old enough to be your father and then some. He has whiskers, turning gray. His face is pleated. You will have to fight down the feeling that you're having a nightmare, and—"

"Archie! It's Nero Wolfe!"

Goddam a woman anyhow. There was absolutely no sense or reason for it. My brain buzzed.

"Sure," I said admiringly. "You do it with mirrors. If it was him, the way I feel about him, the first thing I would do would be to get him a date with

you, huh? Okay, then don't call him Pete, call him
Nero."

"Then who is it?"

"It's a man named Pete Roeder, and I've got to
have a long talk with him that won't get in the papers."

"We could take him to Norway."

"Maybe. We have to discuss Norway. Give me a
ring later in the week and tell me how you feel about
this proposition."

"I'll be out on the sidewalk in ten minutes, less
than that, waiting for my Pete."

"No public announcement."

"Certainly not."

"I'm very pleased with your work so far. We'll
have to get you a social security number. I'll be waiting anxiously at your door."

I hung up and told Wolfe, "All set."

Out of his chair, he grunted. "You overdid it a
little, perhaps? Nightmare, for instance?"

"Yes, sir," I agreed. "I get too enthusiastic."

I glared at him, and he glared back.

Chapter 14

Since I do not intend to use up paper reporting the five-hour conference I had with Wolfe that night in Lily Rowan's living room, I could just as well go on to Wednesday morning, except for one thing. I have got to tell about their arrival at the door of Lily's penthouse apartment on East Sixty-third Street. Wolfe didn't speak and wouldn't look at me. Lily shook hands with me, a form of greeting we hadn't used for I don't know how long, then unlocked the door, and we entered. When her wrap and Wolfe's hat had been disposed of and we passed to the living room, she tossed her firecracker.

"Archie," she said, "I knew darned well that something would happen someday to make up for all the time I've wasted on you. I just felt it would."

I nodded. "Certainly. You'll show a profit on the night even if you feed us sandwiches, especially since Pete is a light eater. He's on a diet."

"Oh," she said, "I didn't mean money, and you can go the limit on sandwiches. I meant the distinction you've brought me. I'm the only woman in America who has necked with Nero Wolfe. Nightmare, my eye. He has a flair."

Wolfe, who had seated himself, cocked his head to frown at her—a first-rate performance.

I smiled at her. "I told Pete what you said on the phone, and he was flattered. Okay, woman of distinction."

She shook her head. "Turn loose, my brave fellow. I've got hold of it." She moved to Wolfe, looking down at him. "Don't be upset, Pete. I wouldn't have known you from Adam, no one would; that wasn't it. It's my hero here. Archie's an awful prude. He has been up against some tough ones, lots of them, and not once has he ever called on me to help. Never! A proud prude. Suddenly he calls me away from revelry—I might have been reveling for all he knew—to get into a car and be intimate with a stranger. There's only one person on earth he would do that for: you. So if I was pretty ardent in the car, I knew what I was doing. And don't worry about me—whatever you're up to, my lips are sealed. Anyway, to me you will always be Pete. The only woman in America who has necked with Nero Wolfe—my God, I'll treasure it forever. Now I'll go make some sandwiches. What kind of a diet are you on?"

Wolfe said through his teeth, "I care for nothing."

"That can't be. A peach? Grapes? A leaf of lettuce?"

"No!"

"A glass of water?"

"Yes!"

She left the room, leering at me as she went by. In a moment the sound of her movements in the kitchen came faintly.

I told Wolfe offensively, "It was you who said we needed a woman."

"It was you who selected her."

"You okayed her."

"It's done," he said bitterly. "So are we. She'll blab, of course."

"There's one hope," I suggested. "Marry her. She wouldn't betray her own husband. And apparently in that one short ride uptown with her—"

I stopped abruptly. The face as a whole was no longer his, but the eyes alone were enough to tell me when I had gone far enough.

"I'll tell you what I'll do," I offered. "I know her quite well. Two things that could conceivably happen: first, you might go to Zeck tomorrow and tell him who you are, and second, Lily might spill it either thoughtfully or thoughtlessly. I'll bet you ten bucks the first happens as soon as the second."

He growled. "She's a woman."

"All right, bet me."

The bet didn't get made. Not that Wolfe came to my point of view about Lily Rowan, but what could the poor son of a gun do? He couldn't even take to the bushes again and start all over. From that point on, though, up to the end, the strain was ten times worse for him than for me. It cramped his style some all that night, after Lily had gone off to bed and we talked in the living room until long after dawn. At six o'clock he went. Probably it would then have been safe for me to go too, since if they were enough interested in him to have posted a sentry outside the building he would almost certainly leave when Roeder did, but probabilities weren't good enough now, not after the picture Wolfe had given me and the program he had drawn up, so I took a good two-hour nap before leaving for Thirty-fifth Street and a bath and breakfast.

At ten o'clock I was at 1019, starting at the phone to get hold of Saul and Orrie and Fred.

I did not like it at all. The way Wolfe was getting set to play it, it looked to me as if we had one chance in a thousand, and while that may be good enough to go ahead on when what you're after is to nail a guy on a charge, and if you muff it the worst you get is a new start under a handicap, it's a little different when a muff means curtains. I had of course told Wolfe all I knew, including Inspector Cramer's visit and advice, but that only made him stubborner. With Zeck on Rackham's tail, through me, it seemed likely that the murderer of Mrs. Rackham might get his proper voltage with Zeck's blessing, and since that was all that Wolfe was committed to, why not settle for it? For now anyway, and then take a good breath. As for commitments, I had one of my own. I had promised myself to see Norway before I died.

So I didn't like it, and I either had to lump it or bow out. I tossed a coin: heads I stick, tails I quit. It landed tails, but I had to veto it because I had already talked to Orrie Cather and he was coming at noon, and I had left messages for Fred Durkin and Saul Panzer. I tossed again, tails again. I tossed once more and it was heads, which settled it. I had to stick.

The tailing of Barry Rackham was a classic, especially after the first week. It was a shame to waste the talents of Saul Panzer on what was actually a burlesque, but it was good to have him around anyhow. I briefed them all together at 1019, Wednesday evening, with Saul perched on a corner of the desk because there were only three chairs. Saul was undersized, inconspicuous all but his nose, and the best all-round man alive. Fred Durkin was big and clumsy, with a big red face, with no Doberman pinscher in him but plenty of bulldog. Orrie Cather was slender and muscular and handsome, just the man to mingle with the guests at a swell dinner party when circumstances called for it. After I had explained the job, with details as required, I supplied a little background.

"As far as you know," I told them, "I'm only doing this for practice. Your only contact is me. There is no client."

"Jesus," Fred remarked, "a hundred bucks a day and more with expenses? I guess you ought to pay in advance."

"Take it up with the NLRB," I said stiffly. "As an employer, I do not invite familiarities from the help."

"Of course," Orrie stated with an understanding smile, "it's just a coincidence that this Rackham was with you once at the scene of a murder. When you got tossed in the coop."

"That's irrelevant. Let us stick to the point, gentlemen. I want to make it clear that I do not actually care a damn where Rackham goes or what he does or who he sees. You are to hang on and report in full, since that's the proper way to handle a dry run, but I don't want anyone to get hurt. If he turns on you and starts throwing rocks, dodge and run. If you lose him, as of course you will, don't bark your shins trying to hurdle."

"You ought to have workmen's compensation insurance," Fred advised. "Then we could be serious about it."

"Do you mean," Saul Panzer asked, "that the purpose is to get on his nerves?"

"No. Play it straight. I only mean it's not life and death—until further notice." I pushed my chair back and got up. "And now I wish to prove that being an employer hasn't changed me any. You may continue to call me Archie. You may come with me to Thirty-fifth Street, where we will find a poker deck, and Fritz will make five, and when we have finished I'll lend you carfare home."

For the record, I lost twelve dollars. Saul was the big winner. One hand, I had three nines and—but I'd better get on.

Rackham was living at the Churchill, in an air-conditioned suite in the tower. During the first week we compiled quite a biography of him. He never stuck his nose outside before one o'clock, and once not until four. His ports of call included two banks, a law office, nine bars, two clubs, a barber shop, seven other shops and stores, three restaurants, three theaters, two night spots, and miscellaneous. He usually ate lunch with a man or men, and dinner with a woman. Not the same woman; three different ones during the week. As described by my operatives, they were a credit to their sex, to the American way of life, and to the International Ladies' Garment Workers' Union.

I took on a little of it myself, but mostly I left it to the help. Not that I loafed. There were quite a few hours with Lily Rowan, off and on, both as a substitute for the trip to Norway, indefinitely postponed, and as a check on the soundness of the estimate of her I had given Wolfe. She caused me no qualms. Once when we were dancing she sighed for Pete, and once at her apartment she said she would love to help some more with my work, but when I tactfully made it plain that the detective business was not on our agenda she took it nicely and let it lay.

There were other things, including the reports on

Rackham to be typed. Late every afternoon Max Christy called at my office to get the report of the day before, and he would sit and read it and ask questions. When he got critical, I would explain patiently that I couldn't very well post a man at the door of Rackham's suite to take pictures of all the comers and goers, and that we were scoring better than eighty per cent on all his hours outside, which was exceptional for New York tailing.

I had the advantage, of course, of having had the situation described to me by their Pete Roeder. They were worried a little about Westchester, but more about the city. Shortly after he had become a millionaire by way of a steak knife, whoever had used it, Rackham had got word to Zeck that he was no longer available for contacts. Brownie Costigan had got to Rackham, thinking to put the bee on him, and had been tossed out on his ear. The stink being raised in Washington on gambling and rackets, and the resulting enthusiasm in the office of the New York County District Attorney, had started an epidemic of jitters, and it was quite possible that if one of my typed reports had told of a visit by Rackham to the DA's office, or of one by an assistant DA to Rackham's suite, Rackham would have had a bad accident, like getting run over or falling into the river with lead in him. That was why Wolfe had given me careful and explicit instructions about what I should report and what I shouldn't.

I had no sight or sound of Wolfe. He was to let me know if and when there was something stirring, and I had been told how to reach him if I had to.

Meanwhile I had my schedule, and on the ninth day, a Friday, the first of September, it called for a move. Things looked right for it. Saul, on instructions, had let himself get spotted once, and Orrie twice, and Fred, without instructions, at least three times. I too had cooperated by letting myself be seen at the entrance of the Crooked Circle one night as Rackham emerged with companions. So Friday at five o'clock, when Saul phoned that the subject had entered the Romance Bar on Forty-ninth Street, I went for a walk, found Saul window-shopping, told him to go home to his wife and children, moseyed along to the Romance Bar entrance, and went on in.

Business was rushing, with as many as five at a table the size of a dishpan. Making no survey, I found a place at the long bar where two customers were carelessly leaving enough room for a guy to get an elbow through, and took the opening. After a while the bartender admitted I was there and let me buy a highball. I took a casual look around, saw Rackham at a table with a pair of males, turned my back that way, and got his range in the mirror.

I did not really expect a bite at the very first try. I thought it might take two or three exposures. But evidently he was ripe. I was in the middle of my second highball when my mirror view showed me the trio getting up and squeezing through the mob to the clear. I dropped my chin and looked at my thumb. They went on by, toward the door, and I turned to watch their manly backs. As soon as they were out I followed, and, on the sidewalk, immediately turned right, thinking to reconnoiter from the shop entrance next door. But I was still two paces from it when there was a voice at my elbow.

"Here I am, Goodwin."

I turned to face him, looking mildly startled. "Oh, hello."

"What's the idea?" he demanded.

"Which one?" I asked politely. "There's so many around."

"There are indeed. You and three others that I know of. Who wants to know so much about me?"

"Search me." I was sympathetic. "Why, are you being harassed?"

Color had started to show in his face, and the muscles of his jaw were called upon. His right shoulder twitched.

"Not here on the street," I suggested. "A crowd will collect, especially after I react. See that man turning to look? You're standing like Jack Dempsey."

He relaxed a little. "I think I know," he said.

"Good for you. Then I'm not needed."

"I want to have a talk with you."

"Go ahead."

"Not here. At my place—the Churchill."

"I think I have a free hour next Tuesday."

"Now. We'll go there now."

I shrugged. "Not together. You lead the way, and I'll tag along."

He turned and marched. I gave him twenty paces and then followed. It takes the strain off of tailing a man to have a date with him, and since we had only a few blocks to go it would have been merely a pleasant little stroll if he hadn't been in such a hurry. I had to use my full stride to keep my distance. As we neared the Churchill I closed in a little, and when he entered an elevator I was there ready for the next one.

He had a corner suite at the setback, which gave him a terrace and also a soundbreak for the street noises. It was cool and quiet in his big sitting room, with light blue summer rugs and pretty pictures and light blue slipcovers on the furniture. While he adjusted venetian blinds I glanced around, and when he was through I told him, "Very nice. A good place for a heart-to-heart talk."

"What will you have to drink?"

"Nothing, thanks. I had my share at the bar, and anyway I don't drink with people I'm tailing."

I was in a comfortable chair, and he pulled a smaller one around to face me. "You've got your own office now," he stated.

I nodded. "Doing pretty well. Of course, summer's the slack season. After Labor Day they'll start coming back and bringing their troubles along."

"You didn't take on that job for Mrs. Frey."

"How could I?" I upturned a palm. "No one would speak to me."

"You can't blame them." He got out a cigarette and lit it, and his hands were almost steady but not quite. "Look, Goodwin. There on the street I nearly lost my head for a second. You're merely doing what you're paid for."

"Right," I said approvingly. "People resent detectives more than they do doctors or plumbers, I don't see why. We're all trying to make it a better world."

"Certainly. Who are you working for?"

"Me."

"Who pays you to work for you?"

I shook my head. "Better start over. Show a gun or a steak knife or something. Even if I'm not hard to persuade, I must keep up appearances."

He licked his lips. Apparently that was his substitute for counting ten, but if so it didn't work, for he sprang up, towering over me, making fists. I moved nothing but my head, jerking it back to focus on his face.

"It's a bad angle," I assured him. "If you swing

from up there I'll duck and hit your knees, and you'll lose your balance."

He held it a second, then his fists became hands, and he stooped to use one of them to recover the cigarette he had dropped on the rug. He sat down, took a drag, inhaled, and let it out.

"You talk too much, Goodwin."

"No," I disagreed, "not too much, but too frankly, maybe. Perhaps I shouldn't have mentioned a steak knife but I was irritated. I might name my client if you stuck needles under my nails or showed me a dollar bill, but your being so damn casual annoyed me."

"I didn't kill my wife."

I smiled at him. "That's a straightforward categorical statement, and I appreciate it very much. What else didn't you do?"

He ignored it. "I know Annabel Frey thinks I did, and she would spend all the money my wife left her —well, say half of it—to prove it. I don't mind your taking her money, that's your business, but I hate to see her waste it, and I don't like having someone always behind me. There ought to be some way I can satisfy you and her that I didn't do it. Can't you figure one out? If it's arranged so you won't lose anything by it?"

"No," I said flatly.

"Why not? I said satisfy you."

"Because I'm getting irritated again. You don't care a damn what Mrs. Frey thinks. What's eating you is that you don't know who is curious enough about you to spend money on it, and you're trying to catch a fish without bait, which is unsportsmanlike. I'll bet you a finif you can't worm it out of me."

He sat regarding me half a minute, then got up

and crossed to a portable bar over by the wall and began assembling a drink. He called to me, "Sure you won't have one?"

I declined with thanks. Soon he returned with a tall one, sat, took a couple of swallows, put the glass down, burped, and spoke. "A thousand dollars for the name."

"Just the name, cold?"

"Yes."

"It's a sale." I extended a hand. "Gimme."

"I like to get what I pay for, Goodwin."

"Absolutely. Guaranteed against defects."

He arose and left the room through a door toward the far end. I decided I was thirsty and went to the bar for a glass of soda and ice, and was back in my chair when he reentered and came to me. I took his offering and counted it by flipping the edges: ten crackly new hundreds.

He picked up his glass, drank, and eyed me. "Well?"

"Arnold Zeck," I said.

He made a little squeaking noise, went stiff for a short count, and hurled the tall glass against the wall, where it smacked into the middle of the glass of a picture, which improved the effect both for the ear and for the eye.

Chapter 15

I admit I was on my feet when it hit. He was so slapdash that there was no certainty about his target, and a well-thrown heavy glass can make a bruise.

"Now look what you've done," I said reproachfully, and sat down again. He glared at me a second, then went to the bar, and with slow precise movements of his hands mixed another long one. I was pleased to note that the proportion of whisky was the same as before. He returned to his chair and put the glass down without drinking.

"I thought so, by God," he said.

I merely nodded.

"Who hired you? Zeck himself?"

"Not in the contract," I objected firmly. "You bought the name, and you've got it."

"I'm in the market for more. I'll take it all."

I frowned at him. "Now I guess I'll have to do some talking. You comfortable?"

"No."

"Listen anyway. I'm taking Zeck's money and I'm crossing him. How do you know I won't cross you?"

"I don't. But I'll top him."

"That's the point exactly; you don't. Who is Zeck and who are you? You know the answer to that. You were taking his money too, up to five months ago, and you know for what. When your wife hired Nero Wolfe to take the lid off of you for a look, you yapped to Zeck and he took aim at Wolfe, and when your wife got it with that steak knife Wolfe took a powder, and for all I know he is now in Egypt, where he owns a house, talking it over with the Sphinx. It was Zeck and you, between you, that broke up our happy home on Thirty-fifth Street, and you can have three guesses how I feel about it. I may like it fine this way, with my own office and my time my own. I may figure to work close to Zeck and get in the big dough, which would mean I'm poison to you, or I may be loving a chance to stick one between Zeck's ribs and incidentally get a nice helping from your pile, or I may even be kidding both of you along with the loony idea of trying to earn the ten grand your wife paid Nero Wolfe. Zeck can guess and you can guess. Do I make myself clear?"

"I don't know. Are you just warning me not to trust you? Is that it?"

"Well, yes."

"Then save your breath. I've never trusted anybody since I started shaving. As for a nice helping from my pile, that depends. How do you earn it?"

I shrugged. "Maybe I don't want it. Guess. I got the impression that I have something you want."

"I think you have. Who hired you and what were you told to do?"

"I told you, Zeck."

"Zeck himself?"

"I would be risking my neck and you know it.

Five grand now, and beyond that we can decide as we go along."

It was a mistake, though not fatal. He was surprised. I should have made it ten. He said, "I haven't got that much here."

"Tut. Send downstairs for it."

He hesitated a moment, regarding me, then got up and went to a phone on a side table. It occurred to me that it would be of no advantage for a clerk or assistant manager to see whose presence in Rackham's suite required the delivery of so much cash, so I asked where the bathroom was and went there. After a sufficient interval I returned, and the delivery had been made.

"I said I don't trust anybody," Rackham told me, handing me the engravings. "But I don't like to be gypped."

It was used bills this time, Cs and five-hundreds, which didn't seem up to the Churchill's standard of elegance. To show Rackham how vulgar it was not to trust people, I stowed it away without counting it.

"What do you want?" I asked, sitting. "Words and pictures?"

"I can ask questions, can't I?"

"Sure, that's included. I have not yet seen Zeck himself, but expect to. I was first approached by Max Christy. He—"

"That son of a bitch."

"Yeah? Of course you're prejudiced now. He was merely scouting. He didn't name Zeck and he didn't name you, but offered good pay for an expert tailing job. I was interested enough to make a date to get picked up on the street that night by a man in a car. He gave—"

"Not Zeck. He wouldn't show like that."

"I said I haven't seen Zeck. He gave me the layout. He said his name was Roeder—around fifty—"

"Roeder?" Rackham frowned.

"So he said. He spelled it—R-o-e-d-e-r. Around fifty, brown hair slicked back, face wrinkled and folded, sharp dark eyes, brown pointed beard with gray in it."

"I don't know him."

"He may be in a different department from the one you were in. He did name Zeck. He said—"

"He actually named Zeck?"

"Yes."

"To you? That's remarkable. Why?"

"I don't know, but I can guess. I had previously been tapped by Max Christy, some time ago, and I think they've got an idea that I may have it in me to work up to an executive job—now that Nero Wolfe is gone. And they figure I must know that Christy plays with Brownie Costigan, and that Costigan is close to the top, so why not mention Zeck to me to make it glamorous? Anyhow, Roeder did. He said that what they wanted was a tail on you. They wanted it good and tight. They offered extra good pay. I was to use as many men as necessary. I took the job, got the men, and we started a week ago yesterday. Christy comes to my office every day for the reports. You know what's been in them; you know where you've been and what you've done."

Rackham was still frowning. "That's all there is to it?"

"That's the job as I took it and as I've handled it."

"You weren't told why?"

"In a way I was. I gathered that they think you might be a bad influence on the District Attorney, and they want to be sure you don't start associating with him. If you do they would probably make a complaint. I suppose you know what their idea is of making a complaint."

The frown was going. "You say you gathered that?"

"I didn't put it right. I was told that in so many words."

"By Roeder?"

"Yes."

The frown was gone. "If this is straight, Goodwin, I've made a good buy."

"It's straight all right, but don't trust me. I warned you. Those are the facts, but you can have a guess without any additional charge if you want it."

"A guess about what?"

"About them and you. This guess is why I'm here. This guess is why I went into that bar so you would see me, and followed you out like a halfwit to give you a chance to flag me."

"Oh. So you staged this."

"Certainly. I wanted to tell you about this guess, and if you were in a mood to buy something first, why not?"

He looked aloof. "Let's have the guess."

"Well—" I considered. "It really is a guess, but with a background. Do you want the background first?"

"No, the guess."

"Right. That Zeck is getting set to frame you for the murder of your wife."

I think Rackham would have thrown another glass if he had happened to have it in his hand, possibly at me this time. His blood moved fast. The color came up in his neck and face, and he sort of swelled all over; then his jaw clamped.

"Go on," he mumbled.

"That's all the guess amounts to. Do you want the background?"

He didn't answer. I went on. "It won't cost you a cent. Take the way I was approached. If it's a plain tailing job with no frills, why all the folderol? Why couldn't Christy just put it to me? And why pay me double the market of the highest-priced agencies? Item. If Zeck has his friends at White Plains, which is far from incredible, and if the current furore is upsetting their stomach, there's nothing they would appreciate more than having their toughest unsolved murder case wrapped up for them. Item. Hiring me is purely defensive, and Zeck and his staff don't function that way, especially not when the enemy is a former colleague and they've got a grudge."

I shook my head. "I can't see it with that background. But listen to this. Roeder came up to my office and stayed an hour, and do you know what he spent most of it doing? Asking me questions about the evening of April eighth! What has that got to do with my handling a tailing job? Nothing! Why should they be interested in April eighth at all? I think they brought me this job, at double pay, just to start a conversation with me and soften me up. It has already been hinted that Zeck might like to meet me. I think that to frame you for murder they've got to have first-hand dope from someone who was there, and I'm elected. I think they're probably sizing me up, to decide whether I'm qualified to be asked to remember something that happened that night which has slipped my mind up to now, at a nice juicy price."

I turned my palms up. "It's just a guess."

He still had nothing to say. His blood had apparently eased up a little. He was staring at my face, but I doubted if he was seeing it.

"If you care to know why I wanted you to hear it," I went on, "you can have that too. I have my weak spots, and one of them is my professional pride. It got a hard blow when Nero Wolfe scooted instead of staying to fight it out, with your wife's check for ten grand deposited barely in time to get through before she was croaked. If the ten grand is returned to her estate, who gets it? You. And it could be that you killed her. I prefer to leave it where it is and earn it. Among other things, she was killed while I was there, and I helped find the body. That's a fine goddam mess for a good detective, and I was thinking I was one."

He found his tongue. "I didn't kill her. I swear to you, Goodwin, I didn't kill her."

"Oh, skip it. Whether you did or didn't, not only do I not want to help frame you, I don't want anyone to frame anybody, not on this one. I've got a personal interest in it. I intend to earn that ten grand, and I don't want Zeck to bitch it up by getting you burned, even if you're the right one, on a fix. Therefore I wanted you to know about this. As I told you, I haven't got it spelled out, it's only a guess with background, and I admit it may be a bum one. What do you think? Am I hearing noises?"

Rackham picked up his drink, which hadn't been touched, took a little sip, about enough for a sparrow, and put it down again. He sat a while, licking his lips. "I don't get you," he said wistfully.

"Then forget it. You're all paid up. I've been known to guess wrong before."

"I don't mean that, I mean you. Why? What's your play?"

"I told you, professional pride. If that's too fancy for you, consider how I was getting boxed in, with Zeck on my right and you on my left. I wanted a window open. If you don't like that either, just cross me off as screwy. You don't trust me anyhow. I merely thought that if my guess is good, and if I get approached with an offer of a leading part, and maybe even asked to help with the script, and if I decided I would like to consult you about it, it would be nice if we'd already met and got a little acquainted." I flipped a hand. "If you don't get me, what the hell, I'm ahead six thousand bucks."

I stood up. "One way to settle it, you could phone Zeck and ask him. That would be hard on me, but what can a double-crosser expect? So I'll trot along." I moved toward the door and was navigating a course through the scattered fragments of glass in the path when he decided to speak.

"Wait a minute," he said, still wistful. "You mentioned when you get approached."

"*If* I get approached."

"You will. That's the way they work. Whatever they offer, I'll top it. Come straight to me and I'll top it. I want to see you anyhow, every day—wait a minute. Come back and sit down. We can make a deal right now, for you to—"

"No," I said, kind but firm. "You're so damn scared it would be a temptation to bargain you out of your last pair of pants. Wait till you cool off a little and get some spunk back. Ring me any time. You understand, of course, we're still tailing you."

I left him.

Several times, walking downtown, I had to rein myself in. I would slow down to a normal gait, and in another block or so there I would be again, pounding along as fast as I could swing it, though all I had ahead was an open evening. I grinned at myself indulgently. I was excited, that was all. The game was on, I had pitched the first ball, and it had cut the inside corner above his knees. Not only that, it was a game with no rules. It was hard to believe that Rackham could possibly go to Zeck or any of his men with it, but if he did I was on a spot hot enough to fry an egg, and Wolfe was as good as gone. That was why I had tried to talk Wolfe out of it. But now that I had started it rolling and there was no more argument, I was merely so excited that I couldn't walk slow if you paid me.

I had had it in mind to drop in at Rusterman's Restaurant for dinner and say hello to Marko that evening, but now I didn't feel like sitting through all the motions, so I kept going to Eleventh Avenue, to Mart's Diner, and perched on a stool while I cleaned up a plate of beef stew, three ripe tomatoes sliced by me, and two pieces of blueberry pie. Even with a full stomach I was still excited. It must have shown, I suppose in my eyes, for Mart asked me what the glow was about, and though I had never had any tendency to discuss my business with him, I had to resist an impulse to remark casually that Wolfe and I had finally mixed it up with the most dangerous baby on two legs, one so tough that even Inspector Cramer had said he was out of reach.

I went home and sat in the office all evening, holding magazines open as if I were reading them. All I really did was listen for the phone or doorbell. When the phone rang at ten o'clock and it was only Fred Durkin wanting to know where Saul and the subject were, I was so rude that I hurt his feelings and had to apologize. I told him to cover the Churchill as usual, which was one of the factors that made it a burlesque, since that would have required four men at least. What I wanted to do so bad I could taste it was call the number Wolfe had given me, but that had been for emergency only. I looked emergency up in the dictionary, and got "an unforeseen combination of circumstances which calls for immediate action." Since this was just the opposite, a foreseen combination of circumstances which called for getting a good night's sleep, I didn't dial the number. I did get the good night's sleep.

Saturday morning at 1019 I had to pitch another ball, but not to the same batter. The typing of Friday's reports required only the customary summarizing of facts as far as Saul and Fred and Orrie were concerned, but my own share took time and thought. I had to account for the full time I had spent in Rackham's suite, since there was a double risk in it: the chance that I was being checked and had been seen entering and leaving, and the chance that Rackham had himself split a seam. So it was quite a literary effort and I spent three hours on it. That afternoon, when Max Christy called to get the report as usual, and sat to look it over, I had papers on my desk which kept me so busy that I wasn't even aware if he sent me a glance when he got to the middle of the second page, where my personal contribution began. I looked up only when he finally spoke.

"So you had a talk with him, huh?"

I nodded. "Have you read it?"

"Yes." Christy was scowling at me.

"He seemed so anxious that I thought it would be a shame not to oblige him. It's my tender heart."

"You took his money."

"Certainly. He was wild to spend it."

"You told him you're working for Mrs. Frey. What if he takes a notion to ask her?"

"He won't. If he does, who will know who to believe or what? I warned him about me. By the way, have I ever warned you?"

"Why did you play him?"

"It's all there in the report. He knew he had a tail, how could he help it, already on guard, after eight days of it? I thought I might as well chat with him and see what was on his mind. He could have said something interesting, and maybe he did, I don't know, because I don't know what you and your friends would call interesting. Anyway, there it is. As for his money, he practically stuffed it in my ear, and if I had refused to take it he would have lost all respect for me."

Christy put the report in his pocket, got up, rested his fingertips on the desk, and leaned over at me. "Goodwin," he asked, "do you know who you're dealing with?"

"Oh, for God's sake," I said impatiently. "Have I impressed you as the sort of boob who would jump off a building just to hear his spine crack? Yes, brother, I know who I'm dealing with, and I expect to live to ninety at least."

He straightened up. "Your chief trouble," he said, not offensively, "is that you think you've got a sense of humor. It confuses people, and you ought to get over it. Things strike you as funny. You thought it would be funny to have a talk with Rackham, and it may be all right this time, but someday something that you think is funny will blow your goddam head right off your shoulders."

Only after he had gone did it occur to me that that wouldn't prove it wasn't funny.

I had a date that Saturday evening with Lily Rowan, but decided to call it off. Evidently I wasn't tactful enough about it, for she took on. I calmed her down by promising to drown myself as soon as the present crisis was past, went home and got my dinner out of the refrigerator, and settled down in the office for another evening of not reading magazines. A little after nine the minutes were beginning to get too damn long entirely when the phone rang. It was Lily.

"All right," she said briskly, "come on up here."

"I told you—"

"I know, but now I'm telling you. I'm going to have company around eleven, and as I understand it you're supposed to get here first. Get started."

"Phooey. I'm flattered that you bothered to try it, but—"

"I wouldn't have dreamed of trying it. The company just phoned, and I'm following instructions. My God, are you conceited!"

"I'll be there in twenty minutes."

It took twenty-two, to her door. She was vindictive enough to insist that there were three television programs she wouldn't miss for anything, which was just as well, considering my disposition. I suppose I might have adjusted to it in time, say ten years, but I was so used to having Wolfe right at hand any minute of the day or night when difficulties were being met that this business of having to sit it out until word came, and then rushing up to a friend's penthouse and waiting another hour and a half, was too much of a strain.

He finally arrived. I must admit that when the bell rang Lily, having promised to behave like a lady, did so. She insisted on opening the door for him, but having got him into the living room, she excused herself and left us.

He sat. I stood and looked at him. Eleven days had passed since our reunion, and I hadn't properly remembered how grotesque he was. Except for the eyes, he was no one I had ever seen or cared to see.

"What's the matter?" I asked peevishly. "You look as if you hadn't slept for a week."

"I'm a little tired, that's all," he growled. "I have too much to watch, and I'm starving to death. So far as I know everything at my end is satisfactory. What about Miss Rowan?"

"She's all right. As you may remember, every week or so I used to send her a couple of orchids of a kind that couldn't be bought. I have told her that the custom may be resumed someday provided we get this difficulty ironed out, and that it depends on her. Women like to have things depend on them."

He grunted. "I don't like to have things depend on them." He sighed. "It can't be helped. I can only stay an hour. Bring me some of Miss Rowan's perfume."

I went and tapped on a door, got no answer, opened it and crossed a room to another door, tapped again, was told to enter, and did so. Lily was on a divan with a book. I told her what I wanted.

"Take the Houri de Perse," she advised. "Pete likes it. I had it on that night."

I got it from the dressing table, returned to the living room, aimed it at him from the proper distance, and squeezed the bulb. He shut his eyes and tightened his lips to a thin line.

"Now the other side," I said gently. "What's worth doing—"

But he opened his eyes, and their expression was

enough. I put the sprayer on a table and went to a chair.

He looked at his wrist watch. "I read the report of your talk with Rackham. How did it go?"

"Fine. You might have thought he had rehearsed it with us."

"Tell me about it."

I obeyed. I felt good, giving him a communiqué again, and since it needed no apologies I enjoyed it. What I always tried for was to present it so that few or no questions were required, and though I was a little out of practice I did well enough.

When I was through he muttered, "Satisfactory. Confound this smell."

"It'll go away in time. Sixty dollars an ounce."

"Speaking of dollars, you didn't deposit what you took from Rackham?"

"No. It's in the safe."

"Leave it there for the present. It's Mrs. Rackham's money, and we may decide we've earned it. Heaven knows no imaginable sum could repay me for these months. I was thinking—"

He cut it off, tilted his head a little, and regarded me with eyes narrowed to slits.

"Well?" I said aggressively. "More bright ideas?"

"I was thinking, Archie. August is gone. The risk would be negligible. Get Mr. Haskins on the phone tomorrow and tell him to start a dozen chickens on blueberries. Uh—two dozen. You can tell him they are for gifts to your friends."

"No, sir."

"Yes. Tomorrow."

"I say no. He would know damn well who they were for. My God, is your stomach more important than your neck? Not to mention mine. You can't help it if you were born greedy, but you can try to control—"

"Archie." His voice was thin and cold with fury. "Nearly five months now. Look at me."

"Yes, sir." He had me. "You're right. I beg your pardon. But I am not going to phone Haskins. You just had a moment of weakness. Let's change the subject. Does Rackham's biting of the first try change the schedule any?"

"You could tell Mr. Haskins—"

"No."

He gave up. After sitting a while with his eyes closed, he sighed so deep it made him shudder, and then came back to black reality. Only a quarter of his hour was left, and we used it to review the situation and program. The strategy was unchanged. At midnight he arose.

"Please thank Miss Rowan for me?"

"Sure. She thinks you ought to call her Lily."

"You shouldn't leave on my heels."

"I won't. She's sore and wants to have a scene."

I went ahead to open the door for him. As I did so he asked, "What is this stuff called?"

"Houri de Perse."

"Great heavens," he muttered, and went.

Chapter 16

Having my own office was giving me a new slant on some of the advantages of the setup I had long enjoyed at Wolfe's place. With a tailing job on, Sunday was like any other day, and I had to be at 1019 at the usual hour, both to type the report and to take calls from the man on the job in case he needed advice or help. It was no longer just burlesque, at least not for me. Even though Rackham knew we were on him, those were three good men, particularly Saul, and I stood a fair chance of being informed if he strayed anywhere out of bounds to keep an appointment. To some extent the tail now served a purpose: to warn me if the subject and the client made a contact, which was somewhat bassackwards but convenient for me.

After a leisurely Sunday dinner at Rusterman's Restaurant, where I couldn't make up my mind whether Marko Vukcic knew that I had my old job back, I returned to 1019 to find Max Christy waiting at the door. He seemed a little upset. I glanced at my wrist and told him he was early.

"This one-man business is no good," he complained. "You ought to have someone here. I tried to get you on the phone nearly two hours ago."

Unlocking the door and entering, I explained that I had dawdled over tournedos à la Béarnaise, which I thought would impress him. He didn't seem to hear me. When I unlocked a desk drawer to get the report, and handed it to him, he stuffed it in his pocket without glancing at it.

I raised the brows. "Don't you want to read it?"

"I'll read it in the car. You're coming along."

"Yeah? Where to?"

"Pete Roeder wants to see you."

"Well, here I am. As you say, this is a one-man business. I've got to stick here, damn it."

Christy was glaring at me under his brow thickets. "Listen, Goodwin, I'm supposed to have you somewhere at four o'clock, and it's five to three now. I waited for you nearly half an hour. Let's go. You can argue on the way."

I had done my arguing, double-quick, while he was speaking. To balk was out of the question. To stall and try to get an idea what the program really was would have been sappy. I got my keys out again, unlocked the bottom drawer, took off my jacket, got out the shoulder holster, slipped it on, and twisted my torso to reach for the buckle.

"What's that for, woodchucks?" Christy asked.

"Just force of habit. Once I forgot to wear it and a guy in an elevator stepped on my toe. I had to cut his throat. If we're in a hurry, come on."

We went. Down at the curb, as I had noticed on my way in, force of habit again, was a dark blue Olds sedan, a fifty, with a cheerful-looking young man with a wide mouth, no hat, behind the wheel. He gave me an interested look as Christy and I got in the back seat, but no words passed. The second the door slammed the engine started and the car went forward.

The Olds fifty is the only stock car that will top a hundred and ten, but we never reached half of that— up the West Side Highway, Saw Mill River, and Taconic State. The young man was a careful, competent, and considerate driver. There was not much conversation. When Christy took the report from his pocket and started reading it my first reaction was mild relief, on the ground that if I were about to die they wouldn't give a damn what my last words were, but on second thought it seemed reasonable that he might be looking for more evidence for the prosecution, and I left the matter open.

It was a fine sunny day, not too hot, and everything looked very attractive. I hoped I would see many more days like it, in either town or country, I didn't care which, though ordinarily I much prefer the city. But that day the country looked swell, and therefore I resented it when, as we were rolling along the Taconic State Parkway a few miles north of Hawthorne Circle, Christy suddenly commanded me, "Get down on the floor, face down."

"Have a heart," I protested. "I'm enjoying the scenery."

"I'll describe it to you. Shall we park for a talk?"

"How much time have we?"

"None to waste."

"Okay, pull your feet back."

The truth was, I was glad to oblige. Logic had stepped in. If that was intended for my last ride I wouldn't ever be traveling that road again, and in that case what difference did it make if I saw where we turned off and which direction we went? There must have been some chance that I would ride another day, and without a chaperon, or this stunt was pointless. So as I got myself into position, wriggling and adjusting to keep my face downward without an elbow or knee taking my weight, the worst I felt was undignified. I heard the driver saying something, in a soft quiet voice, and Christy answering him, but I didn't catch the words.

There was no law against looking at my watch. I had been playing hide and seek, with me it, a little more than sixteen minutes, with the car going now slower and now faster, now straight and now turning left and now right, when finally it slowed down to a full stop. I heard a strange voice and then Christy's, and the sound of a heavy door closing. I shifted my weight.

"Hold it," Christy snapped at me. He was still right above me. "We're a little early."

"I'm tired of breathing dust," I complained.

"It's better than not breathing at all," the strange voice said and laughed, not attractively.

"He's got a gun," Christy stated. "Left armpit."

"Why not? He's a licensed eye. We'll take care of it."

I looked at my watch, but it was too dark to see the hands, so of course we were in out of the sun. The driver had got out, shut the car door, and walked away, if I was any good at reading sounds. I heard voices indistinctly, not near me, and didn't get the words. My left leg, from the knee down, got bored and decided to go to sleep. I moved it.

"Hold it," Christy commanded.

"Nuts. Tape my eyes and let me get up and stretch."

"I said hold it."

I held it, for what I would put at another seven minutes. Then there were noises—a door opening, not loud, footsteps and voices, a door closing, again not loud, still steps and voices, a car's doors opening and shutting, an engine starting, a car moving; and in a minute the closing of the heavy door that had closed after we had stopped. Then the door which my head was touching opened.

"All right," a voice said. "Come on out."

It took acrobatics, but I made it. I was standing, slightly wobbly, on concrete, near a concrete wall of a room sixty feet square with no windows and not too many lights. My darting glance caught cars scattered around, seven or eight of them. It also caught four men: Christy, coming around the rear end of the Olds, and three serious-looking strangers, older than our driver, who wasn't there.

Without a word two of them put their hands on me. First they took the gun from my armpit and then went over me. The circumstances didn't seem favorable for an argument, so I simply stood at attention. It was a fast and expert job, with no waste motion and no intent to offend.

"It's all a matter of practice," I said courteously.

"Yeah," the taller one agreed, in a tenor that was almost a falsetto. "Follow me."

He moved to the wall, with me behind. The cars had been stopped short of the wall to leave an alley, and we went down it a few paces to a door where a man was standing. He opened the door for us—it was the one that made little noise—and we passed through into a small vestibule, also with no windows in its concrete walls. Across it, only three paces, steps down began, and we descended—fourteen shallow steps to a wide metal door. My conductor pushed a button in the metal jamb. I heard no sound within, but in a moment the door opened and a pasty-faced bird with a pointed chin was looking at us.

"Archie Goodwin," my conductor said.

"Step in."

I waited politely to be preceded, but my conductor moved aside, and the other one said impatiently, "Step in, Goodwin."

I crossed the sill, and the sentinel closed the door. I was in a room bigger than the vestibule above: bare concrete walls, well-lighted, with a table, three chairs, a water-cooler, and a rack of magazines and newspapers. A second sentinel, seated at the table, writing in a book like a ledger, sent me a sharp glance and then forgot me. The first one crossed to another big metal door directly opposite to the one I had entered by, and when he pulled it open I saw that it was a good five inches thick. He jerked his head and told me, "On in."

I stepped across and passed through with him at my heels.

This was quite a chamber. The walls were paneled in a light gray wood with pink in it, from the tiled floor to the ceiling, and the rugs were the same light gray with pink borders. Light came from a concealed trough continuous around the ceiling. The six or seven chairs and the couch were covered in pinkish gray leather, and the same leather had been used for the frames of the pictures, a couple of big ones on each wall. All that, collected in my first swift survey, made a real impression.

"Archie Goodwin," the sentinel said.

The man at the desk said, "Sit down, Goodwin. All right, Schwartz," and the sentinel left us and closed the door.

I would have been surprised to find that Pete Roeder rated all this splash so soon after hitting this territory, and he didn't. The man at the desk was not Roeder. I had never seen this bozo, but no introduction was needed. Much as he disliked publicity, his picture had been in the paper a few times, as for instance the occasion of his presenting his yacht to the United States Coast Guard during the war. Also I had heard him described.

I had a good view of him at ten feet when I sat in one of the pinkish gray leather chairs near his desk. Actually there was nothing to him but his forehead and eyes. It wasn't a forehead, it was a dome, sloping up and up to the line of his faded thin hair. The eyes were the result of an error on the assembly line. They had been intended for a shark and someone got careless. They did not now look the same as shark eyes because Arnold Zeck's brain had been using them to see with for fifty years, and that had had an effect.

"I've spoken with you on the phone," he said.

I nodded. "When I was with Nero Wolfe. Three times altogether—no, I guess it was four."

"Four. Where is he? What has happened to him?"

"I'm not sure, but I suspect he's in Florida, training with an air hose, preparing to lay for you in your swimming pool and get you when you dive."

There was no flicker of response, of any kind, in the shark eyes. "I have been told of your habits of speech, Goodwin," he said. "I make no objection. I take men for what they are or not at all. It pleases me that, impressed as you must be by this meeting, you insist on being yourself. But it does waste time and words. Do you know where Wolfe is?"

"No."

"Have you a surmise?"

"Yeah, I just told you." I got irritated. "Say I tell you he's in Egypt, where he owns a house. I don't but say I do. Then what? You send a punk to Cairo to drill him? Why? Why can't you let him alone? I know he had his faults—God knows how I stood them as long as I did—but he taught me a lot, and wherever he is he's my favorite fatty. Just because he happened to queer your deal with Rackham, you want to track him down. What will that get you, now that he's faded out?"

"I don't wish or intend to track him down."

"No? Then what made me so interesting? Your Max Christy and your bearded wonder offering me schoolboy jobs at triple pay. Get me sucked in, get me branded, and when the time comes use me to get at Wolfe so you can pay him. No." I shook my head. "I draw the line somewhere, and all of you together won't get me across that one."

I'm not up enough on fish to know whether sharks blink, but Zeck was showing me. He blinked perhaps one-tenth his share. He asked, "Why did you take the job?"

"Because it was Rackham. I'm interested in him. I was glad to know someone else was. I would like to have a hand in his future."

No blink. "You think you know, I suppose, the nature of my own interests and activities."

"I know what is said around. I know that a New York police inspector told me that you're out of reach."

"Name him."

"Cramer. Manhattan Homicide."

"Oh, him." Zeck made his first gesture: a forefin-

ger straightened and curved again. "What was the
occasion?"

"He wouldn't believe me when I said I didn't
know where Wolfe was. He thought Wolfe and I
were fixing to try to bring you down, and he was just
telling me. I told him that maybe he would like to
pull us off because he was personally interested, but
that since Wolfe had scooted he was wasting it."

"That was injudicious, wasn't it?"

"All of that. I was in a bad humor."

Zeck blinked; I saw him. "I wanted to meet you,
Goodwin. I've allowed some time for this because I
want to look at you and hear you talk. Your idea of
my interests and activities probably has some rela-
tion to the facts, and if so you may know that my
chief problem is men. I could use ten times as many
good men as I can find. I judge men partly by their
record and partly by report, but mainly by my first-
hand appraisal. You have disappointed me in one respect. Your conclusion that I want to use you to find
Nero Wolfe is not intelligent. I do not pursue an op-
ponent who has fled the field; it would not be profitable. If he reappears and gets in my path again, I'll
crush him. I do want to suck you in, as you put it. I
need good men now more than ever. Many people get
money from me, indirectly, whom I never see and
have no wish to see; but there must be some whom I
do see and work through. You might be one. I would
like to try. You must know one thing: if you once say
yes it becomes impractical to change your mind. It
can't be done."

"You said," I objected, "you would like to try.
How about my liking to try?"

"I've answered that. It can't be done."

"It's already being done. I'm tailing Rackham for

you. When he approached me I took it on myself to chat with him and report it. Did you like that or not? If not, I'm not your type. If so, let's go on with that until you know me better. Hell, we never saw each other before. You can let me know a day in advance when I'm to lose the right to change my mind, and we'll see. Regarding my notion that you want to use me to find Nero Wolfe, skip it. You couldn't anyway, since I don't know whether he went north, east, south, or west."

I had once remarked to Wolfe, when X (our name then for Zeck) had brought a phone call to a sudden end, that he was an abrupt bastard. He now abruptly turned the shark eyes from me, which was a relief, to reach for the switch on an intercom box on his desk, flip it, and speak to it. "Send Roeder in."

"Tell him to shave first," I suggested, thinking that if I had a reputation for a habit of speech I might as well live up to it. Zeck did not react. I was beginning to believe that he never had reacted to anything and never would. I turned my head enough for the newcomer to have my profile when he entered, not to postpone his pleasure at seeing me.

It was a short wait till the door opened and Roeder appeared. The sentinel did not come in. Roeder crossed to us, stepping flat on the rugs so as not to slide. His glance at me was fleeting and casual.

"Sit down," Zeck said. "You know Goodwin."

Roeder nodded and favored me with a look. Sitting, he told me, "Your reports haven't been worth what they cost."

It gave me a slight shock, but I don't think I let it show. I had forgotten that Roeder talked through his nose.

"Sorry," I said condescendingly. "I've been sticking to facts. If you want them dressed up, let me know what color you like."

"You've been losing him."

I flared up quietly. "I used to think," I said, "that Nero Wolfe expected too much. But even he had brains enough to know that hotels have more than one exit."

"You're being paid enough to cover the exits to the Yankee Stadium."

Zeck said, in his hard, cold, precise voice that never went up or down, "These are trivialities. I've had a talk with Goodwin, Roeder, and I sent for you because we got to Rackham. We have to decide how it is to be handled and what part Goodwin is to play. I want your opinion on the effect of Goodwin's telling Rackham that he is working for Mrs. Frey."

Roeder shrugged. "I think it's unimportant. Goodwin's main purpose now is to get Rackham scared. We've got to have him scared good before we can expect him to go along with us. If he killed his wife—"

"He did, of course. Unquestionably."

"Then he might be more afraid of Mrs. Frey than of you. We can see. If not, it will be simple for Goodwin to give him a new line." Roeder looked at me. "It's all open for you to Rackham now?"

"I guess so. He told me he wanted to see me every day, but that was day before yesterday. What are we scaring him for? To see him throw glasses?"

Zeck and Roeder exchanged glances. Zeck spoke to me. "I believe Roeder told you that he came here recently from the West Coast. He had a very successful operation there, a brilliant and profitable op-

eration which he devised. It has some novel features
and requires precise timing and expert handling.
With one improvement it could be enormously profitable here in New York, and that one improvement is
the cooperation of a wealthy and well-placed man.
Rackham is ideal for it. We intend to use him. If you
help materially in lining him up, as I think you can,
your share of the net will be five per cent. The net is
expected to exceed half a million, and should be
double that."

I was frowning skeptically. "You mean if I help
scare him into it."

"Yes."

"And help with the operation too?"

"No."

"What have I got to scare him with?"

"Ilis sense of guilt first. He escaped arrest and
trial for the murder of his wife only because the police couldn't get enough evidence for a case. He is
under the constant threat of the discovery of additional evidence, which for a murderer is a severe
strain. If he believes we have such evidence he will
be open to persuasion."

"Have we got it?"

Zeck damn near smiled. "I shouldn't think it will
be needed. If it is needed we'll have it."

"Then why drag him in on a complicated operation? He's worth what, three million? Ask him for
half of it, or even a third."

"No. You have much to learn, Goodwin. People
must not be deprived of hope. If we take a large
share of Rackham's fortune he will be convinced that
we intend to wring him dry. People must be allowed
to feel that if our demands are met the outlook is not

intolerable. A basic requirement for continued success in illicit enterprises is a sympathetic understanding of the limitations of the human nervous
system. Getting Rackham's help in Roeder's operation will leave plenty of room for future requests."

I was keeping my frown. "Which I may or may
not have a hand in. Don't think I'm playing hard to
get, but this is quite a step to take. Using a threat of
a murder rap to put the screws on a millionaire is a
little too drastic without pretty good assurance that
I get more than peanuts. You said five per cent of a
probable half a million, but you're used to talking big
figures. Could I have that filled in a little?"

Roeder reached for a battered old leather brief
case which he had brought in with him and deposited
on the floor. Getting it on his lap, he had it opened
when Zeck asked him, "What are you after, the esti-
mates?"

"Yes, if you want them."

"You may show them to him, but no names." Zeck
turned to me. "I think you may do, Goodwin. You're
brash, but that is a quality that may be made use of.
You used it when you talked with Rackham. He must
be led into this with tact or he may lose his head and
force our hand, and all we want is his cooperation.
His conviction for murder wouldn't help us any; quite
the contrary. Properly handled, he should be of value
to us for years."

The shark eyes left me. "What's your opinion of
Goodwin, Roeder? Can you work with him?"

Roeder had closed the brief case and kept it on
his lap. "I can try," he said, not enthusiastically. "The
general level here is no higher than on the coast. But
we can't get started until we know whether we have

Rackham or not, and the approach through Goodwin does seem the best way. He's so damned cocky I don't know whether he'll take direction."

"Would you care to have my opinion of Roeder?" I inquired.

Zeck ignored it. "Goodwin," he said, "this is the most invulnerable organization on earth. There are good men in it, but it all comes to me. I am the organization. I have no prejudices and no emotions. You will get what you deserve. If you deserve well, there is no limit to the support you will get, and none to the reward. If you deserve ill, there is no limit to that either. You understand that?"

"Sure." His eyes were the hardest to meet in my memory. "Provided you understand that I don't like you."

"No one likes me. No one likes the authority of superior intellect. There was one man who matched me in intellect—the man you worked for, Nero Wolfe —but his will failed him. His vanity wouldn't let him yield, and he cleared out."

"He was a little handicapped," I protested, "by his respect for law."

"Every man is handicapped by his own weaknesses. If you communicate with him give him my regards. I have great admiration for him."

Zeck glanced at a clock on the wall and then at Roeder. "I'm keeping a caller waiting. Goodwin is under your direction, but he is on trial. Consult me as necessary within the routine."

He must have had floor buttons for foot-signaling, for he touched nothing with his hands, but the door opened and the sentinel appeared.

Zeck said, "Put Goodwin on the B list, Schwartz."

Roeder and I arose and headed for the door, him with his brief case under his arm.

Remembering how he had told me, tapping his chest, "I am a D, Archie," I would have given a lot if I could have tapped my own bosom and announced, "I am a B, Mr. Wolfe."

Chapter 17

There was one chore Wolfe had given me which I haven't mentioned, because I didn't care to reveal the details—and still don't. But the time will come when you will want to know where the gun at the bottom of the brief case came from, so I may as well say now that you aren't going to know.

Since filing the number from a gun has been made obsolete by the progress of science, the process of getting one that can't be traced has got more complicated and requires a little specialized knowledge. One has to be acquainted with the right people. I am. But there is no reason why you should be, so I won't give their names and addresses. I couldn't quite meet Wolfe's specifications—the size and weight of a .22 and the punch of a .45—but I did pretty well: a Carson Snub Thirty, an ugly little devil, but straight and powerful. I tried it out one evening in the basement at Thirty-fifth Street. When I was through I collected the bullets and dumped them in the river. We were taking enough chances without adding another, however slim.

The next evening after our conference with Zeck, a Monday, Wolfe and I collaborated on the false bottom for the brief case. We did the job at 1019. Since I was now a B and Roeder's lieutenant on his big operation, and he was supposed to keep in touch with me, there was no reason why he shouldn't come to Thirty-fifth Street for an evening visit, but when I suggested it he compressed his lips and scowled at me with such ferocity that I quickly changed the subject. We made the false bottom out of an old piece of leather that I picked up at a shoe hospital, and it wasn't bad at all. Even if a sentinel removed all the papers for a close inspection, which wasn't likely with the status Roeder had reached, there was little chance of his suspecting the bottom; yet if you knew just where and how to pry you could have the Carson out before you could say Jackie Robinson.

However, something had happened before that: my second talk with Barry Rackham. When I got home late Sunday night the phone-answering service reported that he had been trying to reach me, both at 1019 and at the office, and I gave him a ring and made a date for Monday at three o'clock.

Usually I am on the dot for an appointment, but that day an errand took less time than I had allowed, and it was only twelve to three when I left the Churchill tower elevator at Rackham's floor and walked to his door. I was lifting my hand to push the button, when the door opened and I had to step back so a woman wouldn't walk into me. When she saw me she stopped, and we both stared. It was Lina Darrow. Her fine eyes were as fine as ever.

"Well, hello," I said appreciatively.

"You're early, Goodwin," Barry Rackham said. He was standing in the doorway.

Lina's expression was not appreciative. It didn't look like embarrassment, more like some kind of suspicion, though I had no notion what she could suspect me of so spontaneously.

"How are you?" she asked, and then, to make it perfectly clear that she didn't give a damn, went by me toward the elevator. Rackham moved aside, giving me enough space to enter, and I did so and kept going to the living room. In a moment I heard the door close, and in another moment he joined me.

"You're early," he repeated, not reproachfully.

He looked as if, during the seventy hours since I had last seen him, he had had at least seventy drinks. His face was mottled, his eyes were bloodshot, and his left cheek was twitching. Also his tie had a dot of egg yolk on it, and he needed a shave.

"A week ago Saturday," I said, "I think it was, one of my men described a girl you were out with, and it sounded like Miss Darrow, but I wasn't sure. I'm not leading up to something, I'm just gossiping."

He wasn't interested one way or the other. He asked what I would have to drink, and when I said nothing thank you he went to the bar and got himself a straight one, and then came and moved a chair around to sit facing me.

"Hell," I said, "you look even more scared than you did the other day. And according to my men, either you've started sneaking out side doors or you've become a homebody. Who said boo?"

Nothing I had to say interested him. "I said I wanted to see you every day," he stated. His voice was hoarse.

"I know, but I've been busy. Among other things, I spent an hour yesterday afternoon with Arnold Zeck."

That did interest him. "I think you're a goddam liar, Goodwin."

"Then I must have dreamed it. Driving into the garage, and being frisked, and the little vestibule, and fourteen steps down, and the two sentinels, and the soundproof door five inches thick, and the pinkish gray walls and chairs and rugs, and him sitting there drilling holes in things, including me, with his eyes, and—"

"When was this? Yesterday?"

"Yeah. I was driven up, but now I know how to get there myself. I haven't got the password yet, but wait."

With an unsteady hand he put his glass down on a little table. "I told you before, Goodwin, I did not kill my wife."

"Sure, that's out of the way."

"How did it happen? Your going to see him."

"He sent Max Christy for me."

"That son of a bitch." Suddenly his mottled face got redder and he yelled at me, "Well, go on! What did he say?"

"He said I may have a big career ahead of me."

"What did he say about me?"

I shook my head. "I'll tell you, Rackham. I think it's about time I let my better judgment in on this. I had never seen Zeck before, and he made quite an impression on me." I reached to my breast pocket. "Here's your six thousand dollars. I hate to let go of it, but—"

"Put that back in your pocket."

"No, really I—"

"Put it back." He wasn't yelling now. "I don't blame you for being impressed by Zeck—God knows you're not the first. But you're wrong if you think he can't ever miss and I'm all done. There's one thing you ought to realize: I can't throw in my hand on this one; I've got to play it out, and I'm going to. You've got me hooked, because I can't play it without you since you were there that night. All right, name it. How much?"

I put the six grand on the little table. "My real worry," I said, "is not Zeck. He is nothing to sneer at and he does make a strong impression, but I have been impressed before and got over it. What called my better judgment in was the New York statutes relating to accessories to murder. Apparently Zeck has got evidence that will convict you. If you—"

"He has not. That's a lie."

"He seems to think he has. If you want to take dough from a murderer for helping him beat the rap you must be admitted to the bar, and I haven't been. So with my sincere regret at my inability to assist you in your difficulty, there's your dough."

"I'm not a murderer, Goodwin."

"I didn't mean an actual murderer. I meant a man against whom evidence has been produced in court to convince a jury. He and his accessory get it just the same."

Rackham's bloodshot eyes were straight and steady at me. "I'm not asking you to help me beat a rap. I'm asking you not to help frame me—and to help me keep Zeck from framing me."

"I know," I said sympathetically. "That's the way you tell it, but not him. I don't intend to get caught in a backwash. I came here chiefly to return your money and to tell you that it's got beyond the point where I name a figure and you pay it and then we're all hunky-dory, but I do have a suggestion to make if you care to hear it—strictly on my own."

Rackham started doing calisthenics. His hands, resting on his thighs, tightened into fists and then opened again, and repeated it several times. It made me impatient watching him, because it seemed so inadequate to the situation. By now the picture was pretty clear, and I thought that a guy who had had enough initiative to venture into the woods at night to stalk his wife, armed only with a steak knife, when she had her Doberman pinscher with her, should now, finding himself backed into a corner, respond with something more forceful than sitting there doing and undoing his fists.

He spoke. "Look, Goodwin, I'm not myself. I know damn well I'm not. It's been nearly five months now. The first week it wasn't so bad—there was the excitement, all of us suspected and being questioned; if they had arrested me then I wouldn't have skipped a pulse beat. I would have met it fair and square and fought it out. But as it stretched out it got tougher. I had broken off with Zeck without thinking it through —the way it looked then, I ought to get clean and keep clean, especially after the hearings in Washington, those first ones, and after the New York District Attorney took a hand. But what happened, every time the phone rang or the doorbell, it hit me in the stomach. It was murder. If they came and took me or sent for me and kept me, I could be damn sure it had been fixed so they thought it would stick. A man can stand that for a day or a week, or a month perhaps, but with me it went on and on, and by God, I've had about all I can take."

He had ended his calisthenics with the fists closed tight, the knobs of the knuckles the color of boils. "I made a mistake with Zeck," he said fretfully. "When I broke it off he sent for me and as good as told me that the only thing between me and the electric chair was his influence. I lost my temper. When I do that I can never remember what I said, but I don't think I actually told him that I had evidence of blackmailing against him personally. Anyhow, I said too much." He opened his fists and spread his fingers wide, his palms flat on his thighs. "Then this started, stretching into months. Did you say you have a suggestion?"

"Yeah. And brother, you need one."

"What is it?"

"On my own," I said.

"What is it?"

"For you and Zeck to have a talk."

"What for? No matter what he said I couldn't trust him."

"Then you'd be meeting on even terms. Look straight at it. Could your wife trust you? Could your friends trust you—the ones you helped Zeck get at? Could I trust you? I warned you not to trust me, didn't I? There are only two ways for people to work together: when everybody trusts everyone or nobody trusts no one. When you mix them up it's a mess. You and Zeck ought to get along fine."

"Get along with Zeck?"

"Certainly." I turned a palm up. "Listen, you're in a hole. I never saw a man in a deeper one. You're even willing and eager to shell out to me, a doublecrosser you can't trust, to give you a lift. You can't possibly expect to get out in the clear with no ropes tied to you—what the hell, who is? Your main worry is getting framed for murder, so your main object is to see that you don't. That ought to be a cinch. Zeck has a new man, a guy named Roeder, came here recently from the coast, who has started to line up an operation that's a beaut. I've been assigned to help on it, and I think I'm going to. It's as tight as a drum and as slick as a Doberman pinscher's coat. With the help of a man placed as you are, there would be absolutely nothing to it, without the slightest risk of any noise or a comeback."

"No. That's what got—"

"Wait a minute. As I said, this is on my own. I'm not going to tell you what Zeck said to me yesterday, but I advise you to take my suggestion. Let me arrange for you to see him. You don't have to take up where you left off, a lot of dirty little errands; you're a man of wealth now and can act accordingly. But also you're a man who is suspected by thirty million people of killing his wife, and that calls for concessions. Come with me to see Zeck, let him know you're willing to discuss things, and if he mentions Roeder's operation let him describe it and then decide what you want to do. I told you why I don't want to see you or anyone else framed for that murder, and I don't think Zeck will either if it looks as though you might be useful."

"I hate him," Rackham said hoarsely. "I'm afraid of him and I hate him!"

"I don't like him myself. I told him so. What about tomorrow? Say four o'clock tomorrow, call for you here at a quarter to three?"

"I don't—not tomorrow—"

"Get it over with! Would you rather keep on listening for the phone and the doorbell? Get it over with!"

He reached for his straight drink, which he hadn't touched, swallowed it at a gulp, shuddered all over, and wiped his mouth with the back of his hand.

"I'll ring you around noon to confirm it," I said, and stood up to go. He didn't come with me to the door, but under the circumstances I didn't hold it against him.

So that evening when Wolfe came to 1019 it appeared to be high time for getting the false bottom in the brief case ready, and we went on until midnight, discussing the program from every angle and trying to cover every contingency. It's always worth trying, though it can never be done, especially not with a layout as tricky as that one.

Then the next morning, Tuesday, a monkey wrench, thrown all the way from White Plains, flew into the machinery and stopped it. I had just finished breakfast, with Fritz, when the phone rang and I went to the office to get it. It was the Westchester DA's office.

The talk was brief. When I had hung up I sat a while, glaring at the phone, then with an exasperated finger dialed the Churchill's number. That talk was brief too. Finished with it, I held the button down for a moment and dialed another number.

There had been only two buzzes when a voice came through a nose to me. "Yes?"

"I'd like to speak to Mr. Roeder."

"Talking."

"This is Goodwin. I've just had a call from White Plains to come to the DA's office at once. I asked if I could count on keeping a two o'clock appointment and was told no. I phoned the Churchill and left a message that I had been called out of town for the day. I hope it can be tomorrow. I'll let you know as soon as I can."

Silence.

"Did you hear me?"

"Yes. Good luck, Goodwin."

The connection went.

Chapter 18

I had once sat and cooled my heels for three hours on one of the wooden benches in the big anteroom of the DA's office in the White Plains courthouse, but this time I didn't sit at all. I didn't even give my name. I entered and was crossing to the table in the fenced-off corner when a man with a limp intercepted me and said, "Come with me, Mr. Goodwin."

He took me down a long corridor, past rows of doors on either side, and into a room that I was acquainted with. I had been entertained there for an hour or so the evening of Sunday, April ninth. No one was in it. It had two big windows for the morning sun, and I sat and watched the dust dance. I was blowing at it, seeing what patterns I could make, when the door opened and Cleveland Archer, the DA himself, appeared, followed by Ben Dykes. I have never glanced at faces with a deeper interest. If they had looked pleased and cocky it would probably have meant that they had cracked the case, and in that event all our nifty plans for taking care of Arnold Zeck were up the flue and God help us.

I was so glad to see that they were far from cocky

that I had to see to it that my face didn't beam. I responded to their curt greeting in kind, and when they arranged the seating with me across a table from them I said grumpily as I sat, "I hope this is going to get somebody something. I had a full day ahead, and now look at it."

Dykes grunted, not with sympathy and not with enmity, just a grunt. Archer opened a folder he had brought, selected from its contents some sheets of paper stapled in a corner, glanced at the top sheet, and gave me his eyes, which had swollen lids.

"This is that statement you made, Goodwin."

"About what? Oh, the Rackham case?"

"For God's sake," Dykes said gloomily. "Forget to try to be cute just once. I've been up all night."

"It was so long ago," I said apologetically, "and I've been pretty busy."

Archer slid the statement across the table to me. "I think you had better read it over. I want to ask some questions about it."

I couldn't have asked for a better chance to get my mind arranged, but I didn't see that that would help matters any, since I hadn't the vaguest notion from which direction the blow was coming.

"May I save it for later?" I inquired. "If you get me up a tree and I need time out for study, I can pretend I want to check with what I said here." I tapped the statement with a forefinger.

"I would prefer that you read it."

"I don't need to, really. I know what I said and what I signed." I slid it back to him. "Test me on any part of it."

Archer closed the folder and rested his clasped hands on it. "I'm not as interested in what is in that statement as I am in what isn't in it. I think you ought to read it because I want to ask you what you left out—of the happenings of that day, Saturday, April eighth."

"I can answer that without reading it. I left nothing out that was connected with Mrs. Rackham."

"I want you to read what you said and signed and then repeat that statement."

"I don't need to read it. I left out nothing."

Archer and Dykes exchanged looks, and then Dykes spoke. "Look, Goodwin, we're not trying to sneak up on you. We've got something, that's all. Someone has loosened up. It looks like this is the day for it."

"Not for me." I was firm. "I loosened up long ago."

Archer told Dykes, "Bring her in." Dykes arose and left the room. Archer took the statement and returned it to the folder and pushed the folder to one side, then pressed the heels of his palms to his eyes and took a couple of deep breaths. The door opened and Dykes escorted Lina Darrow in. He pulled a chair up to the end of the table for her, to my left and Archer's right, so that the window was at her back. She looked as if she might have spent the night in jail, with red eyes and a general air of being pooped, but judging from the clamp she had on her jaw, she was darned determined about something. I got a glance from her but nothing more, not even a nod, as she took the chair Dykes pulled up.

"Miss Darrow," Archer told her, gently but firmly, "you understand that there is probably no chance of getting your story corroborated except through Mr. Goodwin. You haven't been brought in here to face him for the purpose of disconcerting or discrediting him, but merely so he can be informed first-hand." Archer turned to me. "Miss Darrow came to us last evening of her own accord. No pressure of any kind has been used with her. Is that correct, Miss Darrow? I wish you could confirm that to Mr. Goodwin."

"Yes." She lifted her eyes to me, and though they had obviously had a hard night, I still insist they were fine. She went on, "I came voluntarily. I came because—the way Barry Rackham treated me. He refused to marry me. He treated me very badly. Finally—yesterday it was too much."

Archer and Dykes were both gazing at her fixedly. Archer prodded her. "Go on, please, Miss Darrow. Tell him the main facts."

She was trying the clamp on her jaw to make sure it was working right. Satisfied, she released it. "Barry and I had been friendly, a little, before Mrs. Rackham's death. Nothing but just a little friendly. That's all it meant to me, or I thought it was, and I thought it was the same with him. That's how it was when we went to the country for the Easter weekend. She had told me we wouldn't do any work there, answer any mail or anything, but Saturday at noon she sent for me to come to her room. She was crying and was so distressed she could hardly talk."

Lina paused. She was keeping her eyes straight at mine. "I can rattle this off now, Mr. Goodwin. I've already told it now."

"That always makes it easier," I agreed. "Go right ahead."

She did. "Mrs. Rackham said she had to talk about it with someone, and she wanted to with her daughter-in-law, Mrs. Frey, but she just couldn't, so there was only me. She said she had gone to see Nero Wolfe the day before, to ask him to find out where her husband was getting money from, and he had agreed to do it. Mr. Wolfe had phoned her that evening, Friday evening, and told her that he had already partly succeeded. He had learned that her husband was connected with something that was criminal. He was helping somebody with things that were against the law, and he was getting well paid for it. Mr. Wolfe advised her to keep it to herself until he had more details. He said his assistant, Mr. Goodwin, would come up Saturday afternoon, and might have more to report then."

"And that Goodwin knew all about it?" Archer asked.

"Well, naturally she took that for granted. She didn't say that Mr. Wolfe told her in so many words that Mr. Goodwin knew all about it, but if he was his assistant and helping with it, naturally she would think so. Anyway that didn't seem to be important then, because she had told it all to her husband. They used the same bedroom at Birchvale, and she said that after they had gone to bed she simply couldn't help it. She didn't tell me their conversation, what they said to each other, but they had had a violent quarrel. She had told him they would have to separate, she was through with him, and she would have Mr. Wolfe go on with his investigation and get proof of what he had done. Mrs. Rackham had a very strong character, and she hated to be deceived. But the next day she wasn't sure she really meant it, that she really wanted to part from him. That was why she wanted to talk about it with someone. I think the reason she didn't want to talk with Mrs. Frey—"

"If you don't mind, Miss Darrow," Archer suggested gently, "just the facts now."

"Yes, of course." She sent him a glance and returned to me. "I told her I thought she was completely wrong. I said that if her husband had been untrue to her, or anything like that, that would be different, but after all he hadn't done wrong to her, only to other people and himself, and that she should try to help him instead of destroying him. At the very least, I said, she should wait until she knew all the details of what he had done. I think that was what she wanted to hear, but she didn't say so. She was very stubborn. Then, that afternoon, I did something that I will regret all my life. I went to Barry and told him she had told me about it, and said I was sure it would come out all right if he would meet her halfway—tell her the whole thing, tell her he was sorry, as he certainly should be—and no more foolishness in the future. And Barry said he loved me."

She weakened a little there for the first time. She dropped her eyes. I had been boring at her with as steady and sharp a gaze as I had in me, but up to that point she had met it full and fair.

"So then?" I asked.

Her eyes lifted and she marched on. "He said he didn't want it to come out all right because he loved me. Shall I try to tell you what I—how I felt?"

"Not now. Just what happened."

"Nothing happened then. That was in the middle of the afternoon. I didn't tell Barry I loved him—I didn't even know I loved him then. I got away from him. Later we gathered in the living room for cocktails, and you and Mr. Leeds came, and we played that game—you remember."

"Yep, I do."

"And dinner, and television afterward, and—"

"Excuse me. That is common knowledge. Skip to

later, when the cops had come. Did you tell them all this?"

"No."

"Why not?"

"Because I didn't think it would be fair to Barry. I didn't think he had killed her, and I didn't know what criminal things he had helped with, and I thought it wouldn't be fair to tell that about him when all I knew was what Mrs. Rackham had told me." The fine eyes flashed for the first time. "Oh, I know the next part. Then why am I telling it now? Because I know more about him now—a great deal more! I don't know that he killed Mrs. Rackham, but I know he could have; he is cruel and selfish and unscrupulous—there is nothing he wouldn't do. I suppose you think I'm vindictive, and maybe I am, but it doesn't matter what you think about me as long as I'm telling the truth. What the criminal things were that he did, and whether he killed his wife—I don't know anything about it; that's your part."

"Not mine, sister. I'm not a cop."

She turned to the others. "Yours, then!"

This would have been a good moment for me to take time out to read my signed statement, since I could have used a few minutes for some good healthy thinking. Here was a situation that was new to me. About all that Barry Rackham's ticket to the electric chair needed was my endorsement, and I thought he had it coming to him. All I had to do was tell the truth. I could say that I had no knowledge whatever of the phone call Nero Wolfe was purported to have made to Mrs. Rackham, but that it was conceivable that he had made such a call without mentioning it to me, since he had often withheld information from me regarding his actions and intentions. You couldn't beat that for truth. On various occasions I had used all my wits to help pin it on a murderer, and here it would take no wit at all, merely tossing in a couple of facts.

But if I let it go at that, it was a cinch that before the sun went down, Rackham would be locked up, and that would ruin everything. The program sunk, the months all wasted, the one chance gone, Zeck sailing on with the authority of his superior intellect, and Wolfe and me high and dry. My wits had a new job, and quick. I liked to think that they had done their share once or twice in getting a murderer corralled: now it was up to them to do more than their share in keeping a murderer running loose and free to keep appointments. Truth was not enough.

There was no time to draw a sketch and see how I liked it. All three of them were looking at me, and Archer was saying, "You can see, Goodwin, why I wanted you to read your statement and see if you left anything out."

"Yeah." I was regretful. "I can also see you holding your breath, and I don't blame you. If I now say that's right, I forgot, Wolfe did phone Mrs. Rackham that Friday evening and tell her that, you've got all you need and hallelujah, I would love to help out, but I like to stick to the truth as far as practical."

"The truth is all I'm asking for. Did you call on Rackham at his apartment yesterday afternoon?"

That punch had of course been telegraphed. "Yes," I said.

"What for?"

"On a job for a client. At first it was a tailing job, and then when Rackham spotted me my client thought I might learn something by chatting with him."

"Why is your client interested in Rackham?"

"He didn't say."

"Who's the client?"

I shook my head. "I don't think that would help you any. He's a man who came here recently from the West Coast, and I suspect he's connected with gambling or rackets or both, but my suspicions are no good at the bank. Let's table it for now."

"I want the name, Goodwin."

"And I want to protect my client within reason. You can't connect him up with the murder you're investigating. Go ahead and start the rigmarole. Charge me again as a material witness and I get released on bail. Meanwhile I'll be wanting my lawyer present and all that runaround. What will it get you in the long run?"

Ben Dykes said in a nasty voice, "We don't want to be arbitrary about it. We wouldn't expect you to name a client if you haven't got one. West Coast, huh?"

"Is Rackham your client?" Archer asked.

"No."

"Have you done any work for him?"

"No."

"Has he given you or paid you any money in the past week?"

That was enough and to spare. I was hooked good, and if the best I could do was flop around trying to wriggle off, the outlook was damn thin. "Oh," I said, "so that's it." I gave Lina Darrow an appreciative look and then transferred it to Archer. "This narrows it down. I've collected for withholding evidence against a murderer. That's bad, isn't it?"

No one answered. They just looked at me.

So I went on. "First, I hereby state that I have no

money from Rackham, and that's all on that for now.
Second, I'm a little handicapped because although I
know what Miss Darrow has in her mind, I don't
know how it got there. She's framing Rackham for
murder or trying to, but I'm not sure whether it's
her own idea or whether she has been nudged. I
would have to find out about that first before I could
decide how I stand. I know you've got to give me the
works, and that's all right, it's your job, you've got all
day and all night for it, but you can take your pick.
Either I clam up as of now, and I mean clam, and you
start prying at me, or first I am allowed to have a
talk with Miss Darrow—with you here, of course.
Then you can have the rest of the week with me.
Well?"

"No," Archer said emphatically.

"Okay. May I borrow some adhesive tape?"

"We know everything Miss Darrow has to say."

"Sure you do. I want to catch up. I said with you
here. You can always stop it if you get bored."

Archer looked at Dykes. I don't know whether he
would have rather had Dykes nod his head or shake
it, but he got neither. All Dykes did was concentrate.

"You gentlemen," I said, "want only one thing, to
crack the case. It certainly won't help if I shut my
trap and breathe through my nose. It certainly won't
hurt if I converse with Miss Darrow in your presence."

"Let him," Lina said belligerently. "I knew he
would deny it."

"What do you want to ask her?" Archer demanded.

"The best way to find that out is to listen." I
turned to Lina. "When I saw you yesterday afternoon, coming out of his apartment, I thought some-

thing was stirring. It was rude the way you went right by me."

She met my gaze but had no comment.

"Was it yesterday," I asked, "that he treated you badly?"

"Not only yesterday," she said evenly. "But yesterday he refused definitely and finally to marry me."

"Is that so bad? I mean, a guy can't marry everyone."

"He had said he would—many times."

"But hadn't you been keeping your fingers crossed? After all, it was kind of a special situation. He knew that you knew something that would get him arrested for murder if you spilled it—not to mention other criminal things, whatever they were. Didn't it occur to you that he might be kidding you along for security reasons?"

"Yes, I—yes, it did, but I didn't want to believe it. He said he loved me. He made love to me—and I wanted him for my husband." She decided that wasn't adequate and improved on it. "I wanted him so much!" she exclaimed.

"I'll bet you did." I tried not to sound sarcastic. "How do you feel about it now? Do you think he ever loved you?"

"No, I don't! I think he was heartless and cruel. I think he was afraid of me. He just wanted me not to tell what I knew. And I began to suspect—the way he acted—and yesterday I insisted that we must be married immediately, this week, and when I insisted he lost his temper and he was—he was hateful."

"I know he's got a temper. Was there any urgent reason for wanting to get married quick, like expecting a visitor from heaven, for instance a baby?"

She flushed and appealed to Archer. "Do I have to let him insult me?"

"I beg your pardon," I said stiffly, "but you seem to be pretty sensitive for a woman who was hell-bent to marry a murderer. Did—"

"I didn't know he was a murderer! I only knew if I told about what Mrs. Rackham told me and what he told me—I knew he would be suspected even more than he was."

"Uh-huh. When the blowup came yesterday, did you threaten to tell what you knew?"

"Yes."

I goggled at her. "You know, sister," I declared, "you should have spent more time thinking this through. You are unquestionably the bummest liar I have ever run across. I thought maybe—"

Dykes broke in. "She says Rackham probably figured he wasn't in much danger, so many months had passed."

"Yeah? That's partly what I mean. Whatever she says, what about Rackham? He's not boob enough to figure like that. He would know damn well that five months is nothing in the life of a murder. He has his choice between marrying this attractive specimen or having her run to you with the ink for his death warrant, and not only does he act heartless and cruel, he actually opens the door for her to go! This guy who had it in him to sneak into the woods at night with a knife to stab his wife to death *and* a fighting dog—he just opens the door for this poor pretty creature to tell the world about it! My God, you would buy that?"

"You can't tell about people," Archer said. "And she has details. Take the detail of the phone call Wolfe made to Mrs. Rackham and what he told her about her husband. Not even a good liar would have that detail, let alone a bum one."

"Nuts." I was disgusted. "No such phone call was made, and Mrs. Rackham never said it was. As for Rackham's having been in with crooks, either he wasn't and sister here invented it, in which case you'd better watch your step, or he was, and sister here got his tongue loosened enough for him to tell her about it. I'm perfectly willing to believe she is capable of that, however bum a liar she may be."

"You say Wolfe didn't make that call to Mrs. Rackham?"

"Yes."

"And he didn't learn that Rackham's income came from a connection with criminal activities?"

"My God, Mrs. Rackham didn't leave our office until afternoon that Friday. And he called her that evening to tell her? When he hadn't moved a finger to start an inquiry, and I hadn't either? He was good, but not that good." I turned to Lina. "I thought maybe you had had a coach for this, possibly got in with some professionals yourself, but not now, the way you tell it. Obviously this is your own baby—I beg your pardon if you don't want babies mentioned —say your own script—and it is indeed a lulu. Framing a man for murder is no job for an amateur. Aside from the idea of Rackham's preferring a jury trial to you, which if I may get personal is plain loco, look at other features. If it had been the way you say, what would Wolfe and I have done after I phoned him that night and told him Mrs. Rackham had got it? Our only interest was the fee she had paid us. Why didn't we just hand it all to the cops? Another little feature, do you remember that gathering that evening? Did either Rackham or his wife act like people who were riding the kind of storm you describe? Don't ask me, I could be prejudiced; ask all the others."

I left her for Archer. "I could go on for an hour, but don't tell me you need it. I don't wonder you grabbed at it, it looked as if it might possibly be the break you had been hoping for, and besides, she had fixed it up with some trimmings that might be very juicy, like the crap about me working for Rackham. I have not and am not, and I have none of his dough. Must I punch more holes in it?"

Archer was studying me. "Is it your contention that Miss Darrow invented all this?"

"It is."

"Why?"

I shrugged. "I don't know. Do you want me to guess?"

"Yes."

"Well—my best one first. Have you noticed her eyes—the deep light in them? I think she's trying to take over for you. She liked Mrs. Rackham, and when she got left that two hundred grand it went to her head. She thought Rackham had killed her—I don't know whether it was a hunch or what—and when time passed and it looked as if he wasn't going to get tagged for it, she decided it was her duty or mission, or whatever word she uses for it, to step in. Having the two hundred grand, she could afford a hobby for a while. That was when she started to put the eyes on Rackham. I expect she thought she could get him into a state where he would dump it all out for her, and then she would not only know she was right but would also be able to complete her mission. But the months went by and he never dumped, and it probably got a little embarrassing, and she got frantic about it, and she must even have got desperate, judging by the performance she finally ended up with. She decided Rackham was guilty, that part was all right, and the only thing lacking was evidence, so it was up to her to furnish it."

I leaned forward at her. "It's not enough to want to do a good deed, you damn fool. Wanting is fine, but you also need some slight idea of how to go about it. It didn't bother you that one by-product was making me out a cheap crook, did it? Many thanks sincerely yours."

She dropped her head into her hands to cover her face, and convulsions began.

They sat and looked at her. I looked at them. Archer was pulling jerkily at his lower lip. Dykes was shaking his head, his lips compressed.

"I suggest," I said modestly, raising my voice to carry over the noise Lina Darrow was making, "that when she quiets down it might pay to find out if Rackham has told her anything that might help. That item about his getting dough from gambling or rackets could be true, if they actually got intimate enough for him to tell her the story of his life."

They kept their eyes on her. She was crying away what had looked like a swell chance to wrap up a tough one, and I wouldn't have been surprised if they had burst into tears too. I pushed back my chair and stood up.

"If you get anything that I can be of any help on, give me a ring. I'll have a crowded afternoon, but word will reach me."

I walked out.

Chapter 19

As I hit the sidewalk in front of the courthouse my watch said 11:17. It was sunny and warm, and people looked as if they felt pleased with the way things were going. I did not. In another few minutes they would have Lina Darrow talking again, and whether she gave it to them straight this time or tried her hand on a revised version, they might decide any minute that they wanted to talk with Barry Rackham, and that could lead to anything. The least it could lead to was delay, and my nerves were in no condition for it.

I dived across the street to a drugstore, found a booth, and dialed Roeder's number. No answer. I went to where my car was parked, got in, and headed for the parkway.

On my way back to Manhattan I stopped four times to find a phone and dial Roeder's number, and the fourth try, at a Hundred and Sixteenth Street, I got him. I told him where I was. He asked what they had wanted at White Plains.

"Nothing much, just to ask some questions about a lead they had got. I'm going to the Churchill to fix it to go ahead with that date today."

"You can't. It has been postponed until tomorrow at the other end. Arrange it for tomorrow."

"Can't you switch it back to today at your end?"

"It would be difficult and therefore inadvisable."

I considered how to put it, in view of the fact that there was no telling who or how many might hear me. "There is a possibility," I said, "that the Churchill will have a vacant suite tomorrow. So my opinion is that it would be even more inadvisable to postpone it. I don't know, but I have an idea that it may be today or never."

A silence. Then, "How long will it take you to get to your office?"

"Fifteen minutes, maybe twenty."

"Go there and wait."

I returned to the car, drove to a parking lot on Third Avenue in the upper Forties, left the car there, and made steps to Madison Avenue and up to 1019. I sat down, stood at the window, sat down, and stood at the window. I wouldn't ring the phone-answering service because I wanted my line free, but after a few minutes I began thinking I better had, in case Roeder had tried for me before I arrived. The debate on that was getting hot when the ring came and I jumped for it.

It was Roeder. He asked me through his nose, "Have you phoned the Churchill?"

"No, I was waiting to hear from you."

"I hope you will have no trouble. It has been arranged for today at four o'clock."

I felt a tingle in my spine. My throat wanted to tighten, but I wouldn't let it. "I'll do my best. In my car?"

"No. I'll have a car. I'll stop in front of your office building precisely at two forty-five."

"It might be better to make it the Churchill."

"No. Your building. If you have to reach me I'll be here until two-thirty. I hope you won't have to."

"I do too."

I pressed the button down, held it for three breaths, and dialed the Churchill's number. It was only ten to one, so surely I would get him.

I did. As soon as he heard my name he started yapping about the message I had sent him, but I didn't want to try to fix it on the phone, so I merely said I had managed to call off the trip out of town and was coming to see him. He said he didn't want to see me. I said I didn't want to see him either, but we were both stuck with this and I would be there at one-thirty.

At a fountain service down on a side street I ate three corned-beef sandwiches and three glasses of milk without knowing how they tasted, burned my tongue on hot coffee, and then walked to the Churchill and took the elevator to the tower.

Rackham was eating lunch, and it was pitiful. Apparently he had done all right with a big glass of clam juice, since the glass was empty and I couldn't see where the contents had been thrown at anything, but all he did in my presence was peck at things— some wonderful broiled ham, hashed brown potatoes, an artichoke with anchovy sauce, and half a melon. He swallowed perhaps five bites altogether, while I sat at a distance with a magazine, not wanting to disturb his meal. When, arriving, I had told him that the appointment with Zeck was set for four o'clock, he had just glared at me with no comment. Now, as he sat staring at his coffee without lifting the cup, I got up and crossed to a chair near him and remarked that we would ride up to Westchester with Roeder.

I don't think I handled it very well, that talk with Barry Rackham, as he sat and let his coffee get cold and tried to pretend to himself that he still intended to eat the melon. It happened that he had already decided that his only way out was to come to some kind of an understanding with Arnold Zeck, but if he had been balky I doubt if I would have been able to manage it. I was so damned edgy that it was all I could do to sit still. It had been a long spring and summer, those five months, and here was the day that would give us the answer. So there are two reasons why I don't report in detail what Rackham and I said there that afternoon: first, I doubt if it affected the outcome any, one way or another; and second, I don't remember a word of it. Except that I finally said it was time to go, and he got himself a man-sized straight bourbon and poured it down.

We walked the few blocks to my building. As we waited at the curb I kept my eyes peeled for a Chevy sedan, but apparently Roeder had been promoted, either that or the Chevy wasn't used for important guests, for when a car nosed in to us it was a shiny black Cadillac. I got in front with the driver and Rackham joined Roeder in the rear. They didn't shake hands when I pronounced names. The driver was new to me—a stocky, middle-aged number with black hair and squinty black eyes. He had nothing whatever to say to anyone, and for that matter neither did anybody else, all the way to our destination. Once on the Taconic State Parkway a car passed and cut in ahead of us so short that it damn near grazed our bumper, and the driver muttered something, and I went so far as to glance at him but ventured no words. Anyway my mind was occupied.

Evidently Rackham had been there before with

his eyes open, for there was no suggestion that he should take to the floor, and of course I was now a B. We left the parkway a couple miles south of Millwood, to the right, followed a curving secondary road a while, turned onto another main route, soon left it for another secondary road, and after some more curves hit concrete again. The garage was at a four-corners a little out of Mount Kisco, and I never did know what the idea was of that roundabout way of getting there. In front it looked like any other garage, with gas-pumps and a graveled plaza, and cars and miscellaneous objects around, except that it seemed a little large for its location. Two men were there in front, one dressed like a mechanic and the other in a summer suit, even a necktie, and they exchanged nods with our driver as we headed in.

The big room we drove into was normal too, like a thousand others anywhere, but a variation was coming. Our car rolled across, past pillars, to the far end, and stopped just in front of a big closed door, and our driver stuck his head out, but said nothing. Nothing happened for thirty seconds; then the big door slowly opened, rising; the driver pulled his head in, and the car went forward. As we cleared the entrance the door started back down, and by the time we had eased across to a stop the door was shut again, and our reception committee was right there—two on one side and one on the other. I had seen two of them before, but one was a stranger. The stranger was in shirt sleeves, with his gun in a belt holster.

Stepping out, I announced, "I've got that same gun under my armpit."

"Okay, Goodwin," the tenor said. "We'll take care of it."

They did. I may have been a B, but there was no

discernible difference between inspection of a B and of an unknown. In fact, it seemed to me that they were slightly more thorough than they had been on Sunday, which may have been because there were three of us. They did us one at a time, with me first, then Rackham, then Roeder. With Roeder they were a little more superficial. They went over him, but not so enthusiastically, and all they did with the brief case was open it and glance inside and let Roeder himself shut it again.

One change from Sunday was that two of them, not one, accompanied us to the door in the rear wall, and through, across the vestibule, and down the fourteen steps to the first metal door. The sentinel who opened and let us in was the same pasty-faced bird with a pointed chin—Schwartz. This time the other sentinel did not stay at the table with his book work. He was right there with Schwartz, and interested in the callers, especially Rackham.

"We're a little early," Roeder said, "but they sent us on in."

"That's all right," Schwartz rumbled. "He's ahead of schedule today. One didn't come."

He went to the big metal door at the other end, pulled it open, and jerked his head. "On in."

Entering, Roeder took the lead, then Rackham, then me. Schwartz brought up the rear. He came in three paces and stood. Arnold Zeck, from behind his desk, told him, in the cold precise tone that he used for everything, "All right, Schwartz."

Schwartz left us. As the door closed I hoped to heaven it was as soundproof as it was supposed to be.

Zeck spoke. "The last time you were here, Rackham, you lost control of yourself and you know what happened."

Rackham did not reply. He stood with his hands behind him like a man ready to begin a speech, but his trap stayed shut, and from the expression of his face it was a good guess that his hands, out of sight, were making a tight knot.

"Sit down," Zeck told him.

Since the seating was an important item of the staging, I had stepped up ahead after we entered and made for the chair farthest front, a little to the left of Zeck's desk and about even with it, and Roeder had taken the one nearest me, to my right. That left, for Rackham, of the chairs near the desk, the one on the other side, and he went to it. He was about twelve feet from Zeck, Roeder about the same, and I was slightly closer.

Zeck asked Roeder, "Have you had a talk?"

Roeder shook his head. "Since Mr. Rackham had never met me before, I thought it might be better for you to explain the proposal to him. Naturally he will want to know exactly how it is to be handled before deciding whether to help with it." He reached to get his brief case from the floor, put it on his lap, and opened it.

"I think," Zeck said, "that you should describe the operation, since you conceived it and will manage it. But you were right to wait." He turned to Rackham. "You remember our last talk some time ago."

Rackham said nothing.

"You remember it?" Zeck demanded. He made it a demand by the faintest possible sharpening of his tone.

"I remember it," Rackham stated, not much above a whisper.

"You know the position you took. Ordinarily that course is not permitted to any man who has been given a place in my organization, and I made an exception of you only because the death of your wife had changed your circumstances. I thought it better to await an opportunity to take advantage of that change, and now it has come—through Roeder here. We want your help and we are prepared to insist on getting it. How do you feel about it?"

"I don't know." Rackham licked his lips. "I'd have to know more about what you want."

Zeck nodded. "But first your attitude. You will need to recognize the existence of mutual interests— yours and mine."

Rackham said nothing.

"Well?" The faint sharpening.

"Damn it, of course I recognize them!"

"Good. Go ahead, Roeder."

Roeder had got some papers from his brief case. One of them fluttered away from him, and I left my chair to retrieve it for him. I believe he did that on purpose. I believe he knew that now that the moment had come every nerve and muscle in me was on a hair trigger, and he was giving me an excuse to loosen them up.

"As I understand it," he said, "we're going to give Rackham a cut, and before I tell him about it I wish you'd take a look at this revised list of percentages. Yours is of course fixed, and I don't like to reduce mine unless it's absolutely unavoidable . . ."

He had a sheet of paper in his hand. With his brief case on his lap, and loose papers, it was awkward for him to get up, so I obliged. I reached, and he handed me the paper, and I had to leave my chair to get it to Zeck. On my way I took a glance at the paper because I thought it was in character to do that, and if I ever needed my character to stay put for another four seconds I did right then. When I extended my hand to Zeck I released the paper an instant too soon and it started to drop. I grabbed at it and missed, and that made me take another step and bend over, which put me in exactly the right position to take him away from there before he could possibly get a toe on one of the buttons under his desk.

Not wanting to knock his chair over, I used my left knee to push him back, chair and all, my right knee to land on his thighs and keep him there, and my hands for his throat. There was only one thing in my mind at that precise instant, the instant I had him away from the desk, and that was the fear that I would break his neck. Since I was in front of him I had to make absolutely sure, not only that he didn't yap, but also that he was too uncomfortable to try things like jabbing his thumbs in my eyes, but God knows I didn't want to overdo it, and bones and tendons are by no means all alike. What will be merely an inconvenience for one man will finish another one for good.

His mouth was open wide and his shark eyes were popping. With my knee on him he couldn't kick, and his arms were just flopping around. And Roeder was there by me, with a wadded handkerchief in one hand and a piece of cord in the other. As soon as he had the handkerchief stuffed tight in the open mouth he moved to the rear of the chair, taking Zeck's right hand with him, and reached around for the left hand. I tried to elude him, and I increased the pressure of my fingers a little, and then he got it.

"Hurry up," I growled, "or I'll kill him sure as hell."

It took him a year. It took him forever. But finally he straightened up, came around to take another look at the handkerchief and poke it in a little tighter, backed up, and muttered, "All right, Archie."

When I took my hands away my fingers ached like the devil, but that was nerves, not muscles. I leaned over to get my ear an inch away from his nose; there was no question about his breathing.

"His pulse is all right," Roeder said, not through his nose.

"You're crazy," Rackham said hoarsely. "Good God! You're crazy!"

He was out of his chair, standing there in front of it, trembling all over. Roeder's hand went to his side pocket for the Carson Snub Thirty, which he had got from the brief case along with the piece of cord. I took it and aimed it at Rackham.

"Sit down," I said, "and stay."

He sank down into the chair. I moved to the end of the desk so as to have him in a corner of my eye while looking at Zeck. Roeder, at my left elbow, spoke rapidly but distinctly.

"Mr. Zeck," he said, "you told me on the telephone two years ago that you had great admiration for me. I hope that what has just happened here has increased it. I'm Nero Wolfe, of course. There are many things it would give me satisfaction to say to you, and perhaps I shall someday, but not now. It is true that if one of your men suddenly opened the door Mr. Goodwin would kill you first, but I'm afraid you'd have company. So I'll get on. Having by your admission matched you in intellect, it's a question of will, and mine has not failed me, as you thought. Confound it, I wish you could speak."

The expression of Zeck's eyes, no longer popping, indicated that Wolfe had nothing on him there.

"Here's the situation," Wolfe went on. "During the two months I've been here in this outlandish guise I have collected enough evidence to get you charged on thirty counts under Federal law. I assure you that the evidence is sound and sufficient, and is in the hands of a man whom you cannot stop or deflect. You'll have to take my word for it that if that evidence is produced and used you are done for, and that it will be immediately produced and used if anything untoward happens to Mr. Goodwin or me. I fancy you will take my word since you admit that I match you in intellect, and to climax these five frightful months with such a bluff as this, if it were one, would be witless. However, if you think I'm bluffing there's no point in going on. If you think I'm bluffing, please shake your head no, meaning you don't believe me."

No shake.

"If you think I have the evidence as described, please nod your head."

No nod.

"I warn you," Wolfe said sharply, "that Mr. Goodwin and I are both ready for anything whatever."

Zeck nodded. Nothing violent, but a nod.

"You assume my possession of the evidence?"

Zeck nodded again.

"Good. Then we can bargain. While I have great respect for the Federal laws, I am under no obligation to catch violators of them. Without compunction I can leave that to others. But I am under an obligation to a certain individual which I feel strongly and which I must discharge. Mrs. Rackham paid me a large sum to serve her interest, and the next day she was murdered. It was clearly my duty to expose her murderer—not only my duty to her but to my own self-respect—and I have failed. With an obligation of that nature I have never accepted failure and do not intend to. Mr. Goodwin, working in my behalf, has been a party to that failure, and he too will not accept it."

Zeck nodded again, or I thought he did, probably to signify approval of our high moral standards.

"So we can bargain," Wolfe told him. "You said day before yesterday that you have evidence, or can easily get it, that will convict Rackham of the murder of his wife. Was that true?"

Zeck nodded. The shark eyes were intent on Wolfe.

"Very well. I believe you because I know what you are capable of. I offer a trade. I'll trade you the evidence I have collected against you for the evidence that will convict Rackham. Will you make the trade?"

Zeck nodded.

"It will have to be more or less on my terms. I can be trusted; you cannot. You will have to deliver first. But I realize that the details of anything as vital as this is to you cannot be settled without discussion, and it must be discussed and settled now. We are going to release your hands and take that handkerchief from your mouth, but before we do so, one more warning. You are to stay where you are until we're finished. If you move toward the floor signals under your desk, or try to summon your men in any other manner, you will die before anyone else does.

Also, of course, there is the evidence that exists against you. You understand the situation?"

Zeck nodded.

"Are you ready to discuss the matter?"

Zeck nodded.

"Release him, Archie," Wolfe snapped.

Needing two hands to untie the cord, I put the Carson Snub Thirty down on the polished top of Zeck's desk. I would have given a year's pay for a glance at Rackham, to see what the chances were, but that might have ruined it. So I put the gun there, stepped around to the rear of Zeck's chair, knelt, and started untying the knot. My heart was pounding my ribs like a sledgehammer.

So I didn't see it happen; I could only hear it. I did see one thing there behind Zeck's chair: a sudden convulsive jerk of his arms, which must have been his reaction to the sight of Rackham jumping for the gun I had left on the desk. More even than a sight of Rackham, to see if he was rising to it, I wanted a sight of Wolfe, to see if he was keeping his promise to duck for cover the instant Rackham started for the gun, but I couldn't afford it. My one desperate job now was to get that cord off of Zeck's wrists in time, and while Wolfe had used the trick knot we had practiced with, he had made it damn tight. I barely had it free and was unwinding the cord from the wrists when the sound of the shot came, followed immediately by another.

As I got the cord off and jammed it in my pocket, Zeck's torso slumped sideways and then forward. Flat on the floor, I slewed around, saw Zeck's contorted face right above my eyes, pulled the handkerchief out of his mouth and stuffed it in my pocket with the cord, slid forward under the desk, and reached for one of the signal buttons.

I didn't know, and don't know yet, whether the noise of the shots had got through the soundproof door or whether it was my push on the button that brought them. I didn't hear the door open, but the next shots I heard were a fusillade that came from no Carson, so I came back out from under the desk and on up to my feet. Schwartz and his buddy were standing just inside the door, one with two guns and one with one. Rackham was stretched out on the floor, flat on his face. Wolfe was standing at the end of the desk, facing the door, scowling as I had never seen him scowl before.

"The dirty bastard," I said bitterly, and I admit my voice might have trembled even if I hadn't told it to.

"Reach up," Schwartz said, advancing.

Neither Wolfe nor I moved a muscle. But Wolfe spoke. "What for?" He was even bitterer than me, and contemptuous. "They let him in armed, not us."

"Watch 'em, Harry," Schwartz said, and came forward and on around behind the desk where I was. Ignoring me, he bent over Zeck's collapsed body, spent half a minute with it, and then straightened and turned.

"He's gone," he said.

Harry, from near the door, squealed incredulously. "He's gone?"

"He's gone," Schwartz said.

Harry wheeled, pushed the door open, and was gone too. Schwartz stared after him three seconds, not more than that, then jumped as if I had pinched him, made for the door, and on through.

I went and took a look at Rackham, found he was

even deader than Zeck, and turned to Wolfe. "Okay, that's enough. Come on."

"No." He was grim. "It will be safer when they've all skedaddled. Phone the police."

"From here?"

"Yes."

I went to Zeck's desk and pulled one of the phones to me.

"Wait." I had never heard him so grim. "First get Marko's number. I want to speak to Fritz."

"Now? For God's sake, *now?*"

"Yes. Now. A man has a right to have his satisfactions match his pains. I wish to use Mr. Zeck's phone to tell Fritz to go home and get dinner ready."

I dialed the operator.

Chapter 20

Three days later, Friday afternoon, I said to Wolfe, "Anyway, it's all over now, isn't it?"

"No, confound it," he said peevishly. "I still have to earn that fee."

It was six o'clock, and he had come down from the plant rooms with some more pointed remarks about the treatment the plants had got at Hewitt's place. The remarks were completely uncalled for. Considering the two journeys they had taken, out to Long Island and then back again, the plants were in splendid shape, especially those hard to handle like the Miltonias and Phalaenopsis. Wolfe was merely trying to sell the idea, at least to himself, that the orchids had missed him.

Fritz might have been a mother whose lost little boy has been brought home after wandering in the desert for days, living on cactus pulp and lizards' tails. Wolfe had gained not an ounce less than ten pounds in seventy-two hours, in spite of all the activity of getting resettled, and at the rate he was going he would be back to normal long before Thanksgiving. The pleats in his face were already showing a tendency to spread out, and of course the beard was gone, and the slick had been shampooed out of his hair. I had tried to persuade him to stay in training, but he wouldn't even bother to put up an argument. He just spent more time than ever with Fritz, arranging about meals.

He had not got home for dinner Tuesday evening after all, in spite of the satisfaction he had got by putting in a call to Fritz on Zeck's phone. We were now cleaned up with Westchester, but it had not been simple. The death of Arnold Zeck had of course started a chain reaction that went both deep and wide, and naturally there had been an earnest desire to make goats out of Wolfe and me, but they didn't have a damn thing on us, and when word came from somewhere that Wolfe, during his association with Zeck, might have collected some facts that could be embarrassing to people who shouldn't be embarrassed, the attitude toward us changed for the better right away.

As for the scene that ended with the death of Zeck and Rackham, we were clean as a whistle. The papers in Roeder's brief case, which of course the cops took, proved nothing on anybody. By the time the cops arrived there had been no one on the premises but Wolfe and me and the two corpses. A hot search was on, especially for Schwartz and Harry, but so far no take. No elaborate lying was required; our basic story was that Wolfe, in his disguise as Roeder, had got in with Zeck in order to solve the murder of Mrs. Rackham, and the climax had come that afternoon when Zeck had put the screws on Rackham by saying that he had evidence that would convict him for killing his wife, and Rackham had pulled a gun, smuggled somehow past the sentinels, and had shot Zeck, and Schwartz and Harry had rushed in and drilled Rackham. It was surprising and gratifying to note how much of it was strictly true.

So by Friday afternoon we were cleaned up with Westchester, as I thought, and therefore it was a minor shock when Wolfe said, "No, confound it, I still have to earn that fee."

I was opening my mouth to ask him how come, when the phone rang. I got it. It was Annabel Frey. She wanted to speak to Wolfe. I told him so. He frowned and reached for his phone, and I stayed on.

"Yes, Mrs. Frey? This is Nero Wolfe."

"I want to ask you a favor, Mr. Wolfe. That is, I expect to pay for it of course, but still it's a favor. Could you and Mr. Goodwin come up here this evening? To my home, Birchvale?"

"I'm sorry, Mrs. Frey, but it's out of the question. I transact business only in my office. I never leave it."

That was a little thick, I thought, from a guy who had just spent five months the way he had. And if she read newspapers she knew all about it—or anyhow some.

"I'm sorry," she said, "because we must see you. Mr. Archer is here, the District Attorney, and I'm calling at his suggestion. We have a problem—two problems, really."

"By 'we' do you mean you and Mr. Archer?"

"No, I mean all of us—all of us who inherited property from Mrs. Rackham, and all of us who were here the night she was killed. Our problem is about evidence that her husband killed her. Mr. Archer says he has none, none that is conclusive—and perhaps you know what people are saying, and the newspapers. That's what we want to consult you about—the evidence."

"Well." A pause. "I'm trying to get a little rest after a long period of overexertion. But—very well. Who is there?"

"We all are. We met to discuss this. You'll come? Wonderful! If you—"

"I didn't say I'll come. All five of you are there?"

"Yes—and Mr. Archer—"

"Be at my office, all of you, at nine o'clock this evening. Including Mr. Archer."

"But I don't know if he will—"

"I think he will. Tell him I'll be ready then to produce the evidence."

"Oh, you will? Then you can tell me now—"

"Not on the phone, Mrs. Frey. I'll be expecting you at nine."

When we had hung up I lifted the brows at him. "So that's what you meant about earning that fee? Maybe?"

He grunted, irritated that he had to interrupt his convalescence for a job of work, sat a moment, reached for a bottle of the beer Fritz had brought, grunted again, this time with satisfaction, and poured a glass with plenty of foam.

I got up to go to the kitchen, to tell Fritz we were having company and that refreshments might be required.

Chapter 21

I was mildly interested when the six guests arrived—a little early, five to nine—in such minor issues as the present state of relations between Annabel Frey and the banker, Dana Hammond, and between Lina Darrow and the statesman, Oliver Pierce, and whether Calvin Leeds would see fit to apologize for his unjust suspicions about Wolfe and me.

To take the last first, Leeds was all out of apologies. The spring was in his step all right, but not in his manners. First to enter the office, he plunged himself down in the red leather chair, but I figured that Archer rated it ex officio and asked him to move, which he did without grace. As for the others, there was too much atmosphere to get any clear idea. They were all on speaking terms, but the problem that brought them there was in the front of their minds, so much so that no one was interested in the array of liquids and accessories that Fritz and I had arranged on the table over by the big globe. Annabel was in the most comfortable of the yellow chairs, to Archer's left; then, working toward me at my desk,

Leeds and Lina Darrow; and Hammond and Pierce closest to me.

Wolfe's eyes swept the arc.

"This," he said, "is a little awkward for me. I have met none of you before except Mr. Leeds. I must be sure I have you straight." His eyes went along the line again. "I think I have. Now if you'll tell me what you want—you, Mrs. Frey, it was you who phoned me."

Annabel looked at the DA. "Shouldn't you, Mr. Archer?"

He shook his head. "No, you tell him."

She concentrated, at Wolfe. "Well, as I said, there are two problems. One is that it seems to be supposed that Barry Rackham killed his wife, but it hasn't been proven, and now that he is dead how can it be proven so that everyone will know it and the rest of us will be entirely free of any suspicion? Mr. Archer says there is no official suspicion of us, but that isn't enough."

"It is gratifying, though," Wolfe murmured.

"Yes, but it isn't gratifying to have some of the people who say they are your friends looking at you as they do." Annabel was earnest about it. "Then the second problem is this. The law will not allow a man who commits a murder to profit by it. If Barry Rackham killed his wife he can't inherit property from her, no matter what her will said. But it has to be legally proven that he killed her, and unless that is done her will stands, and what she left to him will go to his heirs."

She made a gesture. "It isn't that we want it—the rest of us. It can go to the state or to charity—we don't care. But we think it's wrong and a shame for it to go to his people, whoever will inherit from him.

It's not only immoral, it's illegal. It can't be stopped by convicting him of murder, because he's dead and can't be tried. My lawyer and Mr. Archer both say we can bring action and get it before a court, but then we'll have to have evidence that he killed her, and Mr. Archer says he hasn't been able to get it from you, and he hasn't got it. But surely you can get it, or anyhow you can try. You see, that would solve both problems, to have a court rule that his heirs can't inherit because he murdered her."

"You have stated it admirably," Archer declared.

"We don't want any of it," Lina blurted.

"My interest," Pierce put in, "is only to have the truth fully and universally known and acknowledged."

"That," Wolfe said, "will take more than me. I am by no means up to that. And not only my capacities, but the circumstances themselves, restrict me to a much more modest ambition. I can get you one of the things you want, removal of all suspicion from the innocent, but the other, having Mrs. Rackham's bequest to her husband set aside, is beyond me."

They all frowned at him, in their various fashions. Hammond, the banker, protested, "That doesn't seem to make sense. What accomplishes one accomplishes the other. If you prove that Rackham killed his wife—"

"But I can't prove that." Wolfe shook his head. "I'm sorry, but it can't be done. It is true that Rackham deserved to die, and as a murderer. He killed a woman here in New York three years ago, a woman named Delia Montrose—one of Mr. Cramer's unsolved cases; Rackham ran his car over her. That was how Zeck originally got a noose on Rackham, by threatening to expose him for the murder he did commit. As you know, Mr. Archer, I penetrated some distance—not very far, but far enough—into Zeck's confidence, and I learned a good deal about his methods. I doubt if he ever had conclusive evidence that Rackham had killed Delia Montrose, but Rackham, conscious of his guilt, hadn't the spine to demand a showdown. Murderers seldom have. Then Rackham got a spine, suddenly and fortuitously, by becoming a millionaire; he thought then he could fight it; he defied Zeck, who, taking his time, retorted by threatening to expose Rackham for the murder of his wife. The threat was dangerous and effective even without authentic evidence to support it; there could of course be no authentic evidence that Rackham killed his wife, because he didn't."

They all froze, still wearing the frowns. Knowing Wolfe as I did, I had suspected that was coming, so I was taking them all in to get the impact, but there wasn't much to choose. After the first shock they all began to make noises, then words came, and then, as the full beauty of it hit them, the words petered out.

All but Archer's. "You have signed a statement," he told Wolfe, "to the effect that Zeck told Rackham he could produce evidence that would convict him of murder, and that Rackham thereupon shot Zeck. Now you say, in contradiction—"

"There is no contradiction," Wolfe declared. "The fact of Rackham's innocence would have been no defense against evidence manufactured by Zeck, and Rackham knew it. Innocent as he was—of this murder, that is—he knew what Zeck was capable of."

"You have said that you think Rackham killed his wife, but that you have no proof."

"I have not," Wolfe snapped. "Read your transcripts."

"I shall. And you now say that you think Rackham did not kill his wife?"

"Not that I think he didn't. I know he didn't, because I know who did." Wolfe flipped a hand. "I've known that from the beginning. That night in April, when Mr. Goodwin phoned me that Mrs. Rackham had been murdered, I knew who had murdered her. But I also knew that the interests of Arnold Zeck were involved and I dared not move openly. So I— but you know all about that." Wolfe turned to me. "Archie. Precautions may not be required, but you might as well take them."

I opened a desk drawer and got out the Grisson .38. My favorite Colt, taken from me in Zeck's garage antechamber, was gone forever. After a glance at the cylinder I dropped the Grisson in my side pocket and as I did so lifted my head to the audience. As if they had all been on one circuit, the six pairs of eyes left me and went to Wolfe.

"I don't like this," Archer said in a tight voice. "I am here officially, and I don't like it. I want to speak to you privately."

Wolfe shook his head. "It's much better this way, Mr. Archer, believe me. We're not in your county, and you're free to leave if it gets too much for you, but—"

"I don't want to leave. I want a talk with you. If you knew, that night, who had killed Mrs. Rackham, I intend to—"

"It is," Wolfe said cuttingly, "of no importance what you intend. You have had five months to implement your intentions, and where are you? I admit that up to three days ago I had one big advantage over you, but not since then—not since I told you of the package I got with a cylinder of tear gas in it,

and of the phone call from Mr. Zeck. That brought
you even with me. It was after noon on a Friday that
Mrs. Rackham left here after hiring me. It was the
next morning, Saturday, that I received that package
and the phone call from Zeck. How had he learned
about it? Apparently he even knew the amount of
the check she had given me. How? From whom?"

I was not really itching to shoot anybody. So I got
up and unobtrusively moved around back of them, to
the rear of the chair that was occupied by Calvin
Leeds. Wolfe was proceeding.

"It was not inconceivable that Mrs. Rackham had
told someone else about it, her daughter-in-law or
her secretary, or even her husband, but it was most
unlikely, in view of her insistence on secrecy. She
said she had confided in no one except her cousin,
Calvin Leeds." Wolfe's head jerked right and he
snapped, "That's correct, Mr. Leeds?"

Being back of Leeds, I couldn't see his face, but
there was no difficulty about hearing him, since he
spoke much too loud.

"Certainly," he said. "Up to then—before she
came to see you—certainly."

"Good," Wolfe said approvingly. "You're already
drawing up your lines of defense. You'll need them."

"What you're doing," Leeds said, still too loud, "if
I understand you—you're intimating that I told Zeck
about my cousin's coming here and hiring you. You're
intimating that in front of witnesses."

"That's right," Wolfe agreed. "But it's not vital to
me; I mention it chiefly to explain why I suspected
you of duplicity, and of being involved in some way
with Arnold Zeck even before Mr. Goodwin left here
that day to go up there. It draws attention to you, no
doubt of that; but it is not primary evidence that you

murdered your cousin. The proof that it was you who killed her was given to me on the phone that night by Mr. Goodwin."

There were stirrings and little noises. Leeds ignored them.

"So," he said, not so loud now, "you're actually accusing me before witnesses of murdering my cousin?"

"I'm accusing you of that, yes, sir, but also I'm accusing you of something much worse than that." Wolfe spat it at him. "I'm accusing you of deliberately and ruthlessly, to protect yourself from the consequences of your murder of your cousin for the money you would inherit from her, thrusting that knife into the belly of a dog that loved you and trusted you!"

Leeds started up, but hadn't got far when my hands were on his shoulders, and with plenty of pressure. He let down. I moved my hands to the back of his chair.

Wolfe's voice was cold and cutting. "No one could have done that but you, Mr. Leeds. In the woods at night, that trained dog would not have gone far from its mistress. Someone else might possibly have killed the dog first and then her, but it wasn't done that way, because the knife was left in the dog. And if someone else, permitted to get close to her, had succeeded in killing her with a sudden savage thrust and then defended himself against the dog's attack, it is not believable that he could have stopped so ferocious a beast by burying the knife in its side without himself getting a single toothmark on him. You know those dogs; you wouldn't believe it; neither will I.

"No, Mr. Leeds, it could have been only you. When Mr. Goodwin went on to your house and you stayed out at the kennels, you joined your cousin on her walk in the woods. I doubt if the dog would have permitted even you to stab her to death in its presence; I don't know; but you didn't have to. You sent the dog away momentarily, and, when the knife had done its work on your cousin, you withdrew it, stood there in the dark with the knife in your hand, and called the dog to come. It came, and despite the smell of fresh blood, it behaved itself because it loved and trusted you. You could have spared it; you could have taken it home with you; but no. That would have put you in danger. It had to die for you, and by your hand."

Wolfe took a breath. "To this point I know I am right; now conjecture enters. You stabbed the dog, of course, burying the blade in its belly, but did you leave the knife there intentionally, to prevent a gush of blood on you, or did the animal convulsively leap from you at the feel of the prick, jerking the knife from your grasp? However that may be, all you could do was make for home, losing no time, for you must show yourself to Mr. Goodwin as soon as possible. So you did that. You said good night and went to bed. I don't think you slept; you may even have heard the dog's whimpering outside the door, after it had dragged itself there; but maybe not, since it was beneath Mr. Goodwin's window, not yours. You pretended sleep, of course, when he came for you."

Leeds was keeping his head up, but I could see his hands gripping his legs just above the knees.

"You used that dog," Wolfe went on, his voice as icy as Arnold Zeck's had ever been, "even after it died. You were remorseless to your dead friend. To impress Mr. Goodwin, you were overcome with emotion at the thought that, though you had given the dog to your cousin two years ago, it had come to your doorstep to die. It had not come to your doorstep to die, Mr. Leeds, and you knew it; it had come there to try to get at you. It wanted to sink its teeth in you just once. I say you knew it, because when you squatted beside the dog and put your hand on it, it snarled. It would not have snarled if it had felt your hand as the soothing and sympathetic touch of a trusted friend in its last agony; indeed not; it snarled because it knew you, at the end, to be unworthy of its love and trust, and it scorned and hated you. That snarl alone is enough to convict you. Do you remember that snarl, Mr. Leeds? Will you ever forget it? Your old friend Nobby, his last words for you—"

Leeds' head went forward, dropping, and his hands came up to cover his face.

He made no sound, and no one else did either. The silence darted around us and into us, coming out from Leeds. Then Lina Darrow took in a breath with a sighing, sobbing sound, and Annabel got up and went to her.

"Take him, Mr. Archer," Wolfe said grimly. "I'm through with him, and it's about time."

Chapter 22

I'm sitting at a window overlooking a fiord, typing this on a new portable I bought for the trip. In here it's pleasant. It's late in the season for outdoors in Norway, but if you run hard to keep your blood going you can stand it.

I got a letter yesterday which read as follows:

Dear Archie:

The chickens came from Mr. Haskins Friday, four of them, and they were satisfactory. Marko came to dinner. He misses Fritz, he says. I have given Fritz a raise.

Mr. Cramer dropped in for a talk one day last week. He made some rather pointed comments about you, but on the whole behaved himself tolerably.

I am writing this longhand because I do not like the way the man sent by the agency types.

Vanda peetersiana has a raceme 29 in. long. Its longest last year was 22 in. We have found three snails in the warm room. I thought of mailing them to Mr. Hewitt but didn't.

Mr. Leeds hanged himself in the jail at White Plains yesterday and was dead when discovered. That of course cancels your promise to Mr. Archer to return in time for the trial, but I trust you will not use it as an excuse to prolong your stay.

We have received your letters and they were most welcome. I have received an offer of $315 for the furniture in your office but am insisting on $350. Fritz says he has written you. I am beginning to feel more like myself.

My best regards,
NW

I let Lily read it. "Darn him anyhow," she said. "No message, not a mention of me. My Pete! Huh. Fickle Fatty."

"You'd be the last," I told her, "that he'd ever send a message to. You're the only woman that ever got close enough to him, at least in my time, to make him smell of perfume."

The World of
Rex Stout

Now, for the first time ever, enjoy a peek into the life of Nero Wolfe's creator, Rex Stout, courtesy of the Stout Estate. Pulled from Rex Stout's own archives, here are rarely seen, never-before-published memorabilia. Each title in "The Rex Stout Library" will offer an exclusive look into the life of the man who gave Nero Wolfe life.

In the Best Families

On June 6, 1950—mere days after Rex Stout had finished writing *In the Best Families*—Merwin Hart appeared before the House's Select Committee to Investigate Lobbying Activities and alleged that Stout was a Communist. Stout's letter to the committee chair, clarifying the situation, is reproduced here. The same year, Senator Joe McCarthy would begin making widespread allegations of Communist infiltration in the United States. Stout, through both Freedom House and the Author's League, would become an outspoken critic of McCarthyism.

June 16, 1950

Representative Frank Buchanan
Chairman, Select Committee to
Investigate Lobbying Activities
House of Representatives
Washington 25, D. C.

Dear Mr. Buchanan:

I am informed that on June 6 Mr. Merwin K. Hart testi-
fied before your committee to the effect that "Rex
Stout, executive head of Friends of Democracy, was for-
merly a member of the board of editors of the Communist
magazine, The New Masses".

Mr. Hart and two or three other individuals, and also
a couple of newspapers, especially the Chicago Tribune,
continue to make this charge, although they have been
carefully and completely informed of the facts -- which
are:

1) At the time the magazine New Masses was started,
in 1924, it was in no sense Communist. I contributed
some money to help get it started, and was put on the
executive board, not the board of editors.

2) After attending a few of the monthly meetings of
the executive board, I and two other members became
aware that a strong effort was being made to have the
magazine adopt the Communist line. The three of us
strenuously opposed that effort.

3) When, eighteen months after the magazine was
started, it became apparent that the Communist fac-
tion was practically in control of the editorial

policy of the magazine, I resigned, along with my two
colleagues.

It is ironic that one of the many occasions, in the past
third of a century, on which I have opposed communism,
should be used by Mr. Hart and others to imply that I was
once pro-Communist — although, as I say, they have been
informed of the facts, which are on record, and therefore
they know the charge is false.

Since Mr. Hart's testimony is a part of your committee's
record, I would greatly appreciate it if this letter
could be made also a part of the record, and its contents
communicated to the members of your committee.

                                Respectfully,

                                Rex Stout

rs:bt

Rex Stout's NERO WOLFE

A grand master of the form, Rex Stout is one of America's greatest mystery writers. Now, in this ongoing program dedicated to making available the complete set of Nero Wolfe mysteries, these special collector's editions feature new introductions by today's best writers and never-before-published memorabilia from the life of Rex Stout.

Ask for these books at your local bookstore or use this page to order.

Please send me the books I have checked above. I am enclosing $_____ (add $2.50 to cover postage and handling). Send check or money order, no cash or C.O.D.'s, please.

Name _____

Address _____

City/State/Zip _____

Send order to: Bantam Books, Dept. BD 17, 2451 S. Wolf Rd., Des Plaines, IL 60018
Allow four to six weeks for delivery.
Prices and availability subject to change without notice.   BD 17 1/96

BANTAM MYSTERY COLLECTION

____57204-0 **KILLER PANCAKE** Davidson • • • • • • • • • • • • • • $5.50

____56860-4 **THE GRASS WIDOW** Peitso • • • • • • • • • • • • $5.50

____57235-0 **MURDER AT MONTICELLO** Brown • • • • • • • • $5.99

____57300-4 **STUD RITES** Conant • • • • • • • • • • • • • • • $5.99

____29684-1 **FEMMES FATAL** Cannell • • • • • • • • • • • • $5.50

____56448-X **AND ONE TO DIE ON** Haddam • • • • • • • • • $5.99

____57192-3 **BREAKHEART HILL** Cook • • • • • • • • • • • • $5.99

____56020-4 **THE LESSON OF HER DEATH** Deaver • • • • • • • $5.99

____56239-8 **REST IN PIECES** Brown • • • • • • • • • • • • • $5.50

____56976-7 **THESE BONES WERE MADE FOR DANCIN'** Meyers • • $5.50

____57456-6 **MONSTROUS REGIMENT OF WOMEN** King • • • • • $5.99

____57458-2 **WITH CHILD** King • • • • • • • • • • • • • • $5.99

____57251-2 **PLAYING FOR THE ASHES** George • • • • • • • • $6.50

____57173-7 **UNDER THE BEETLE'S CELLAR** Walker • • • • • • $5.99

____56793-4 **THE LAST HOUSEWIFE** Katz • • • • • • • • • • $5.99

____57205-9 **THE MUSIC OF WHAT HAPPENS** Straley • • • • • $5.99

____57477-9 **DEATH AT SANDRINGHAM HOUSE** Benison • • • • $5.50

____56969-4 **THE KILLING OF MONDAY BROWN** Prowell • • • • • $5.99

____57191-5 **HANGING TIME** Glass • • • • • • • • • • • • • • $5.99

Ask for these books at your local bookstore or use this page to order.

Please send me the books I have checked above. I am enclosing $_____ (add $2.50 to cover postage and handling). Send check or money order, no cash or C.O.D.'s, please.

Name _____

Address _____

City/State/Zip _____

Send order to: Bantam Books, Dept. MC, 2451 S. Wolf Rd., Des Plaines, IL 60018
Allow four to six weeks for delivery.
Prices and availability subject to change without notice.   MC 5/97

JOSEPH WAMBAUGH

"Joseph Wambaugh's characters have altered America's view of police."—*Time*

"Wambaugh is a master artist of the street scene."—*Publishers Weekly*

"Wambaugh is a writer of genuine power."
—*The New York Times Book Review*

Nobody writes about cops better than Wambaugh!